THE SLEEPWALKER

IAN BLACKWOOD

INKUBATOR
BOOKS

For Diane and Rebecca

Published by Inkubator Books
www.inkubatorbooks.com

Copyright © 2025 by Ian Blackwood

ISBN (eBook): 978-1-83756-564-1
ISBN (Paperback): 978-1-83756-565-8
ISBN (Hardback): 978-1-83756-566-5

Ian Blackwood has asserted his right to be identified as the author of this work.

THE SLEEPWALKER is a work of fiction. People, places, events, and situations are the product of the author's imagination. Any resemblance to actual persons, living or dead is entirely coincidental.

No part of this book may be reproduced, stored in any retrieval system, or transmitted by any means without the prior written permission of the publisher.

PROLOGUE

Even at eleven years of age, I knew my parents were crazy. But I never knew they were crazy enough to kill me.

I can't remember much about my father, but I can remember he seemed to hate everything and everyone. Apart from my mother. He adored her, and she adored him. My mother told me they met on a month-long retreat in Goa run by some guru who guaranteed to "cleanse and empty one's body, mind and inner spirit" – her words. They returned from the course "coupled" – they didn't believe in marriage – nor apparently in contraception, as I was born eight months later.

I was a mistake. And I knew from as early as five years of age that I was what you might call an "unwanted guest" in their house. At best they tolerated me; most times they, well ... excluded me.

At school I was a loner. And lonely. I was that weird kid with weird parents who lived in a cottage on the edge of the village where the curtains never opened.

In December 1999, when I was eleven, and my weird parents seemed to become weirder and weirder, they told me terrible things were going to happen on the eve of the millennium, and we had to be prepared. I asked them what they meant, but they wouldn't tell me.

Then on New Year's Eve my father came into my bedroom. He said something like, "It's tonight. The evil spirits will arrive at midnight." He told me that when I woke up in the morning, it would be ... as he called it: "A new dawning. A new millennium." And he said something about how my spirit will "soar away". And he told me I mustn't leave my room no matter what I heard.

They turned out my light at 9 p.m. But I couldn't sleep. I was too nervous, too afraid.

I heard the village church clock strike eleven. Then listened as it struck on each quarter. I waited. God, I remember those last fifteen minutes ticked by so slowly.

And then suddenly it was midnight. I counted along with each strike: nine ... ten ... eleven ... twelve.

And on the twelfth stroke I heard a gunshot echoing around the house. I screamed, jumped out of bed. I was panicking, didn't know what to do. I ran to my bedroom door. But it was locked. I started screaming and screaming before tugging open the wardrobe, dragging my row of clothes off the rail, throwing them onto the wardrobe floor, diving under them and pulling the wardrobe door to. I can remember it so clearly.

My heart was pounding; I could hear every beat. I was breathless. Then I heard my bedroom door squeak open, a click as he switched on the overhead light, and my father's voice asking, "Where are you? Come on, it's time. Where are you?"

I could hear him stalking around the bedroom. Suddenly

the wardrobe door was pulled open. And then he spoke. "Don't be afraid. It's time."

I remember I hardly recognised his voice; it was like ... like robotic and distant.

I was so scared. I was shaking. And I knew something bad was going to happen to me, so I started to plead, "Please no, please, please no—"

And then he shot me. My eardrums, they felt like they exploded, and as I let out this scream, I felt a hot, searing pain in my right arm.

Another gunshot and I passed out.

CHAPTER ONE

NOW

I was exhausted. I'd been in surgery all day. As I opened my locker, I caught a reflection of my face in the small mirror stuck to the inside of the door. My eyes looked tired, dark grey shadows under them. When I first met Nick, he'd told me that I had the most amazing hazel eyes. I told him to fuck off. It turned out he wasn't a bullshitter after all. He'd immediately blushed and apologised.

I grabbed my light, fawn jacket and my black Radley handbag, changed my flat sensible shoes into my two-inch boots, slammed the locker door and locked it with the keypad. I turned into the long, empty corridor. It was quiet on the fourth floor, and my heels clicked on the cream tiles. I decided to pop into the ward at the end of the corridor to check on a patient. I pulled open the swing doors. The hospital was silent apart from the echoing sound of grunting and snoring patients.

I stopped at the first private room on my left. The sign on the door read "Mr Rick Walker". I swung open the door and entered.

Rick Walker was eighteen, and he was fast asleep, snoring. I was about to turn and exit when he woke and sat up in bed, eyes blinking, then staring, vacant.

"It's okay, Rick, go back to sleep," I said gently.

And his eyes closed, and he fell back in his bed with a thud.

I watched him for a moment before I turned and quickly left the room, back into the long corridor and towards the lift.

The lift was one floor above me. I pressed the call button to go down. Waited. The lift didn't move from the fifth. I pressed the button again, impatient. Then again. I heard footsteps coming along the corridor towards me. When I looked, there was no one. I pressed the lift button once more. The lift still hadn't moved from the fifth floor. Finally, I gave up.

Next to the lift was an exit door with a stair logo printed on it. I decided to walk down to the basement car park.

I pushed open the door with the flat palm of my hand. It was quite heavy, and when I stepped inside, it slammed to with a thud. The staircase was dimly lit with overheard LED lights; the walls were bare, grey concrete building blocks; the stairs uncarpeted; and my footsteps echoed as I made my way down to the basement.

I'd just reached the first floor when I heard a door slam on the stairs above me and the sound of footsteps descending. I paused.

The footsteps paused.

I called out, "Hello?" but there was no answer, so I continued, my steps more urgent, holding on to the banister as I scurried down.

I reached the ground floor, paused. No sound of other

footsteps above me. A sense of relief. Hospitals can be creepy places at night, but even so.

I'm being ridiculous, I thought.

One more flight of stairs to the basement, when suddenly the lights went out. I gave a little cry, more of a curse. I fished inside my handbag for my phone.

Then I froze.

I could hear the footsteps again. But much closer. My shaky hands fumbled inside my bag until I grasped my phone, took it out and pressed on the torch icon.

I called out again, "Hello, who's there?" and shone my torch up the flight of stairs. The sound of the footsteps stopped. I shone the torch down and in front of me, and I could see the exit door to the car park just below.

I beamed the torch on to the exit door and ran down the last few steps, pulled on the handle and pushed hard against the door with my shoulder and burst into the car park. I smashed the door behind me and started walking briskly, trying not to panic, towards my BMW, which was parked to my right. There were no other cars in the spacious underground car park.

I approached my car, felt in my handbag for the keys, when suddenly I heard the slam of the exit door. I stopped, turned sharply. The car park was dim and shadowy, but I caught a fleeting glimpse of a figure darting behind a concrete pillar. I called out again, "Who's that? Who is it?"

I felt a panic rise inside my chest, my heart starting to thump. My hands were trembling as I searched for my keys. Eventually I found them at the bottom of the handbag, pulled them out. I was about to zap open the car, but my hands were shaking so much I dropped the keys. I was standing over a drain, and the keys clattered onto the slats of the grid and were now dangling precariously. I bent down to pick them up, but my trembling hands nudged the keys between the slats, and with a tinkle they disappeared into the drain below. I cursed and was about to crouch down on my knees to see if I could retrieve them when I heard a heavy, deep, asthmatic breathing noise, and I realised a figure was standing on the other side of the car.

I jumped up, cried out, "What you doing? You're following me? Who are you?"

The figure stepped away from the car so that I had a vague outline of him. He was tall, over six feet, wearing a dark trench coat that reached down to his ankles, and a hoodie, pulled low over his face. He didn't speak, but he moved a step closer, and as he did, I saw in his hand the gleam from the blade of a long knife.

I panicked. I knew I had to get out of the car park, so I ran from the car towards the ramp up to the ground level, where I could escape.

"Help! Someone help me, please," I screamed as I dashed up the ramp. But then I half stumbled as the heel on my right foot buckled. I'd forgotten to zip the boot up. I tugged off both boots, threw them away, glanced up and saw that the figure was advancing slowly towards me, not running.

I was up the ramp in seconds. No one around, no cars parked on this level either. My foot stepped on a piece of broken glass, and I cried out but didn't stop running.

I ran towards the exit barrier but suddenly stopped in my tracks. I screamed out in frustration, "NO!"

Beyond the barrier the security grilles were locked. I ducked under the exit barrier, ran to the grilles, grabbed them with both hands, started shaking them, screaming,

"Help! Help!" but the car park exit was up a dark side alley. No one was passing; no one was within earshot.

I started crying in frustration and helplessness, rattling the grilles like a trapped prisoner. I heard the footsteps behind me quicken. I turned, and he was only metres away. Panic notched up to a level of hysteria as I started to cry and scream even more. "What are you doing? Who are you? Get away! Stay away!"

His face was hidden in shadow under his hoodie, but I could see his eyes – dark black irises, the whites luminous and startling.

Desperate, I glanced this way and that, in the forlorn hope of a way out. Yet I felt unable to move as if my feet were super-glued to the ground.

Then he spoke, and his voice was detached, metallic: "There's no way out. There's no hope." And he raised his knife.

"No. Please no. I'm a doctor. I'm a doctor! Who are you?"

"I am your worst nightmare," he whispered.

As the knife flashed towards my throat, I just had time to catch sight of the wooden handle with its distinctive hallmark.

It was of a unicorn.

I SPRANG UPRIGHT IN BED, clutching at my throat and screaming. Next to me, Nick also shot bolt upright while my Yorkshire terrier, Samson, was perched on the end of the bed, barking.

I was gasping for air, tears streaming down my face, still

screaming. Nick put his arm round me, cradled and comforted me, "Ellie, Ellie, it's okay, it's okay." He kissed the top of my head – my hair clinging together with sweat – and wiped away my tears with the palm of his hand. And eventually I calmed, and my breathing evened out. "Was it the same dream?" Nick asked.

I nodded. "I'm afraid to go back to sleep."

"Let's go and have a drink," Nick suggested.

I nodded, pulled back the duvet and swung my legs over the side of the bed. However, when I stood up, I cried out.

"What is it?" Nick asked.

"My foot."

I sat back down on the edge of the bed and pulled my leg up to inspect the sole of my foot. A small splinter of glass was sticking out of it, dried blood surrounding it.

"Christ! I've got glass stuck in my foot!"

"Let me have a look," Nick said as he shot round to my side of the bed. He kneeled, inspected it. "It's only small, but I think I can get hold of it."

He managed to grab it with his forefinger and thumb, pulled, and it slid out. He placed it in the palm of my hand. "How the hell did that get there?"

And then I remembered. In my dream. Where I stepped on the broken glass. *Now that is weird*, I thought. Frightening.

Nick picked up on my mood. "What is it?"

"In my nightmare, when I was being chased, I took my boots off to run; then I stepped in some broken glass."

"Wow. Weird. But that doesn't answer the question of how you got the glass in your foot in the first place," Nick said.

"No. It's a bit spooky." My mind was swirling now, and

there was no way I would be able to sleep. After Nick had dabbed some antiseptic cream and stuck a plaster over the small cut, we went downstairs.

It was when we entered the kitchen that both of us started, and I grabbed Nick's hand, squeezing tightly.

Lying on the floor near the island was a broken wine glass, and leading to the door, where we were now standing, frozen, was a trail of bloody footprints.

CHAPTER TWO

It was now just after 3 a.m. Nick and I were sitting on high-backed stools opposite each other at the island in our spacious kitchen diner. Samson was sitting at my feet, somewhat confused about the time.

Nick was pouring me a brandy in a crystal glass.

"I can't remember. I can't remember coming downstairs," I said, stressed. "Taking a wine glass, dropping it, standing in the broken glass, I can't remember any of it."

"You must have been sleepwalking."

"I can't remember that I've ever sleepwalked. Ever."

"You could have been sleepwalking in the past without knowing," Nick suggested.

"I don't know. Possible."

Nick poured himself a small one, clinked glasses, knocked his back in one. I sipped mine. "Anyway, the nightmare, was it the same one?" he asked.

"Similar."

"Did he catch you this time?"

I nodded. "And it was far more real than I've ever had

before. It was my hospital, my locker on the same floor. But the first really spooky bit, when I walked into the ward, I checked on one of the patients, and it was Rick Walker."

"That is so spooky. You're kidding?"

I shook my head.

RICK WALKER CAME into the Royal for an emergency appendectomy that I performed by keyhole surgery. However, during the procedure, it was discovered that an abscess had developed, so I had to cut a three-inch incision in the lower right-hand side of the abdomen for open surgery to remove the affected appendix. The operation seemed to go fine, and he was returned to the ward.

My best friend, Penny, was the ward sister on the night shift, and overnight Rick Walker developed an infection in the operating wound. Penny needed to greatly increase the level of antibiotics, but unfortunately she was called to an emergency on A&E, a multiple-vehicle accident, and she forgot to update the dosage on Rick's chart and on the computer. By the time I started the morning shift, a MRSA infection had led to bacteraemia in his blood, which then quickly developed to sepsis. I pumped him with vancomycin, placed him on a ventilator, but within twenty-four hours he went into septic shock, and in spite of all my efforts, he died.

I was devastated.

Rick Walker's father sued the hospital for negligence, plus the doctor in charge at the time of his death. Me.

I was eventually absolved of all responsibility for Rick's death.

Penny was equally devastated. She had wanted to come

forward and explain to the disciplinary committee how her negligence had set off the chain reaction that led to Rick's death, but I told her to stay out of it. In effect, I covered for her. Penny had been disciplined two years earlier, and I'd suggested she didn't want another black mark on her record.

"It was a mistake any one of us could have made, Penny," I told her.

"You shouldn't be taking this," she replied.

"Well, I am, and that's the end of it."

"God, Ellie, what can I say?"

"Nothing."

Penny had hugged me gratefully. "Thank you," she whispered, "but it's not right."

"We won't talk about it again, Penny. Okay?"

And we never had.

But the whole episode had stressed me out. I knew I wasn't responsible for Rick's death, rather it was a set of unfortunate circumstances. But I still felt huge guilt. And after Rick died, I couldn't sleep. It's always upsetting when a patient dies, but when it is an eighteen-year-old with his whole life in front of him, it is doubly upsetting.

I'd suffered from very real, recurring nightmares for many years, ever since my parents died. But after Rick Walker's death, he started appearing in my nightmares, his face ghostly, his eyes dead and accusing.

Nick and I had been married just over a year when Rick Walker died. We should have been basking in our "honeymoon period". But instead, I disappeared inside myself. I didn't feel comfortable enough to talk to Nick about my feelings or my nightmares. And I was permanently tired, sometimes irritable and constantly anxious. It was like being locked away in a cell with no windows, no door. No escape.

No way in for Nick. And only I could find a way out. I kept telling myself I shouldn't be like this, I'm a doctor. But I felt inadequate, and I didn't know why. I also knew if one of my patients had such feelings, I would refer them to counselling.

At work I was coping, disguising my anxieties, focusing my mind totally during surgery, petrified of making an error. And no one at the Royal noticed the tumble-dryer turmoil swirling inside my head. But it required huge effort and concentration, so when I arrived home, I was totally exhausted; I flopped, jelly-like and uncommunicative.

At the same time, I lost my libido. Sex had never been the most important part of a relationship for me. It was never a driving force – unlike most of the men I'd dated. I hated doing it, but I'd faked more orgasms than a porn star. But now, only months married, when most couples still expect to be shagging as energetically as randy rabbits, I was apologising to Nick that I was too tired and had too much on my mind. Since then, we'd had sex once in the last month.

Of course, I knew what was wrong. I was suffering from clinical depression, something that had plagued my life on and off since my teens. I remember as early as thirteen when I'd be laughing in a group of friends but couldn't understand why inside I was still feeling sad.

Once I'd started studying medicine, however, I understood the sadness inside me. But I'd never told anyone, so I'd never been officially diagnosed. I'd controlled it, and in bad bouts where I became totally overwhelmed – like now – I controlled it by self-prescribing medication. I knew this wasn't right, but it worked for me, especially as I came off it whenever my life was back in control.

No one knew, not even Nick.

I felt real guilt about not telling Nick. Surely I should be sharing all my problems with the person I love? But it was a secret I'd carried with me for many years, and I feared how Nick would react if he knew. I feared it might change the fabric of our relationship.

When the disciplinary committee of the GMC exonerated me, I hoped my depression would lift, that my nightmares would become less real and frightening. And although the verdict was a huge relief, and I felt in control enough to come off the Prozac, the nightmares continued. Rick Walker disappeared from most of them or became peripheral, but he was replaced by a more sinister and terrifying figure that pursued me, hunted me down.

"SO RICK WALKER suddenly woke up, stared at me, his eyes, I don't know, weird ..."

"Shit! That's scary!" Nick said

"Then I left quickly and went down to our basement car park. But the lift wouldn't come. I had to walk down the stairs. Someone was following me. My car was parked in exactly the same spot as in real life. And I dropped my keys, and suddenly there he was. I ran. But I was trapped in the car park, couldn't get out."

"And the knife?"

"Yes. Our kitchen knife. Same unicorn."

There was a block of knives sitting on the breakfast bar. I went to pull one out, but it was missing.

"Where's the unicorn knife?"

"No idea," Nick replied. "I used it last night to cut up some onions when I made the spag bol, but I thought I'd put it back."

He looked in the dishwasher. The previous night's dirty dishes were there but no unicorn knife.

"So where is it, Nick?" I asked, perturbed.

"I've no idea," he said, and paused before adding, "We'll look for it tomorrow. I know it's weird, but it'll be around somewhere."

Nick poured himself another finger of brandy, slugged it back, slammed down the glass, and turned his head to me, looking directly into my eyes, and I knew he was about to broach a subject that had been off-limits through the last two stressful months. His eye contact was intense.

"Nick ..." I warned him.

"Ellie, please, I know this isn't the right time to talk about ... about us ... about you ... the nightmares—"

"No, it isn't," I interrupted.

"But it's affecting me and you," Nick persisted. "It's affecting our relationship. So I do think we need to talk. Openly. About what we, what ... what we both need to do ... and after what's happened tonight—"

He was about to continue, but I raised my palm.

"You're right, it isn't the right time. It's turned three a.m., and I'm in theatre at nine tomorrow."

Nick wasn't giving up so easily. "Things have been tough for you at work. You *have* been under huge stress."

I turned my face away.

"D'you think you should talk to one of your colleagues, you know, who specialises in something like this?" Nick suggested.

I was appalled. "You mean someone from the psychiatric department!"

Nick shrugged.

This was exactly the reason I'd never told Nick about my

dark moments. Everything I ever did would then be defined by the blackness. I was sure Nick would try to be understanding and sympathetic, but any crisis in our marriage and the black question mark would be hanging over us.

And if word filtered up to the CEO that I was having therapy sessions, with the implication that I was possibly unstable, I could be placed on temporary leave, and long term it could affect my future career prospects. I wasn't willing to chance it. I was a good doctor. And I had ambitions. I aspired to be a consultant surgeon.

"Nick, I've just been a bit down because of everything that's been going on. And as for my nightmares, you know I've had them for years. They're just nightmares!"

"Okay, okay ..."

"I mean, Nick, how could you even suggest that?"

"I'm sorry, I'm sorry. Come on, sweetheart." Nick backed off. "Let's go back up. You look exhausted."

He took my hand, and I followed him without objecting.

Once we were in bed, he crooked his arm around me. I nestled close in, and he said, "I'll stay awake until you're asleep, promise."

I don't know if Nick did stay awake, but I was so exhausted I must have fallen asleep in minutes – and gone straight back into a nightmare where I was chased by the same hooded figure down a never-ending alleyway.

AT BREAKFAST THE FOLLOWING MORNING, I was shattered. But I was already up and dressed when Nick entered the kitchen wearing only his boxer shorts and T-shirt, his hair uncombed and wild. I'd had a quick shower, slapped on a dab of make-up, and was looking quite fresh.

"Hi," I said, "You look tired, Nick."

"I'll be fine," he replied. "My first appointment's not until eleven. I'll just chill out here and take Samson for a walk. Are you okay? No more nightmares once you got back to sleep?"

"No. It was fine, thanks," I lied.

I went to Nick, kissed him on the cheek and ruffled his already unruly hair. "You were great for me last night."

He shrugged as if to say, "It's okay."

"And I'll come out of this very soon. And I know, me and you, we're going to be fine," I assured him.

Though I wasn't sure I actually believed a word I'd said.

Before I left, I ran upstairs to clean my teeth in the bedroom ensuite, and I realised the bed hadn't been made.

I pulled back the duvet, noticed speckles of blood on the sheet where my foot had leaked, dragged off the fitted sheet. I tugged the pillows away – and I jumped back in horror at what I saw there.

Lying under the pillow was the unicorn knife.

CHAPTER THREE

I stared down at the knife. How *did* it get there? Did I take it upstairs when I was sleepwalking and hide it under my pillow? There was no other explanation.

It was worrying. No, it was more than worrying. It was frightening.

While asleep, I'd dropped a glass in the kitchen, stood on the splintered shards, then carried the unicorn knife up to my bedroom and placed it under my pillow.

I couldn't recall any of it. That was freaky. What else was I capable of doing while sleepwalking?

I didn't tell Nick about the knife. Instead I sneaked it into the kitchen and slid it into a drawer, then called out to him as he was drinking coffee in the dining area, "Hey, Nick, found the unicorn knife in this drawer."

His head swivelled round. "Really? I must have put it there without thinking."

If only he had.

As I picked up my bag from a stool on the breakfast bar

and was about to leave, Nick stood, approached me. "Hey, Ellie, don't forget tonight, that party at my office?"

"Oh shit. Yes. Forgot. Okay. I'll try to stay awake for it."

I walked out of the kitchen into our expansive square hallway, with its parquet floor and walls that I'd decorated in an expensive grey square webbing design. Our front door had four small diamond-shaped windows. My keys were hooked up on the wall; I plucked them off and exited through a smaller door on the right. This led into our garage, large enough for three cars, but there were just two, my BMW Gran Turismo and Nick's Lexus. I fobbed the garage doors, and as they lifted, bright sunshine flooded in, casting shadows across both cars.

My car was unlocked. I slid in, dropped my handbag on the passenger seat. The car started the first time, and I reversed out onto our large private stone drive, flower borders on three sides. I enjoyed gardening. It somehow soothed me. Our double iron gates were permanently left open.

Our house was a detached 1930s mock-Tudor style off a quiet street in Didsbury, Manchester. I say "our" house, but technically it was my house. After my parents died tragically, the money from the sale of their house, plus their savings, was put in a trust for me until I reached eighteen. When the inheritance was released, I was sensible, first buying a plush modern penthouse in central Manchester and paying my way through medical school before selling the penthouse and investing in my current house.

It was before 7.30 a.m., so the traffic along Wilmslow Road into Manchester was light; too early for the build-up of the school run. It was a bright, cloudless morning for once, and I reached into the glove compartment and took out my spare pair of sunglasses.

I loved my job, and I knew I was good at it. In theatre, I was totally focused, calm, completely in control. I loved the interaction with my patients, I was at ease with them, and they seemed to trust, respect and, I felt, like me.

What frightened me most was the possibility of the nightmares and the bouts of depression seeping into my working life and impinging on my ability to perform at the highest level.

This hadn't happened yet ...

As I entered the hospital's underground car park, it was difficult to push these thoughts away when my previous nightmare was still so real. I slowed the car down, glancing at the open grilles, physically shivering as I remembered grabbing and shaking those grilles in my nightmare.

And the image of the unicorn knife lying under my pillow – it kept popping into my head.

I drove down the ramp where in my nightmare I'd stepped on the broken glass, before sliding between two cars into my designated car space. When I climbed out of the car, I held on to my keys tightly, glancing down to where, in my nightmare, I'd dropped the keys. There was no drain there.

I walked across to the lift and saw that a printed sign was taped on the doors: "Lift not in operation". I cursed, moved across to the emergency stairs and tugged open the door. I felt just a tinge of nervousness that I tried to dismiss. The overhead lights were on, and they seemed bright compared to my dream. I started to climb to ground level, then level one and two. I paused a second for breath, and as I did, I heard the slam of the emergency door below me.

I jumped, and although I told myself I was being silly, I

quickened my steps up the final flight, and was relieved when I pushed open the door and entered my floor.

I was walking up the corridor towards the locker room when behind me I heard the smash of the stair door. I whirled round so quickly that Dr Ben Carson stopped in his tracks, startled. It was he who must have been following me up the stairs.

I nodded. He returned the nod. I carried on walking. At the locker-room door, I turned, glanced back, and Dr Carson was still there; he hadn't moved, and he was staring after me.

He looked away quickly, clearly embarrassed; then he turned and walked the opposite way down the corridor.

Dr Carson was the head of the psychiatric department: mid-forties, small, around five feet five; an intense look with dark piercing eyes. He made me feel uncomfortable, especially when I found myself alone with him, for example, in a lift. He seemed a little creepy, and I never knew what to say to him. Ironically, he wasn't great at small talk. I didn't feel such unease with any other colleagues.

There was no one in the locker room. I tapped in the keypad number, took off my coat – the same one I had been wearing in my nightmare – hung it up in the tall locker before placing my bag inside. I glanced at my phone and decided I had time for a quick coffee before surgery.

As I was leaving, I paused. The thought of the unicorn knife was bugging me, my mind still spinning with the image of the blade lying under my pillow.

THE CAFETERIA on the fourth floor was quiet. As I

helped myself to a cappuccino from the machine, a voice called out, "Ellie."

It was Penny, my best friend. We'd met in freshers' week at Manchester Uni Medical School. Penny was on the nursing course, and we immediately hit it off and then shared a flat. She'd even moved in as my lodger when I bought the penthouse.

Penny was tall and elegant, with long blonde hair that was currently tied up in a bun ready for surgery. She'd recently transferred over to become theatre sister. She was the same age as me, but she wasn't married, and she'd had a string of disappointing relationships. She was currently dating a guy called Tom. I hadn't met him yet, but Penny was adamant that "this could be the one", but as I pointed out, it wasn't the first time she'd said that.

Penny was sitting with Dr James Underwood, who was an anaesthetist. He was late thirties, a widower. His wife had committed suicide just over a year ago. He openly talked about it; how he'd arrived home late from work and found her dead in their bedroom. She'd taken an overdose. I was really touched by how he described the helplessness, the guilt and the irony of being a doctor yet not seeing how desperately unhappy she was. He had seen no signs, he told us. He carried huge guilt that he was unable to save the person he was closest to, the person he loved the most in the world.

How desperate must she have been? Not even to have spoken to James about her depression. She must have felt so lonely, a hopelessness to her life, utter desolation.

Of course I was aware of the irony, but I wasn't like that. Okay, I hadn't spoken to Nick, I hadn't opened up to him about my bouts of depression, but I didn't need to. I'd always coped. I had real meaning in my life. There was no way I could ever contemplate suicide.

James had huge charm, and in looks he reminded me of the first doctor I'd ever dated, who was also a charmer, but he knew it. James was gentler, seemed kinder. All the nurses adored him, and the younger doctors hung on his every word. He had that rare ability to say no to someone without ever offending.

I took my coffee across to them and sat down.

"You okay?" Penny asked.

"Yes, why?" I answered.

"You look tired."

"No, I'm fine. Had one of those nightmares but got back to sleep no bother," I said.

Penny knew the history of my very real nightmares, and I'd also mentioned it to James.

"Not still getting them *every* night?" he asked.

"Not every night, no. Last night wasn't so bad," I lied. "But often, I wake up in the middle of it; then when I get back to sleep, I return in the middle of the same nightmare," I told them.

"Oh, I'm the exact opposite," Penny said. "I dream Timothée Chalamet's making love to me, I wake up, then I can't get back into that dream. A fine example of coitus interruptus!"

I laughed. James smiled but then said to me, "Okay, we all have nightmares, and most times we deal with them ... but this is clearly affecting your life, Ellie; you have to do something."

"James, yes, it's affecting my life, but I'm not out of control. And it's certainly not affecting my work."

I spoke as if this was a question, and I took a sideways, quizzical glance at James for support.

"No, no, no." James backtracked. "It certainly isn't. Ellie, you're fantastic at your job; everyone knows that ..."

I smiled, nodded a thank you.

"Look, Ellie, I'm no expert, but I've read up on extreme nightmares. You've not just come off any form of medication?" he asked.

"No." Again, I wasn't being exactly truthful. "Nor am I suffering from post-traumatic stress disorder," I told him.

"Ellie's done all the research, James," Penny said.

"So you know that seventy per cent of patients successfully reduce recurring nightmares through behavioural therapy?"

"Yes."

He nodded. "So ... have you thought about it?" he continued.

The thought of Dr Carson or some other shrink delving into my psyche made me shiver. Who knew what might be unearthed?

"And, Ellie, I know you've had these nightmares on and off for years, but have they become more extreme since the Rick Walker case?"

I was thrown for a second by the directness of his question, and I could see Penny shift uneasily in her chair. I knew Penny still felt the weight of guilt for Rick Walker's death. But did she have sleepless nights? If she did, she'd never mentioned them to me.

"No," I said defensively. James was staring at me, as if he could see right through me, and I added, "Well, maybe a little."

"So it is possible you could be suffering from a form of PTSD?"

I didn't want to answer. I'd constantly assured myself I wasn't the sort of person who suffered PTSD. Yes, Rick Walker had played on my mind, and of course he would – his death had taken up so much of my life earlier in the year. Of course, I knew I was blameless, and the inquiry had cleared me of any negligence. So why would this bring back the nightmares? No, I definitely did not have PTSD.

I thought about telling James and Penny about the sleepwalking, but decided against it. I needed to think it through on my own because the implications were scary.

The sound of James's bleeper interrupted my thoughts. "Okay, guys, let's get our skates on. Theatre in ten." He stood up, smiled warmly down at me. "Take it easy, Ellie; finish your coffee; see you down there," he said, and walked off.

Penny gave me a meaningful smile, raising one eyebrow.

"What?"

"He likes you," she said with a twinkle.

"Stop it! He knows I'm a happily married woman."

"Are you, though?"

And as Penny stood, turned and spun away, she winked at me.

"See you down there."

Why did she say that about my marriage? Was it a flippant, throwaway comment, or could she see something in me that I couldn't?

PENNY and I were scrubbing up. We had donned our surgical gowns, masks and head coverings, removed rings from fingers, and we were standing next to each other at twin sinks. We'd washed our hands, cleaned out our fingernails and were now scrubbing our hands and arms to the elbow with the surgical sponge.

"How are things with you and ... Tom, isn't it?" I asked.

"Yeah." Penny paused before shaking her head.

"What?"

"I found out the other night" – she took a deep breath – "he's married."

"You're kidding!" I was genuinely shocked. "Bastard. So you've finished with him?"

Penny looked away.

"You've not?"

"Ellie, I love him."

"Penny, for God's sake," I said before adding as an observation, "He won't leave his wife. They never do. Bloody hell, Penny, what are you like?"

"I know, I know, I know," she said, then added, "But ..."

"But what?"

She paused, looked me closely in the eyes. "I sense that there's something not quite right between you and Nick."

After her previous flippant remark, this threw me further. I hesitated before forcing a smile. "Penny, me and Nick are great. Honestly."

My friend just nodded, not pursuing it any further.

And I was glad; we both needed to concentrate on something far more important than our love-life woes.

CHAPTER FOUR

It had been a long day, and I was knackered. The last thing I needed was one of Nick's office socials. I approached the lift. Fortunately, it was now working. I heard the slam of a door further down the corridor. I spun round. No one there.

The lift was on the fifth floor. I pressed the call button to go down. Waited. The lift didn't move. I pressed the button again. Then again. I heard footsteps coming along the corridor towards me. Looked around. No one there. I pressed the lift button once more. The lift still hadn't moved.

This was spooky. It exactly mirrored my nightmare. But this time I knew I absolutely wasn't asleep. I pressed the call button again. The lift wasn't moving. I felt impatient, irritable, but I was determined I wouldn't walk down the stairs. *Stay composed, patient,* I told myself.

But still the lift never moved. Finally, I gave up. I had no choice. I had to take the stairs.

I pushed open the door with the flat palm of my hand. The staircase was well lit; the walls were bare, grey concrete building blocks; the stairs uncarpeted; and my footsteps echoed as I made my way down to the basement.

It was all identical to my nightmare.

I'd just reached the first floor when I heard a door slam on the stairs above me and then the sound of footsteps descending.

I paused. The footsteps paused.

I called out, "Hello?" but there was no answer, so I continued, more urgently, holding on to the banister as I scurried down. Heart pounding, breath short and fast. What was happening? This was too weird.

I reached the ground floor, paused. No sound of other footsteps above. A sense of relief. "I'm being ridiculous," I murmured to myself.

One more flight of stairs to the basement. I was expecting the lights to go out as in the nightmare. So I anticipated this and felt in my bag for my phone, but didn't need it. They stayed on. I listened again for the footsteps. Nothing. I really was being ridiculous. But then, as I was about to continue downwards, I suddenly heard them: the thud of heavy footsteps now running fast down the stairs.

A sharp intake of breath, almost a gasp, near panic.

I dashed down the last few steps, pushed hard with my shoulder against the door and burst into the car park. The door smashed behind me, and I ran towards my BMW. There were about a dozen other cars in the underground car park.

But no one else around; no other hospital staff.

As I approached my car, I heard the slam of the car park exit door. I stopped, turned sharply. The lighting was dim and shadowy, but I caught a fleeting glimpse, an outline of a figure. I called out, "Hello. Who's that? Who is it? Hello?"

This was way too close to my nightmare. I felt the panic rise inside my chest, my heart thumping. Hands trembling as I searched for the car keys. Eventually found them at the bottom of my handbag, pulled them out. I was just about to zap open the car, but my hands were so shaky I dropped the keys, bent, snatched them up.

I'd started to climb in the car when I saw the lights of a white car; could have been a Kia Sportage or a Qashqai, I wasn't sure. It was parked behind a pillar in a bay near the stair door, and the indicators flashed on and off as the driver's remote opened its doors. I heard the car door being tugged open and smash to and then the start of an engine.

I relaxed. The nightmare had really spooked me out. I was being silly, utterly ridiculous. I took a moment until my breathing eased, then started up the BMW, pushed it into reverse, but as I backed up, the warning reverse alarm started beeping urgently like a sprinter's heartbeat, faster and faster. I stamped on the brakes, glanced in the mirror.

The white car was half parked across the bay, blocking my way out. I couldn't see the driver.

I was confused. I pushed my fist on the horn. The car never moved. Pressed again, fist jammed on it until eventually the car pulled away.

I reversed quickly, glanced both ways. No sign of the car. Must have exited the car park.

I drove up the ramp onto the ground-floor exit, towards the barrier, half expecting the grille to be shut. It wasn't. But then as I pulled up at the barrier, I saw in the mirror that the white car was driving slowly towards me, its headlights on full beam, blinding me in the reflection. Panicked, my heart jumped. As I opened my window to slot in my pass, my hands shaking, I dropped it by the side of the car. I had to open the door, stretch down, grab the pass from the floor, before slamming the door.

In the rear-view mirror, the white car was inches behind me.

I stretched to slot in my pass, but the car bumped into the back of mine, jolting me, so I fumbled and missed the slot. I reached to slot the pass in again. The white car reversed and drove harder into my rear so I was shunted forward. But fortunately, the pass slipped in, and the barrier opened. I didn't wait to retrieve my pass – once the barrier rose, I squealed away.

Tyres screeching, I reached the junction, slamming the brakes on at the last second, all the time glancing in my mirror. As I turned right, slipping into the traffic out of Manchester and towards Didsbury, I caught a glimpse of the car as it emerged through the barrier. I accelerated, overtook a labouring Fiat Punto, eyes half on the road and half in the mirror. Then I saw the white car turn left at the junction away from me and towards Manchester city centre.

I indicated and pulled over, slowly blew in and out, controlling my breathing, calming myself until I relaxed, letting out a huge sigh of relief.

Sat at the side of the road, I rang Nick and told him of the incident.

"You're kidding?"

"No."

"Are you okay?" he asked, concerned.

"Bit shaken up. But physically I'm okay."

"D'you think I should call the police?" Nick offered.

I paused before answering. I'd thought about this before ringing Nick. But what could they do? I didn't see the car registration number, nor did I catch a glimpse of the driver, so I didn't know whether it was a man or a woman. It was a white car; that was all I knew. There was one CCTV camera positioned at the entrance to the car park, but this had been vandalised only the previous month and had not yet been repaired.

I explained all this to Nick.

"But why would someone do that to you?" he asked.

"No idea," I lied, my voice calm.

Except I wasn't calm, but I wasn't about to tell Nick my suspicions. After the disciplinary hearing and being confronted by Rick Walker's dad, where he accused me of negligence and made it very clear he thought I should be struck off, I was sure he'd begun stalking me. I felt instinctively that someone was watching me. I felt unease, a sense of foreboding. I never saw anyone. But I knew.

When I'd told Nick, he was somewhat dismissive.

"So you haven't actually seen anyone following you?" he'd asked.

"No, I just sense it."

"Right. Okay." He'd paused, thinking about it. "You know," he'd continued, "this whole disciplinary committee has really upset you, and I can't blame you. It's put you on edge. It was bound to. But I'm sure if someone was really following you, you'd have seen them."

So I wasn't now about to trust Nick's response to my being targeted and shunted. After a silence, Nick came up with a response. "Maybe the driver was pissed off because you were blasting your horn at them when they were – maybe accidentally? – blocking your car park space."

"It's possible, I suppose."

But I didn't believe it. So who could have done it? Who

had a grudge against me that would compel them to behave like that?

None of the staff at the Royal; none of my colleagues. I knew I was popular as a colleague and a friend.

So it had to be Rick Walker's father. There was no other explanation.

But then another thought struck me. Nick's previous girlfriend, Natasha, used to drive a white car. And she'd been totally obsessed with Nick.

But as quickly as I thought about it, I dismissed it. We'd been married a year, and Nick hadn't heard from Natasha in all that time.

I pondered this before concluding, no, it definitely had to be Rick Walker's dad. If so, I was determined to do something about it. I'd taken his abuse because I felt guilty when, in fact, I told myself for the millionth time, I had nothing to feel guilty about.

CHAPTER FIVE

We took a taxi into the centre of Manchester where Nick's office block was located. It was a forty-storey building in Deansgate Square, and the company occupied the first two floors. For tonight, they had hired out the roof terrace with its spectacular views of the city skyline.

Nick was wearing a dinner suit, bow tie with a white jacket; I wore a sleek black long dress. I supposed we looked the perfect couple.

As we climbed out of the taxi, Nick paid, and before we made our way into the foyer of the building, he took my hand, held me back. "Ellie, thanks for coming, I know you don't always enjoy these events," he said.

I thought that was nice, so I smiled and squeezed his hand as we approached the glass-fronted foyer, the double doors opening automatically.

The truth was, I totally hated social occasions like these. I smiled a lot, nodded, made the occasional non-controversial comment, but inside my guts were churning.

From the outside, no one would guess. No one could

guess the stress and heavy load I carried with me almost constantly. I rarely met any of Nick's colleagues socially, so when I did, I felt awkward; my smile stayed fixed, but I had little in common with them, so I found the small talk stilted.

The only time my inner cement mixer was calmed was when I was in theatre or talking to a patient about a diagnosis. Those were the times when I felt most comfortable, where I felt in total control.

My job meant everything to me.

Did it mean more than my relationship with Nick? It worried me that I was actually asking that question – especially after just over a year of marriage.

As these thoughts whirled round my head, I caught Nick staring at me as we entered the lift.

"You look miles away," he said.

"Work," I said with a tight smile.

The all-glass lift seemed to swallow us up as it shot straight to the roof terrace, where it spewed us out onto the expansive, impressive terrace. A waiter in a smart black suit, purple waistcoat and matching dickie bow met us.

"A glass of champagne, madam, sir?" he proffered from the tray of flutes he was holding.

We both smiled, nodded a thank you and took one each. The terrace was already busy. It was late September, and the evenings were already cool, so stainless-steel gas heaters, shaped like the Eiffel Tower, the bright flames shooting up their centres, were dotted around the terrace. Most people stood in small groups, around the warm bright glow, talking animatedly. There were several waiters, all dressed like Mr Champagne, some offering more bubbly, others carrying trays of canapés, striving to be unobtrusive while offering their tasters to the groups.

A six-piece jazz band played in the far corner.

I could see Nick's eyes darting round, head turning right and left as if he were watching a tennis match, taking in the huddled groups of guests, so I said, "Nick, why don't you go and circulate? I'll be fine. It's lovely up here. I'll just take in the views."

"Are you sure?" he answered.

"Of course. Go on. I'll join you later."

There was a hint of relief on his face. But I didn't mind; I was thankful to be on my own. "Thanks, Ellie. I'll just, you know, talk to some of my colleagues."

I smiled and watched him wander off to a group of smartly dressed young men and women in their twenties, who greeted him warmly. At the centre of the group was Nick's PA, Ursula. She was the same age as Nick, petite, bobbed hair, gaunt face with strong, fierce blue eyes. Intensely loyal to Nick, she'd been his PA long before Nick and I had started seeing each other. At first I'd been suspicious of their closeness but no longer. As Nick joined the group, Ursula kissed him on the cheek and hugged him longer than seemed necessary. Actually, I felt quite sorry for her. As far as I knew, she hadn't been in a relationship all the time she'd been Nick's PA. She obviously had a huge crush on him.

I wandered to the side of the terrace where I could look down across the vista of the city.

There was thick four-foot-high security glass around the whole terrace. But it didn't impair the views: they were stunning. Opposite I could see the Hilton, its forty-seven storeys dwarfing even this rooftop terrace. And far below me, the street lights glowed like fairy lights on a Christmas tree, while dinky-sized cars crawled bumper to bumper along

Deansgate. And weaving through the whole city was the thin grey ribbon of the Manchester Ship Canal.

I was taking all this in and didn't hear him approach me.

"Not thinking of throwing yourself off, are you?"

I spun round. It was Pete, my ex before Nick. He was holding two glasses of champagne.

I forced a sarcastic smile. "Pete, how lovely to see you!"

"I've always loved your sarcasm ... amongst other things." He offered me the spare glass of champagne. "Like another?"

I took it. "Thanks." And I placed my empty glass on a nearby chrome table.

"Has Nick abandoned you?" Pete asked.

"Not at all. I'm loving the views. And he's over there."

We both turned, and I pointed to the group Nick had approached earlier, but he was no longer there.

"Well, he was."

I scanned the terrace and spotted Nick in a corner, talking earnestly to a very beautiful woman in her early twenties, tall, willowy, long blonde hair. She seemed to be hanging on to his every word, her head nodding like a dog in the back window of a car. And when she replied, she was very tactile, touching his arm with each sentence.

Pete picked up my hint of disapproval. "Her name's Clarissa, joined our sales team two months ago, and already she's outselling all the men."

And I replied dryly, "I wonder how she manages that."

Pete laughed. "Meow." Then he paused, looked closely at me. "And how are you, Ellie?" he asked, like it was a loaded question.

"Okay," I told him, not wishing to expand the conversation.

"You look tired."

"I've had a long day in surgery."

So will you please go away and leave me alone, being the very clear subtext.

"Nick told me about the nightmares," Pete continued.

I blanched at the thought of Nick discussing me with Pete. *What else has he told him? I* thought. *How our sex life has dried up and it's all my fault?*

Then Pete leaned in close and whispered in my ear, "You never had nightmares when you were seeing me."

"Pete, *you* were my nightmare. My worst nightmare."

At this, he simply laughed loudly, his head rolling back. "Always loved your sense of humour."

"Thank you. Just trying to think exactly what I loved about you. Finding it difficult to come up with anything," I told him, no hint of a smile or sense of irony.

"Yeah, yeah, yeah," he replied.

"Nice talking to you."

I squeezed out a smile before turning my back on him and returning to scan the glittering Manchester skyline.

God, I thought, *how could I ever have fallen for that creep?*

CHAPTER SIX

TWO YEARS EARLIER

I was hosting a dinner party in my open-plan penthouse with its floor-to-ceiling windows, bifold doors and large wrap-around balcony.

Sitting with me round the black gloss dining table were Pete and, opposite him, Nick with his girlfriend, Natasha, who was leaning into Nick, her arm draped across his shoulders, occasionally stroking his hair. She had flame-red hair, wild but beautiful, with a pretty slightly freckled face covered by heavy make-up. But it was her eyes that were most striking, green and startling.

Pete was in full flow, telling a story.

I knew I looked slightly bored, which I was, as I'd heard the story several times.

"So it was my sister's leaving party, and course it was full of medical people, and I saw this gorgeous woman standing in a group of doctor types ..."

I rolled my eyes.

"Well, you are gorgeous, Ellie," Natasha complimented.

"Oh, thank you, Natasha."

"So I chatted to my sister, got the lowdown on her, and when I went into the kitchen for another drink, I pounced. Introduced myself ... you know ... with that killer smile ..."

I did a big overreacting yawn. Everyone laughed. But the yawn was actually genuine. In truth, the story says more about Pete than me. Over the years, I'd had a string of boyfriends, but they mostly fell into a very similar category: they had false charm, huge confidence but basically were downright shallow. Pete was one of them.

I knew what my problem was in attracting the "wrong" type of man; it was only the good-looking, narcissistic charmers who had the confidence to approach me. I supposed I was sort of ... aloof ... a bit intimidating. It was only men like Pete who found my demeanour a challenge they couldn't resist. It was a persona I had created in my late teens, an extra layer I thought might protect against the all-enveloping blackness inside me. It didn't. All it did was place an emotional barrier between me and the outside world.

I grew bored of these types of men very quickly. I was now bored with Pete. He was not only a terrible flatterer but also an incorrigible flirt. He was great on big romantic gestures like whisking me off to Paris on a whim – without first checking whether I was on call all weekend. It was like being a passenger in a Ferrari with no seat belt being driven by someone who was high on one too many glasses of champagne ... exhilarating, scary and ultimately too exhausting.

And recently he'd tried to persuade me to do something that totally nauseated me.

Pete's voice droned on. "So I told Ellie I was head of sales for an advertising company but admired anyone working in the NHS and said to her, 'I know, with your shifts at the hospital, you often work weekends ... but are you free this weekend?' And she said ..."

Pete paused, looked at me to pick up the story. But I was miles away.

"Ellie ...?"

"Er, sorry ...?"

"It's your line, when I asked if you were free that weekend, you said, 'That's a bold' ... go on ..." he encouraged.

I gave a huge inward sigh. "That's a bold ... that's a bold question coming from a man who's obviously very shy."

Pete laughed and continued, "Typical sarcastic Ellie. So I said, 'Jan told me you were single. Which amazed me. So I thought I'd better make a move quickly ...'"

Why did I fall for such corn? I thought.

"So then I said, 'Are you free this Saturday?' And she answered, 'Probably not,' and I said, 'Oh, that's a shame cos I've got two tickets to see Lady Gaga at the Manchester Arena, and my mate Nick can't make it.' Jan had told me Ellie loved Lady Gaga."

Natasha laughed. This story was for her because Nick had also heard it.

"But the thing was, Natasha, I actually didn't have any tickets, I don't really like Lady Gaga, and I had to spend a fortune buying two tickets off a tout!"

Pete roared with laughter at his own story; Natasha joined him.

Nick and I shared a look, and Nick raised one eyebrow that made me smile.

"Best money I ever spent!" Pete finished.

When they stopped smiling and laughing, Natasha spoke up.

"Nick and I are thinking of going to Venice this Easter."

"Really?" I replied. "Have you been before?"

"No. Neither of us."

I noticed as Nick shifted uncomfortably in his seat, eased slightly away from Natasha.

"You'll like it," I said.

"Is it as romantic as they say?" Natasha asked.

"Depends who you go with," Pete answered with a twinkle.

"Exactly!" Natasha replied, her green eyes bright. "We're really looking forward to it, aren't we, Nick?"

"It's not definite yet," he said, an edge of unease in his voice.

"Yes, it is; we agreed."

"Well, not exactly."

Natasha's green eyes narrowed; the brightness disappeared as she looked across the table to me and Pete.

"And do you know why we're going?"

Pete and I shook our heads. This was starting to feel uncomfortable.

"Shall we tell them, Nick?"

Nick looked puzzled. "Tell them what?"

Natasha looked round the table, again to bring in me and Pete. "The surprise!" she cried out like a game show host.

A confused Nick stumbled, "Errr …"

"I'll tell them." Natasha paused for effect. "The reason we're going to Venice … the reason is … to celebrate our engagement!"

She looked around at us all as if waiting for applause.

"Really?" I replied. "Wow."

Nick looked totally ill at ease as Pete said, "You kept that quiet, mate."

"Listen—" Nick started before being interrupted by Natasha.

"No, no, let me finish, sweetheart. You're the first people we've told. I wasn't going to say anything yet ... but I'm so excited, and you're our very best friends ..."

That was news to me. My best friends were all health workers.

Natasha then reached down under the table to retrieve her handbag, and as she opened it, she said, "So I wanted to share it with you ..."

She took out a ring box.

I could see the panic in Nick's eyes as he warned, "No, Natasha. Stop. Don't do this."

But Natasha ignored him. "And this is my engagement ring! Da-daaaa!"

And she opened the box to reveal a white gold ring encrusted with a sapphire surrounded by a cluster of small diamonds.

But then everyone's attention was on Nick as he suddenly let out a huge groan, covered his face with his hands and spluttered, "Oh for fuck's sake!"

Pete and I looked at each other, both of us confused and slightly embarrassed.

Natasha immediately chided, "Nick!"

I was squirming. Then Pete asked, "What's going on?"

"We're not engaged," Nick said firmly.

"We are!" Natasha shouted back.

I could see that Nick was trying desperately to stay calm as he answered firmly, "Natasha, we're not. And we're not going to Venice."

Natasha exploded, her green eyes flashing, "Oh yes, we are!"

"We're not," Nick replied, still composed.

But Natasha continued to rant as Pete and I looked on in horror. "We are! I've booked the flights!"

At this, Nick was thrown. "You're kidding," he said bluntly. Then he turned to the rest of the table. "This is the first I know about it. And she bought the ring herself."

"Nick!" Natasha screamed, her voice a warning.

"She did."

"Did you?" Pete asked, with his usual tactless bluntness.

Natasha simply let rip in a high-pitched shriek, "WE ARE ENGAGED! And we're getting married in the summer!"

Nick didn't flinch. He waited until he was sure Natasha wasn't continuing her rant; then when he did speak, he was composed, his voice firm.

"Natasha, I've told you I don't want to get engaged. I certainly don't want to get married. In fact, for the last few weeks I've been trying to finish with you, but you won't listen; you're in complete denial. So I'm saying this now in front of my friends so that they're witnesses. Natasha, you and I are finished. Full stop."

Nick had hardly stopped speaking when Natasha snatched up the cheese knife that lay on the bread board next to her and screamed, "NOOOOOOO!"

And she rammed the long, sharp blade of the knife into the cheeseboard, where it stood upright, quivering like an arrow.

The room fell silent in total shock and huge embarrassment. Natasha was breathing heavily, her shoulders heaving up and down, head bowed, staring into her lap.

No one spoke for some time.

I thought, *This is the last dinner party I'm ever having,*

before reaching across the table and tugging the knife from the cheeseboard, out of Natasha's reach.

Finally, Natasha lifted her face. She looked calmer, like all the fight had left her.

"I'm sorry," she began, her voice soft. "I apologise." She paused briefly before continuing, "I apologise for Nick's rude behaviour." She stood up. "Come on, Nick, I think we need to go home."

And she stared down at him. Nick didn't move. His head was bent, staring at the cheeseboard in shock and disbelief.

"Nick, I'm talking to you; don't ignore me," she said, speaking rather like a teacher to a naughty pupil. When Nick didn't reply or move, Natasha continued, "Nick, we need to talk about this at home ... sort it out ... the misunderstanding."

Without looking up, Nick mumbled, "It's no misunderstanding."

"Of course it's a misunderstanding. And if we go now and talk about it privately, I'll forgive you ... for how you're behaving in front of our friends."

Nick didn't answer. Pete and I continued to be utterly mortified, our eyes fixed, staring down at the tabletop as if all answers to the world's problems lay before us.

"Just going to ignore me, are you?" Natasha went on. "You know you're showing us up in front of our friends, don't you?"

Nick had been motionless throughout this exchange, but now he jerked to life, like a puppet whose strings have suddenly been pulled, and he stood up, looked across at Pete.

"Pete, can I stay at your place tonight?" he asked.

This was a dilemma Pete wasn't expecting.

"Er ... yeah. Yeah, I suppose. I mean, yeah, course you can," he managed to answer.

But now the volcanic rage inside Natasha erupted once again.

"No! No, no, no!" she screamed.

Nick stayed calm. "I've had enough, Natasha. Enough. We're finished. I want you to move out of my place in the next twenty-four hours."

"No! Don't do this to me. Please, Nick, please don't do this to me."

I listened as Natasha's tone changed abruptly from anger to pleading, and she looked helpless, lost.

I watched her face as it crumbled, and suddenly she looked like a child. And my heart went out to her. She must love Nick so much. Maybe not a healthy love, maybe obsessive, but there was no doubt the passion she felt for Nick.

I had never felt such passion for any man in the whole of my life.

"I'm sorry, but I need you to move your things out, Natasha," Nick insisted.

Natasha pleaded some more. "No! I love you, Nick. I really love you."

"I'm sorry, Natasha, this isn't working," Nick continued, unmoved by her desperate pleas. "So you need to move your clothes out, back into your own flat."

You never know what goes on inside a relationship, and maybe, I thought, Nick was acting so cold and detached because, as he said, Natasha wouldn't listen to him. And if it was true, how desperate was it for Natasha to go out and buy her own engagement ring? I felt a surge of pity for her. I couldn't fathom what was going on between them, but it was pretty uncomfortable viewing.

Nick was now standing. He nodded to Pete. "Come on."

Nick walked towards the door. Pete stood, followed, paused and turned back to me. "I'll ring you tomorrow."

I nodded.

But now Natasha ran to Nick and grabbed hold of him, trying to hug him, all the time screaming, "NO! I love you!" He managed to push her away, and he and Pete were about to make their escape when to my absolute horror Natasha ran to the patio doors, slid them open, rushed to the balcony and started to climb on the railing.

"Oh shit!" Nick mumbled. "Holy fuck."

The three of us ran after Natasha, following her out on to the balcony. Natasha was balanced precariously on the railing, holding on to an upright metal post.

"Natasha, come on, get down from there," I said firmly, looking up at her.

"No. Not until Nick apologises. Not until he tells me he's sorry and we're going home together," Natasha demanded, her eyes not meeting mine.

"Natasha, stop being so bloody dramatic and get down from there," Nick snapped.

"I'll jump, I will," Natasha threatened. "I'll jump."

"You won't," Nick said.

"I will. Unless you promise—"

"I'm not promising anything," Nick interrupted.

"Okay, then I'll jump."

Nick didn't reply at first. Eventually he nodded and said, "Okay, Natasha. Go on. Jump."

I saw the confusion and panic in Natasha's eyes. This wasn't the response she'd expected from Nick.

"Go on. Do it." Nick challenged her.

I was alarmed, not sure that was the right thing to say to her. "Nick ..." I warned. "Please."

"No, I'm not having this," he said, his voice rational and steady. "We're finished, Natasha. Let me make myself quite clear ... we're finished. If you want to jump ... you go ahead. But threatening me, blackmailing me, it won't work. So if you want to jump, you jump."

And then Pete spoke, also alarmed. "Christ, Nick!"

"I mean it, Natasha. Go ahead and jump."

Natasha was completely thrown, uncertain. I looked at Nick, then glanced at Natasha. "Natasha," I urged as kindly as I could, "please don't listen to Nick. Do not jump. Please, please come down from there. But do not jump."

A moment, then Natasha's defiance seemed to crumble. I edged closer towards her as she started to shake, tears streaming down her cheeks.

I was now within arm's length of her. I held out my hand.

"Take my hand, Natasha."

Natasha shook her head. She peered down over the edge.

"Do not look down!" I barked. "Just take my hand. Natasha, look at me."

She shook her head again.

But then without a second's warning, Nick leaped forward, and before Natasha could react, he'd grabbed her round the waist and dragged her off the rail.

Natasha started screaming and kicking, lashing out. But Nick didn't flinch; he simply pulled her back inside. Pete and I followed, and I locked the terrace doors.

CHAPTER SEVEN

Nick and Pete had left without further drama.

Natasha blew her nose on a tissue before she said, "God knows what you think of me."

I had no answer to that.

"I'm not crazy, you know. I know that was a stupid, crazy thing to do, and it was pathetic, but ... I love Nick. I've never felt like this about anyone. And I know I'm my own worst enemy. I'm possessive, I know I'm possessive, but I can't help it."

I really did feel sorry for her. I nodded and squeezed her hand.

"You know how you told me you've had vivid nightmares on and off for most of your adult life?" Natasha asked, and I nodded, wondering where this was going. "I have nightmares too. About Nick. About him leaving me. And they're so real."

"I'm sorry, Natasha. Nightmares are horrible especially when they are so intense and vivid," I answered sympathetically.

Then Natasha asked a very weird question. "Have you ever killed someone in your nightmare?"

"Er, no. Never," I answered cautiously.

"I have. I've killed Nick."

My eyes widened, and I didn't know what to say.

The silence was broken as a phone rang in the bathroom. My phone was lying on the table, so I was confused as to whose phone it could be. When I went into the bathroom, I saw the phone lying on the edge of the bath. It was Pete's.

I answered it. "Hello."

It was Nick, and he said, "As you guessed, Pete's left his phone behind."

"Okay, Nick. I'll take it into the Royal tomorrow, so he can pick it up from there."

There was a pause before Nick asked, "How's Natasha?"

"Calmer," I answered.

"Thanks, Ellie. Sorry we ruined your evening."

"It's okay," I answered grudgingly, because to be honest, it wasn't okay at all.

I hung up, and when I returned to the living space, the room was empty.

Natasha had gone, and the front door was left open.

Then I saw, lying on the dining table, scrawled on a paper napkin:

Sorry, Ellie. And thank you for listening. You're a good friend.

I went across to shut the door, and as I did, Pete's phone pinged.

It was a text. I glanced at it. It was from someone called "Leah":

> Thanks for last night. Let's do it again sometime. Coen.

The bastard, I thought. Ironically I was going to finish with him last weekend after what he tried to make me do, but I'm so bloody polite that I put it off because of this dinner party we'd already got lined up. I'm so stupid; I should have followed my instincts.

Then an idea hit me.

I emailed him and suggested the next day we go for Sunday lunch in Didsbury, where I'd return his phone before I went into work. He emailed me from his laptop about an hour later. He said he couldn't wait.

Nor could I.

THE ROYAL OAK was buzzing when I arrived. Pete was already there, and he smiled and stood and was about to kiss me when I pulled away. He frowned as if to ask what was wrong. I took out his phone.

"I've left a message for you." His brow furrowed, confused. "Listen, I'll play it to you."

I put it on speaker and turned the volume up to full.

"Hi, Pete. I don't know who Leah is, and I don't care, and I'm not finishing with you because you've been shagging her …"

The tables nearby fell deadly quiet. Pete looked alarmed, speechless.

"No, the reason I'm finishing with you is because of what you wanted to do to me last weekend. It made me feel sick. You are a disgusting low-life sleaze bag."

And with that, I threw his phone onto his lap, turned and walked calmly but briskly between the silent tables.

I could sense everyone thinking, "What the hell did he do to her?"

CHAPTER EIGHT

Around two months after I finished with Pete, I received a phone call. "Hi, Ellie, it's Nick here."

"Hello, Nick, this is a surprise."

"Yeah. Been meaning to ring for a bit. Look, I'm sorry about you and Pete …"

"It's okay … er, what did he tell you?" I asked tentatively but intrigued.

"He said he'd met someone else, so he finished with you."

I gave a wry smile to myself. "Oh, did he?"

"Anyway, I'm sorry … I'm sorry for the way he treated you. It wasn't right. I mean, you didn't deserve that. You deserved more respect."

Nick was hesitant. And I couldn't understand why he was suddenly ringing me up, expressing sympathy two months later.

"Thank you," I answered without explaining the truth. And then there was silence on the line before I asked, "Nick, are you still there?"

"Yeah, sorry." He sounded nervous. "Hmm, I was

wondering ... I was wondering if you fancied going for a drink?"

I wasn't expecting that. I eventually answered, "How's Natasha? Did she move out?"

"Yes," Nick replied. "She's moved back into her flat, with her friend."

"And she's accepted that it's all over between you?" I asked.

Nick hesitated before adding, "I need someone to talk to, Ellie. Please come for a drink. I'll tell you all about it."

We met on a quiet Monday night in a pub around the corner from the hospital, which was convenient for me, as I'd been working late. When I arrived, Nick was already sitting in a corner, a full pint in front of him. He stood up as soon as I entered, an anxious smile breaking out on his face.

"Thanks for coming, Ellie; what would you like?"

"Dry white wine, thanks, Nick."

Once he'd returned with my wine, he raised his pint, and we chinked glasses and said cheers before I asked, "That night round at my place. Did you really know Natasha wouldn't jump?"

"Of course. I wouldn't have told her to jump if I'd thought there was any chance she would."

I nodded, smiled. I was relieved. It had been playing on my mind.

"I'd only been going out with her for just over four months," Nick continued. "And the first month was great. She was brilliant. We had a fantastic time. But then she moved in with me, sort of by stealth, and it slowly changed."

"In what way?"

"I suddenly had no space, no breathing room. Like if I didn't get back home from work at the same time every day, she'd want to know where I'd been, what I was doing. And working in sales, you never know when you'll finish. Plus at the end of the day, I'd want to unwind, go for a pint with the guys from work. She didn't like that."

"Did you talk to her about it? Sort of ... confront it?"

He shrugged. "Well, yeah."

"And?"

"She never listened. Or she'd say, 'Fine, yes,' agree with me, and then the next day would be no different. And it quickly got worse. I couldn't go out anywhere without her. She became so possessive, jealous, controlling, I felt completely stifled. And I thought, I've got to sort this; I've got to get her out of my life."

It was at this moment that the door of the pub swung open. It was so quiet in the bar, we heard the smash of the door, and automatically we both looked across.

Natasha had just entered.

"Shit," Nick mouthed.

Natasha didn't look across at us. She strode across to the bar, ordered a gin and tonic. Then after she paid, she took a sip of her drink, sat on a bar stool and swivelled round in our direction. She raised her glass to us and then never took her eyes off us, her face expressionless.

Nick spoke first, in a whisper. "She's been doing this ever since we split up. I knew she was following me earlier, but I thought I'd lost her."

"Obviously not. D'you want to leave?" I asked.

"I won't be intimidated by her," Nick answered. "Let's finish our drinks, take our time; then we leave."

But as the minutes ticked by, sipping on my wine, I felt increasingly uncomfortable. It was difficult to hold a conversation especially as Natasha did not take her eyes off us for one second. As soon as I finished the final drop of my wine, I stood up.

As Nick stood, he said, "I'll see you outside. I'm having a word with her. This has to stop."

I was determined to follow his example, to not be intimidated. I walked slowly to the door, edging between the empty tables. I didn't look at Natasha, but as I pulled open the bar door, I sneaked a glance over my shoulder.

Nick was at the bar, his face pushed close to Natasha, talking quietly, his finger emphasising each word. Natasha wasn't answering. She didn't say a word. Her haughty defiance seemed to have drained away from her entire body.

Nick was only a minute, and when he emerged from the bar, his cheeks were flushed.

I said, "I'm going home. I'm not getting involved in any of this. Ring me; we'll arrange a drink another time."

"Ellie, I'm so sorry," he said.

"It's okay," I answered.

"Do you need a taxi or …?"

"No. I'm fine."

He nodded, hesitated, raised his hand in an awkward gesture of goodbye, and we both turned and walked in opposite directions.

I walked quickly, shoulders slightly hunched against the rain that had just started. I took a quick glance behind me as I rounded a corner. No sign of Natasha. I didn't think she'd follow me rather than follow Nick, but with her obsessive, jealous nature, it was still a possibility.

It was quiet, and my heels echoed on the wet pavement. I turned right, and I could see my block of flats at the end of the road, looming up over the rows of modern terraced houses.

My pace quickened as I neared my apartment block. My phone rang in my pocket. I took it out. It was Penny, but I didn't take the call. My mind was too loaded with the events in the pub.

I started to cross the road.

A car horn blasted.

I jumped back on the kerb, heart thumping, almost tripping up on my heels.

I saw that the car was a white Kia Sportage.

As the car swept past, the driver waved a friendly hand at me.

Natasha.

CHAPTER NINE

I weaved my way between the guests, passing a waiter and swapping my second empty glass for a full flute before heading towards the far side, where Nick was still talking to Clarissa. Out of the corner of his eye, Nick saw me approaching, and he pulled away from Clarissa, smiling in my direction. "Clarissa," he said, "I'd like you to meet my beautiful wife, Ellie."

Clarissa turned: huge, fixed smile, perfectly white even teeth, high cheekbones, startling blue eyes. "Lovely to meet you, Ellie," she said as she offered her hand.

I smiled, took her hand. It was as limp as a fish.

"Clarissa's only been with us a couple of months."

"So I believe," I replied. "Pete was telling me."

"Oh right." Nick smiled awkwardly before adding, "Shall we get some nibbles?"

"Lovely," I said, forcing a smile and turning to Clarissa. "Nice to meet you."

THE REST of the evening passed in a haze. As was so often the case on occasions like these, where I knew very few people, I drank too much. I had vague memories of stilted conversations with Nick's dull colleagues and a particularly strained exchange with Nick's boss, Craig, and his wife, Gwen, both late forties, he with a perma-tan, Gwen with a tight, doll-like face from an unsubtle overuse of Botox and fillers.

By ten o'clock I was quite drunk, very tired and needed to go home.

We were standing in a group of young people who worked with Nick. The chat was all work-based, and I zoned out. I felt like a partially deaf person listening to a conversation with their hearing aid switched off; I was in a foggy, indistinct layer of meaningless words. Without realising it, I let out a huge yawn, and as the circle of faces turned in my direction, wrenching me out of my inner world, I said quickly, "Oh sorry. I'm so sorry, I've been in surgery since nine this morning, and I think it's just caught up with me."

Nick turned to me. "D'you want me to take you home, Ellie?"

"No, no," I replied. "It's too early but ..." I paused. "But would you mind if I went back?" My head turned a 180-degree circle, taking in the surrounding faces. "I am so sorry. It's such a great evening, I feel really bad ..." Then I turned back to face Nick. "But you stay on. I'll get a taxi home," I told him.

I could see Nick was unsure what he should do. I knew he wanted to stay longer, but he probably felt bad about not coming home with me.

In the end he said, "Are you sure?"

"Absolutely, Nick. You stay. I insist."

IT WAS ONLY when Nick was helping me into the lift and I slightly stumbled that I realised how deeply drunk I was. He'd ordered a cab on his account, and it was waiting outside the entrance. He opened the passenger door, took my arm to guide me in, and once I'd slumped back in the seat, he slammed the door and waved me goodbye.

The taxi pulled away, swept past a white car, and I glanced out the window and locked eyes with the driver, who smiled at me.

It was Natasha. In the same Kia Sportage as before.

I hadn't seen her in over a year. What was she doing parked outside Nick's workplace? Was it merely a coincidence or something more sinister? Surely she couldn't still be obsessed with Nick after all this time.

I quickly convinced myself it must have been a weird coincidence, and within two minutes my eyelids drooped, my head lolled. With the mixture of alcohol, extreme weariness and the motion of the taxi, I slipped into a shallow sleep, and the outside world became a foggy echo.

I WAS JOLTED awake by the blast of the horn and the slam of brakes. I was disorientated at first, my eyes taking seconds to focus. It appeared a car had jumped the lights, cutting across the taxi.

I was unnerved, but I settled back into my seat, fully awake now as I squinted my eyes, peered out the window to see how far from home I was.

But I didn't recognise the road. From Manchester, we should have been travelling along the busy Wilmslow Road, past the university, through Fallowfield, Withington and then into Didsbury. But this road was quiet. There were hardly any cars.

I leaned forward to talk to the driver. "Excuse me. Where are we?"

The driver peered through his mirror at me, his eyes dark and unresponsive. Silence.

I tried again, my voice a little slurry. "Sorry, I don't recognise this area; can you please tell me where we are?"

Again he didn't answer. I glanced at my watch. It was nearly eleven o'clock. Didn't Nick put me in the taxi just after ten? Something was wrong. Even in rush hour it shouldn't take longer than thirty minutes or so to reach Didsbury. I leaned forward again, tapped on his window. "Can you answer me, please? I should be home by now; where are we?"

When he didn't answer, I felt pure panic rising. Suddenly the car swung off the road, and I was flung sideways. Now he was driving up a narrow, bumpy track. I started banging on his window with my fist. "Where are we? Where are you taking me?"

Ahead, the track widened out, and in front of me I could see a derelict warehouse, black against the sky, its windows smashed or cracked, the roof half collapsed. In my panic, I pulled on the door handle, but it was locked. My breathing quickened, I was half crying, half screaming as the driver suddenly stamped on the brakes. I almost fell off my seat but then tugged again on the door handle. If I could escape before the driver climbed out, I could make a dash. But the door was still locked.

The driver was out now. He seemed big, over six feet, thick set. He tugged his hoodie up before he opened the door.

I started screaming.

"Who are you?" I shouted. "Who are you? What d'you want?"

CHAPTER TEN

Even now, after all these years, everything is so clear. I can't actually remember how long I was unconscious, but when I came to, I was still covered by my clothes. My right arm was really throbbing, and when I touched it, the whole of my pyjama sleeve felt warm and sticky.

Before I dared move, I listened. There was no sound throughout the house. Total silence. So slowly, I pulled the bundle of clothes off me, sat up and peered out from the wardrobe into my bedroom, where the ceiling light was still switched on.

Then I saw him lying in front of the wardrobe. His body was like ... twisted. I couldn't see his face, but the gun was lying next to his body. I crawled out of the wardrobe on all fours and stood up, wincing at the pain in my arm.

Oh, God.

I looked down at my father's body, and I gasped. He was unrecognisable. The whole of the front of his face was ... well, it was ... it was just a mass of red flesh. His nose was gone, but his eyes were still there, vacant and scary, as if shocked at what he'd done.

I didn't feel upset. In fact I was glad. I was glad he was dead. Because I hated him. I'd hated him from the moment I had feelings. And he'd tried to kill me. He'd never loved me. What sort of person wants to kill their only child? He was a monster.

I suddenly remembered my mother. I skirted round my father's body, noticed the wall behind him, blood splattered like a Jackson Pollock painting (though obviously I had no idea who Jackson Pollock was at eleven years of age). I left my bedroom; I walked up the corridor to my parents' bedroom. I realised my arm was dripping blood and leaving a trail of dotted red spots behind me.

The pyjama sleeve on my upper arm had been ripped by the bullet. I cautiously pulled up the sleeve until I could see my wound. There was a red ridge of flesh that was oozing blood. The bullet must have just grazed me. I pulled down the sleeve and carried on towards my mother's bedroom.

The door was open, and when I entered, I immediately saw her lying there in a heap, a large hole in her chest, surrounded by a pool of her own blood. Her eyes were shut, and her arms spread wide in a crucified position. Despite the gory scene, she looked peaceful as if in sleep, as if she had invited her death.

For a second I felt tears prickling my eyes, though I didn't let out a sound. She'd been kinder than my father. But she hadn't protected me. She'd never stood up for me. She was weak. I wiped away the one tear that had managed to escape.

And in that moment I made a decision. I wouldn't be weak. I wouldn't be like her. Yes, I was alone now, but I'd stay strong. And I'd think only of myself. I would be selfish. If I was to survive, I needed to be selfish. And I would do anything to survive. Nothing would stop me.

I had to get out of the house. I needed help. I took one last look at my mother, went downstairs, pulled on my trainers, which I'd left by the front door, and grabbed my duffel coat from the stand in the hall. I could slip only my left arm in the coat, as my right arm was too painful to move. I pulled the coat over my right shoulder and left the house. I remember I didn't lock up.

Outside, the air was cold and the road down to the village slippery. I ran as fast as I could, gripping my right arm. I nearly fell a couple of times.

I knew where I was going. I'd glanced at the clock in the hall before I left. It was almost 1.30 a.m. I would make my way down the hill to the village hall, where the New Year's Eve party was about to finish.

The village hall was at the far end of the cottages on the right next to the church. As I got closer, I could hear the live music.

I could see a group of people standing outside the hall, some smoking, others standing with drinks. I ran quicker, and when I was closer, I started screaming for help. I screamed as loud as I could, and I saw all their heads turn to me. I saw the panic on their faces. I saw two of the men run towards me, and as they reached me, I collapsed at their feet.

Over the years, from the moment my father shot me, I've played the scenario again and again in my head and in my dreams. I've never been able to leave it behind.

THE SLEEPWALKER   67

WHEN I WOKE, *I wasn't sure where I was. I looked around and recognised the mullion windows. I'd seen them many times from the outside.*

I was in the rectory. Someone had changed me into pyjamas that weren't my own. I felt the throbbing in my arm, and I pulled up the sleeve on the pyjamas. My wound had been bandaged up.

The curtains were open, and the sun was streaming in. It was a beautiful New Year's morning. And I thought, I'm safe now.

The door opened, and I quickly shut my eyes, but in that split second I recognised the people who had entered. It was the vicar and his wife, Keith and Vicky.

They were kind people. I'd met the vicar at the church when the school held their Christmas and Easter services. He was good-hearted and funny, and his wife helped out at school when she wasn't working in Manchester as a nurse at the Royal. I had always fantasised about being their child rather than my real parents' child.

The only problem was, they had a daughter. Her name was Rachel, and she was in my class, and she was the meanest girl in the school. I could never understand how a girl like Rachel could have parents who were so warm and gentle. She didn't deserve them.

The vicar and his wife started talking about me, whispering. I can't remember exactly what they said, but they were clearly feeling really sorry for me and were appalled at what my parents had done. They were worried about what was going to happen to me. They seemed to think I might be taken into care, and I remember I wanted to open my eyes and scream, "No!" But then one of them, I'm not sure if it was the vicar or his wife, suggested they could take me in. And I wanted to say, "Yes, yes, please yes."

A bit later a police officer came to interview me (he was the kind local policeman who always gave road safety and Stranger Danger talks at our school). I told him the story exactly as it happened.

Vicky and Keith returned. Vicky sat on the edge of the bed, took my hand and explained how they would like me to move in with them, if Social Services agreed, and how would I feel about that? And I burst into tears, and Vicky hugged me tightly in a way I had never been hugged in all my life.

When I eventually pulled away, I asked if Rachel would be okay about me moving in, and they said she'd be fine.

But I knew she wouldn't be fine.

That night I heard them talking to Rachel, and I crept out on to the landing where I could hear the conversation. Rachel was shouting and saying she wasn't having "that weird kid" living with them.

Then I heard the vicar speak, and he said something about God and being kind and loving. Next I heard the door slam as Rachel stormed out of the house, shouting that she was going to leave home.

I hope you do, I thought as I snuck back to my bed.

BUT RACHEL DIDN'T MOVE OUT, and in front of her parents, she was as sweet as anything to me. But when we were alone, when we were in school together, she was nasty.

But everything was about to change.

It was February, and I'd been living there for two months.

I was in the rectory garden, sitting on a bench next to the pond. I loved it there, as it was so peaceful.

It was late afternoon when I heard her approaching, and she started on me in that mean voice of hers. So I told her to leave me alone, but, instead, she pushed me. Two hands against my chest, and I fell over. I got up and told her not to do it again.

But she pushed me harder and laughed. And I thought, I'm not having that, so I went to her and pushed her in the chest with all my strength, and she fell backwards. Her legs hit the low stone wall that surrounded the pond, and she toppled over into the water. In the centre of the pond was a stone ornament of two angels, and the back of her head smashed against one of the angels. There was a moment's look of surprise in her eyes before they closed, and her head disappeared under the water. She didn't fight or flap her arms around because, I realised, she was unconscious, and the rest of her body sank, almost in slow motion.

I watched. I was pleased. It served her right. I continued to watch, and I waited. Her head didn't surface. When I thought I had waited long enough, I started screaming.

CHAPTER ELEVEN

It was around one thirty when Nick arrived home to find me sitting up in bed, wide awake but in deep shock. My breaths came short and fast as if I was gasping for oxygen. My face was screwed up in confusion, eyes wild, hysterical, my body shaking, and rivulets of black mascara streaked my cheeks.

Nick put his arms round me, cuddled me, then asked, concerned, "What is it, Ellie? What's happened? Another nightmare?"

I shook my head vigorously.

"So what is it?" he asked again.

I shook my head once more, slowly this time.

"Please, Ellie," Nick implored. "Please tell me?"

Finally, in a whispered voice like a frightened little girl, I said, "Nick, I've been sexually assaulted."

Nick's face was a picture of shock. It was the shock of disbelief. And I knew exactly what he was thinking. That it was a nightmare. That it never actually happened. But I also knew he'd play along with me so as not to upset me. That was why, when he spoke, it was a gentle probing.

"How, Ellie? How did it happen?"

So, in a small, patient voice, I explained how the taxi driver didn't take me straight home but had driven to a deserted warehouse. How he stopped, dragged me from the taxi and pulled me screaming into the derelict building. And I described how he threw me on the ground, and that was when I passed out.

Nick was looking at me, nodding sympathetically. Eventually he asked, "You said when you passed out, but don't you really mean when you woke up?"

There! I knew it! It was the wrong thing to say.

My voice rose. "No, this wasn't a dream, Nick, it was real!"

"Are you absolutely sure, Ellie, because it does sound like one of your nightmares?" Nick continued to speak gently.

I was frustrated at Nick's lack of understanding about the gravity of what had happened to me, and I yelled at him, "Did you not hear me, Nick? I've been sexually abused, possibly raped! It wasn't a fucking dream!"

"Okay, okay," Nick apologised. "But just think about it … I mean how … how did you get home?"

"I … I don't know! I was unconscious! Stop!" I raised my palm. "This is exactly why most women don't go to the police when they've been raped, cos no one believes them! But you're my husband, the least I can expect is some fucking support and understanding!"

My voice was high-pitched, angry, frustrated. Then, just as suddenly, my anger dissolved into a flood of tears.

Nick looked so hopeless. Out of his depth.

He let me cry. The heaving and gasping eventually eased, and he put his arm gently round me.

But he didn't know what to say to me.

His brow was creased up in confusion. So he asked tentatively, "What ... what I don't understand, I still don't understand ... how, how you did you get home? Surely the taxi driver didn't, didn't drop you off, not after he ...?"

I turned my head away, unable to answer. I didn't know how I'd got home. Maybe ... maybe afterwards ... he put me back into his taxi, took me home and ... I didn't know. So I said nothing.

"Ellie, darling." Nick spoke again softly. "Darling, honestly, don't get mad at me, but honestly, it has to be a dream."

"You don't believe me? Are you saying I'm fucking lying?"

"No ..."

"Are you saying I'm making all this up? It wasn't a fucking dream, Nick. Just get that into your stupid head." I was almost spitting at him I was so angry. "For the last time, it wasn't a dream!"

"Okay, okay." Nick raised both palms up, placating me, before adding, "I'm sorry. I'm sorry, Ellie, but I'm confused."

I'd had enough. I rolled back the duvet and lifted my legs over the side of the bed.

"What are you doing?"

"I can't sleep here. If my own husband doesn't believe me, I'm not sharing a bed with him."

"Ellie, please no."

But I blanked him, trailing out of the bedroom and smashing the door behind me.

I WENT into the spare room, but my sleep was restless and disturbed. Ghost images of the shadowy figure dragging me from the taxi invaded my dreams, replaying and replaying as if caught in a loop of terror. I knew I should go to the police, but if my husband didn't believe me, why would they?

I awoke around five in the morning, confused, uncertain where I was, until the previous evening came back to me.

No matter how hard I tried, I couldn't return to sleep. I sat up, propped myself up on two pillows. I needed to clarify my thoughts, assess what had happened and how it had happened. I had to hold it together better than last night with Nick when he got home. I needed to be objective and not be swamped by the overwhelming raw emotions that I'd exposed to Nick.

I turned it over and over in my head. How could I have been so drunk that I couldn't remember how I arrived home? I couldn't remember how I even opened my front door or found my way to bed. How could that happen?

And then it struck me. And when it did, it seemed so obvious.

I must have been slipped flunitrazepam – Rohypnol – the so-called "date rape" drug. And when I started thinking back to the evening at the party, the moment when it had all started jumped out at me.

Pete had slipped it in my champagne before he handed it to me. It was just the sort of stupid, puerile, dangerous trick that he'd find hilarious.

And Pete had form. It was what had finished us off. That weekend where he'd tentatively suggested we should experiment with Rohypnol. I'd told him to piss off.

But he didn't give up. "Go on, it could be fun, Ellie," he said.

"Oh yeah, who for?"

"You could look on it as an experiment," he'd said.

"What d'you mean?"

"You must have some patients who've been drugged and date raped. If you take it, you'll understand exactly what they've been going through. You can empathise with them."

I was appalled. "Pete, you can fuck off, you bloody perv!"

And I turned and walked out. It should have been for good. But on reflection, finishing with him in the crowded pub was far more satisfying.

Now he'd done this to me. For a laugh. For revenge. And I thought, *I bet on Monday he'll be asking Nick how I was after the party.*

But now there had been consequences. The taxi driver had seen how out of it I was; he must have decided to take advantage. And I was so far gone, I couldn't remember the details, not even whether it had been the driver who brought me home after.

But Pete, Pete had to pay for these consequences.

The bastard. The total bastard. I'd find the proof I needed; then I'd have it out with him. No, I'd sue him. I'd fucking sue him!

I was thinking logically now. Thinking what I needed to do. I must first take a urine sample. I knew that flunitrazepam stays in the blood for several days. I also knew someone at the Sexual Assault Referral Centre in Manchester GMP, Philippa. We'd trained together, but Philippa had left to train with the police rape unit.

I'd take in a urine sample, plus the clothes I was wearing, and I'd ask Philippa to examine me.

I also needed to contact the taxi company. Nick would have their number. I'd find out who the driver was and the times he'd picked me up and dropped me off at home. And once I'd got that evidence, I would go to the police.

I felt emotionally very delicate, teetering on a cliff edge, exposed, vulnerable, and, worst of all, blindsided by an overwhelming fear that my body had been invaded. But at least now I had something to focus on.

It was just after 7 a.m., and I dragged myself out of bed. My head still felt fuzzy, and when I stood up, I had to steady myself against the bed.

I crept into the bedroom, where Nick was belching out a throaty snore that happened each time he drank too much. I grabbed my clothes from the previous evening, which were screwed into a ball on the floor. I crept out, carrying the bundle of clothes, padded downstairs into the kitchen, took out a black bin liner from under the sink and tossed last night's clothes into it.

Samson was pestering me for food. I fed him, let him out the back door, then filled the kettle for an instant coffee, too tired and lazy to make fresh.

I was desperate for a shower, but I knew that would have to wait.

I dug out a plastic sample bottle from my workbag. Squatted over the downstairs toilet, holding the bottle with thumb and forefinger, but even so, more of the urine spilled onto my hands than in the bottle. I was never into penis envy, but it was moments like this that an appendage would be a distinct advantage.

I went back upstairs. Nick was still dead to the world. His phone lay on the bedside cabinet next to him. I scrolled through his call list, found the taxi number that he'd rung at 21.45 the previous evening and copied it into my own phone.

I quietly dressed into jeans, a Nike hoodie and trainers.

I'd decided not to wake Nick. I'd also made the decision not to mention the Rohypnol for two reasons; I knew his reaction would be one of incredulity and disbelief. But secondly, I felt deeply embarrassed and ashamed of the whole episode.

It was now almost 9 a.m. It was a Saturday, so I wasn't sure if Philippa would be in SARC, but I gave her a call on her personal mobile. It answered after one ring.

"Hey, Ellie, how are you?"

I made my voice sound a lot brighter than I felt. "Yeah, I'm great, thanks," I lied.

And as soon as I spoke, questions and doubts erupted inside my head, and the sober reality of what I was now doing hit me harder than the hangover that still throbbed inside my skull.

What if I was wrong? What if Pete never drugged my drink? What if it really was all a nightmare? Then. No, that was no nightmare. But still, I thought, caution might be the better option.

"Haven't seen you for ages, Ellie; how you doing? We must meet up," Philippa continued cheerfully.

"Yeah, we must. We'll arrange something, Philippa. But the reason I was ringing ... well, it's ... it's for a friend. Last night she thinks she was slipped flunitrazepam in her drink, and she can't remember exactly what happened to her, but I think it's not good."

"Oh wow, Ellie, that's bad."

"I know. Anyway, before she goes to the police, she's given me a urine sample, so I was just wondering—"

"Ohh, Ellie, it's Saturday morning," Philippa interrupted.

"I know, I know ..."

"But ..." She hesitated. "Look ... look, I tell you what ... okay, drop it off. There's a good mate who works in the lab; she's in at the moment. I'll see if she can check it for you as an emergency," she suggested.

"Oh, Philippa, that would be brilliant. And we'll fix something up in the next week or so."

"Great. See you in a bit."

I DROPPED OFF THE SAMPLE. I did have the opportunity to tell Philippa the truth; there was no friend. The friend was me. But I couldn't do it.

So instead of pushing it to the next stage – a forensic examination of my clothes and subjecting myself to a vaginal swab – I decided I'd wait for the results.

I was desperate to take a shower. Before I left home, I had used a wipe to remove the worse of my make-up and streaked mascara, but I could smell my stale, dried sweat and sour perfume. Personal hygiene would have to wait.

I settled into a corner of Idle Hands Coffee in Dale Street with a large cappuccino and took out my phone and rang the taxi firm.

"Hello, Happy Home Taxis." The voice was East European, possibly Polish.

"Hi there." I tried to sound upbeat and friendly when, in fact, I was feeling the opposite, and there was a slight quaver to the edge of my voice. "Wonder if you can help. I was picked up by one of your drivers last night from Deansgate Square at around or just after ten p.m., taking me to Moorland Road in Didsbury. Can you let me know who the driver was and what time I was dropped off, please?"

This was obviously a strange request. "Hmm, oh right. Hmm, I have only just started this shift. I will have to check the records for last night and ring you back?"

"That's fine. Ring me on this number, please. Thank you. And my name's Dr Ellie Thompson." I always dropped in "doctor" if I wanted a quick response or to be taken seriously.

I WAS on to my second cappuccino and had finished off a blueberry muffin when the call came in. I'd saved the number into my phone, and I felt a surge of anxiety as I answered.

"Hello?"

"Dr Thompson?"

"Yes."

"It is Stefan here. From Happy Home Taxis. I have checked now. The pickup was 22.06 exactly, and your driver was Sam."

I didn't reply at first. I took in the name. Sam. I visualised him, remembered the back of his head, his hoodie up, his dark eyes watching me in his rear-view mirror. I remembered his huge, shadowy outline after he jumped from the taxi, opened the passenger door and grabbed me by the arm.

"Dr Thompson," Stefan prompted, "are you still there?"

"Yes. Yes, sorry. And what time did he drop me off home?" I asked nervously.

"Sorry, Dr Thompson. Sam, she is a girl. Sam is a girl. Though she's sometimes mistaken for a boy, she has short hair, often wears a hoodie. And the records show that Sam dropped you off at 10.32 precisely." Stefan paused when I didn't reply. "Dr Thompson, you still there?"

But I couldn't answer. I'd dropped my phone onto my lap, dazed. I could hear Stefan's distant voice calling my name. I lifted the phone to my ear. "Sorry," I replied almost in a whisper.

"And Dr Thompson, I spoke to Sam. She remembered you, said you fell asleep on the way home. Said she could hardly wake you when you arrived home, so she helped you into your house. Is that helpful, Dr Thompson?"

I nodded, as if Stefan could see me, before answering weakly, "Yes, thank you. Thank you very much."

As my phone slipped out of my hand, my heart started thumping, and I gasped for air, unable to make sense of what I'd just been told.

CHAPTER TWELVE

When the call came through, I was driving home along Wilmslow Road through Rusholme. I pulled over outside an Indian takeaway that was just opening. I answered the call, but I knew what the result would be.

"Ellie, I've some good news for your friend," Philippa said. "The test was negative. No trace of flunitrazepam was found in her urine. She can rest assured."

"Thank you, Philippa," I answered weakly. "I'll let her know."

I was about to drive on when another call came through. This time it was Nick.

"Where are you, Ellie? I woke up, and you weren't there."

I paused a second before answering. "I needed to clear my head about last night. I'm on my way home now."

"And are you all right?"

"I'll see you in about ten minutes," I said without answering Nick's question.

I didn't immediately drive on. I sat there, my mind

churning over, thinking how much I could bear to tell Nick. I was embarrassed when I thought about how I'd behaved the previous evening.

But I could deal with that.

What I couldn't deal with, what concerned me and what totally scared me, was the fear that I was unable to distinguish between a nightmare and reality, the inability to discern when I was awake and when I was dreaming.

The implications were alarming.

I was just about to drive on when suddenly the image of Natasha sitting in a parked car shot into my head.

Was it indeed Natasha I saw as the taxi pulled away? In my foggy, drunken state, the image had been pushed to the back of my mind.

If it was Natasha, what was she doing there? Was she indeed stalking me and Nick? And could it be Natasha's Kia Sportage that had shunted my car when I left the hospital?

I decided to make a detour on my way home. I wasn't sure if Natasha lived in the same flat as eighteen months ago, but I was about to find out.

Natasha had lived in a flat along Alexandra Road South directly opposite the park, and immediately I turned left onto the road, I could see the block of flats on my right.

And there, parked up alongside a couple of other cars, was the Kia Sportage.

I parked on the left opposite the flats and the cars. I felt a little nervous as I crossed the road. I'd decided first to inspect Natasha's car. If she'd shunted my red BMW, the front of her car would be damaged, dotted with specks of red paint.

But as soon as I bent down and peered at the front of the Sportage, I could see no damage whatsoever. And Natasha would not have had time to have it repaired and spray-painted.

In some ways I was relieved. There was now no need to confront her, although I would still like to know what she was doing parked outside Nick's office.

I was just about to cross back to my car, waiting for a blue van to pass me, when a voice called out.

"Ellie?"

I turned, and emerging from the front entrance of the flats was Natasha, dressed in dusky pink leggings and a matching top, ready for a jog in the park.

I started. "Oh. Hello, Natasha."

"What are you doing?" she asked, an edge to her voice.

"I was ... I was just passing and ... well, I'll be honest ... we saw each other last night and ... we did see each other, yes?" I asked hesitantly.

"Yes, we did. What an amazing coincidence!" Natasha suddenly gushed. "My boyfriend works on the third floor for an insurance company. I was waiting to pick him up," she explained.

"Oh right, yes. Yes, what a coincidence. I ... I was about to pop in and see how you are ... but obviously you're off for a run," I said, anxious to escape.

"Yes. Anyway, I'm fine. How are you?" Natasha asked.

"Yes. Good."

There was an awkward silence.

"Well, I'd better ..." I was about to cross to my car.

"And Nick? How's Nick?" Natasha asked before I could move away.

"Yeah. He's okay," I said, accompanied by a tiny, uncomfortable smile.

"And your nightmares, how are they?" Natasha asked, completely catching me off guard.

"Er ... hmm ... why d'you ask?" I managed, nervous.

"I remember you telling me, and I told you I also suffered from nightmares," Natasha reminded me.

"That's right. And how are your nightmares?" I asked, deflecting.

"Gone. Not had them for months," she said.

"Same," I lied, desperate to leave. "Anyway, I'd better ... let you get on with your run."

"See you, Ellie."

Natasha said it in such a way that it wasn't a bright farewell greeting but a statement. As I climbed into my car, I watched Natasha start running, through the gate into the park.

So had Natasha been stalking me? Or maybe she'd been stalking Nick. But at least I knew hers wasn't the white car that had harassed and bumped me.

I wasn't sure whether to mention it to Nick and eventually decided against it.

There were things I needed to tell Nick, but I wouldn't mention Rohypnol, the knife under the pillow or my visit to Philippa.

He'd think I was one step away from madness.

CHAPTER THIRTEEN

"I don't actually remember getting out of the taxi, going into our house or getting into bed. But what's really scary, Nick, is this going to happen again? What if it happens again? What if I can't tell my real life from my nightmares? What if they become indistinguishable?"

"Wow, Ellie, I don't know what to say."

I was sitting in the kitchen at the breakfast bar opposite Nick, a fresh coffee in front of me.

Nick thought some more before suggesting, "I suppose ... I suppose it's an extension of the sleepwalking. So that when the driver dropped you off, helped you in, you were actually still asleep."

"Nick ... I was so sure earlier it wasn't a nightmare; I was totally, totally sure. And I'm sorry for shouting at you."

"That's okay." He shrugged.

"But I'm scared, Nick. I'm scared that I won't know when I'm in a dream and when something's really happening to me."

I knew Nick had never been good at handling any form

of emotional crisis, neither big nor small. And I was sure this one seemed very big indeed to him. As it did to me. He just couldn't cope with bubbling emotions in either himself or, worse, in other people. He wanted everything to be on an even keel, smooth running, no crisis. No mess. He was like that at work too.

The more I got to know him, the more I wondered if we were right for each other. And I thought, what a terrible assessment to make after only one year of marriage. I was being unfair on him – and on us as a couple.

Or was I?

"I can see it must be frightening," he eventually managed, inadequately.

It was such an understatement, it only helped to add to my misgivings.

Nick avoided talking about my nightmare evening for the rest of the day; he simply acted as if the previous night had never happened.

I was fond of Nick, which in itself was faintly damning. But when I asked myself how much I loved him, my answer always seemed oddly inadequate. Yes, I loved him, but not passionately. Did I ever love him passionately in our early days? I couldn't give an unequivocal yes. He was different from all the other men I'd dated, and I can't deny that he was just what I needed after the deceptions of Pete. He'd always seemed caring and considerate, yet somehow ...

After our disastrous first "date", if you could call it that, I never followed Nick up, and I didn't hear from him. To be honest, I wasn't really interested.

About two months later I decided to join a local dating website. I wanted to broaden my social life beyond the boundaries of my work. I went on a couple of unsatisfactory dates. Then, out of the blue, I received an invitation for a date from Nick. He had actually joined the dating site only a few weeks before me.

He left a message.

Your photo doesn't do you justice. My mad stalker has backed off. Want to try again?

And we did. And I enjoyed the date, enjoyed his company.

But I certainly didn't love him obsessively in the way Natasha had loved him; I worried I was incapable of loving anyone wholeheartedly and unconditionally. I feared it wasn't in me. I supposed I loved him in my own way, whatever that was. And whatever it was, it sounded a bit pathetic.

ON SATURDAYS we usually had a routine. We chilled in the morning – a long lie-in, reading the papers online, followed by brunch, cooked by Nick. Afterwards, we'd take Samson out for a walk in Didsbury Park, a beautiful park with a rare Green Flag Award.

Then in the afternoon we'd do the week's shopping at the Tesco in Parrs Wood Lane, a trip that I hated. But it was necessary because on weekdays when we arrived home from work, we were either too late to shop or too tired.

But this Saturday was not a usual day. And it was about to take a turn for the worse.

"Ellie, I can't go shopping this afternoon," Nick told me, a look of apologetic anguish creasing his face.

"Oh, you're kidding," I replied. "Why?"

Nick hesitated, knowing my reaction. "Pete and I ... Pete and I have arranged for a round of golf," he said, and he shrugged an apology.

"You've what?"

"Weeks ago. And he reminded me about it last night," he told me.

"Nick, you know how I hate shopping, especially at the checkout, packing on my own. It's the sort of stress I can do without. You'll have to cancel," I told him.

"Ellie, I can't, it's all arranged. And last night the boss said he'd join us as well, so I can't, I really can't cancel."

AFTER KNOWING what I'd been through in the last twenty-four hours, how could Nick even think about abandoning me for a round of bloody golf? I needed support, not to be left on my own.

Even so, an hour later Nick had left for his golf, and I was reversing out of our garage to do the hateful shop. I was still fuming. The heavy hangover had settled into a gentle nagging throb at both my temples.

At the head of Moorland Road, I turned left onto Wilmslow Road and towards Didsbury village. I glanced in my mirror, and two cars back I saw a familiar white car. I told myself to stop being paranoid. There were thousands of cars like that.

At the traffic lights in Didsbury village, I turned left onto School Lane. I casually glanced again in my mirror. The white car had also turned; it was now behind a red Fiat Uno. The lights by Parrs Wood pub were on red. I pulled up, indicating a right turn into Parrs Wood Lane. I looked in my mirror. The white car was not indicating.

Once the lights changed, I made the turn and noted that the white car, the model unclear in the flash of white, carried through the lights along School Lane. I breathed in heavily.

The Tesco superstore was up on my left. As I pulled into the car park, I groaned. It was heaving. There would be long queues at the checkouts. I drove round until I found a parking space, reversed into it, snatched my bundle of bags for life from the passenger seat, and as I eased out of the car, I couldn't help glancing at the car park entrance. There was a blue car entering the parking area, followed by a silver car, but no white car had followed me in.

I grabbed a trolley, the largest kind; I would fill it to overflowing. I pushed it through the automatic doors.

I WAS HALFWAY through my shop when I had this innate sense that I was being watched. I stopped, quickly half-turned to peer over my shoulder. A traffic jam of trolleys, like dodgem cars at a fair, glided between each other, while hands grasped for milk, juice, cheese. Not a single shopper showed any interest in me.

But as I turned into the next aisle, that feeling never left me. I stopped the trolley, turned back, then suddenly popped my head round the corner and down the aisle I'd just left. It was rather comical, like a child's game – now you see me, now you don't. I scanned the sea of bustling shoppers, a throng of differing heights and sizes, but no one appeared to be watching or following me.

As I queued up at the checkout, I glanced behind me,

then at the queues either side of me, but I didn't recognise any faces. I was annoyed at myself for being so unnecessarily edgy and nervous.

By the time I'd packed all the shopping and the bags were piled one on top of the other in the trolley, I was sweating, beads across my forehead, clammy under my armpits, as I struggled to dig my purse from my handbag, then the credit card, which seemed glued to its compartment in my purse.

I didn't mind that it was raining when I left the store; I was just relieved to be out of the claustrophobic aisles and grateful to breathe in the moist, damp air. I was concentrating hard on keeping the heavy trolley under control as its weight swayed it one way then another.

I traversed left and up the third parking lane where my car was parked halfway along. As I reached it, I pushed the trolley into the gap between my car and a Range Rover, the trolley swinging out of control for a second and nearly sliding into the massive SUV.

I happened to glance up and caught a glimpse of what looked like a white Kia Sportage exiting the car park. I brushed the thought aside and took out my keys from my jacket pocket, zapped open the car. I was about to flip open the boot when I noticed that my front nearside tyre was flat.

I cursed, went across to the tyre. I could change the tyre myself, but I was reluctant. Because of my work, my hands are extremely precious to me. What if I had an accident unfastening too-tight wheel nuts or because I hadn't placed the jack correctly and the car dropped as I was easing on the spare? I shuddered at the thought. I was about to bend down to inspect the damage when I heard a voice, "Ellie?"

I looked over. Dr Underwood was standing at the front of my car, holding a carrier bag.

"James."

He nodded to the overflowing trolley. "Shopping for tonight's meal?"

I smiled. "Got a flat," I replied, pointing to the front tyre.

"Oh heck. Let's have a look." He came round the side and bent down at my feet, looked at the tyre. "Oh dear," he said.

"What?"

"The tyre's been slashed. See here." He pointed to two deep cut marks on the rim of the tyre. "Looks like it was deliberate."

My heart surged, a sudden rise of fear. "Seriously?"

"Yes. Have you checked your other tyres?" he asked.

"Er, no," I managed, my voice tight at the back of my throat. "This rear tyre seems okay."

James walked round the front of the car, and he noticed that the driver's side tyre was also flat. "This one's down," he said. He kneeled to inspect it. "Slashed as well."

"God!" I muttered.

"You don't expect vandals round here. Not in broad daylight in a Tesco car park."

I couldn't answer. I knew this wasn't some random vandal. It was whoever's been stalking me.

CHAPTER FOURTEEN

James was inspecting the front tyre more closely. "The problem you've got, Ellie, we could change one of the tyres for your spare, but you still wouldn't be able to drive. Plus, I think the tyres are irreparable. You'll need two new tyres. Is Nick around to pick you up?"

"No. He's out on the bloody golf course!"

James thought for a moment, then said, "I'm parked over there." He pointed across to the next aisle. "Let's transfer your shopping into my car, and I'll drop you home. You'll have to leave yours here."

"Thanks, James," I said.

WHEN JAMES PARKED UP, he insisted on carrying almost all my shopping bags inside.

As we entered the kitchen, I started unpacking, and he asked, "Want some help?"

"No, thanks. I know where everything goes. You can put the kettle on if you fancy a tea or a coffee?"

"Great." He smiled. "I would love a tea."

We sat opposite each other in the conservatory that is off the kitchen diner, overlooking the garden. Little red fuchsia bells creeping around the edges of the conservatory were still in bloom, but the rest of the garden was dying back for the winter apart from the thick green leylandii at the far end of the lawn.

I sat in a deep cushioned rattan armchair, while James sank into its matching settee.

He told me he only lived five minutes from Tesco, which I sort of knew, and he'd just popped in for a few items.

"Lucky for me I bumped into you," I said.

He nodded, smiled, sank deeper into the sofa. "How was Nick's office social?" he asked.

I'd told James and Penny about it on the Friday at work and how I really wasn't looking forward to it. I rolled my eyes in answer. "I was in the wrong mood for it, and I was tired. I went home early."

I paused. How much should I tell James? Could I trust him?

I felt a sudden, urgent need to talk about it and guessed he might possibly be a more understanding listener than Nick.

So I took a deep breath and told him the whole story: the taxi journey home, the nightmare I thought was real, including my morning's foolish trip to Philippa with my urine sample; that last one really was something I couldn't tell Nick.

James nodded, listened intently without interrupting,

and when I'd finished, he said, "Ellie, I am sorry. It must be so distressing for you."

"It's scary because it's almost as if my real life and my dreams are like, well, merging." And I felt ridiculous as soon as I said it, so I added, "I mean, I know they're not, and that's ludicrous and not logical …"

"But it seems like that," he finished.

"Yes. And I think the reason why I feel they're so … so absolutely real is … well, you know in a normal dream nothing is logical, nothing is like in real life. You could be, for example, at home, but somehow in the dream it doesn't look anything like your home. Or you could have people in your dream who you haven't seen for years and weren't that special to you. It's non-logical, a bit like … I suppose it's like … like looking at yourself in a cracked mirror, with pieces of the glass missing, a distorted image that isn't quite you."

"A bit like a Picasso portrait?" James added.

"Well, yeah."

James nodded and waited for me to continue.

"But my dreams, my nightmares aren't like that. They are totally, totally real. I look the same and wear the same clothes. My house is exactly as it is in real life; my car is the same, my parking space, my office, my desk, even the hospital. So that when I wake up, because they are so real, it's difficult to know if the events in my dreams really happened or not."

I stopped. James didn't answer at first. It was so silent in the house, and all we could hear was the ticking of the grandfather clock in the hall and the chirpy whistle of a couple of sparrows outside on the patio.

Should I tell him about the sleepwalking?

He picked up his mug of tea from the glass-topped coffee

table that separated us, took a sip, then said, "I know you were reluctant to see Dr Carson …"

"I was … I am," I replied.

"But I'll tell you something." He hesitated before adding, "I've had sessions with him."

I was taken by surprise. "Really?"

"It was after my wife died. I wasn't coping very well. I felt such terrible guilt because I didn't know why she'd done it. And why I didn't pick up on the signs of her depression. I couldn't sleep at night, suffered from terrible nightmares, Ellie. But not real like yours."

"I'm so sorry," I said genuinely.

He shrugged. "So, to a certain extent, I understand because I was also reluctant to talk to him," he continued.

He looked at me, waited for my response.

"James, there's something else I haven't mentioned."

He nodded, encouraging me to continue.

"I've been suffering from somnambulism. I think the incident in the taxi was an example of me sleepwalking. But there's been a more concerning incident that I don't really know how to deal with."

I paused.

"Go on," he encouraged.

And I told him about the broken glass in the kitchen, the splinter in my foot and the missing knife. But I also told him about finding the knife under my pillow, and immediately James looked truly alarmed.

"Oh, Ellie, that is really dangerous," he said.

"I know, I know. I've been worried sick. I haven't even been able to tell Nick about the knife under the pillow."

"You could be a danger to yourself, Ellie. I mean,

carrying a knife upstairs in your sleep, stepping on broken glass ..."

"Or I could be a danger to someone else," I added, a thought that had been bugging me ever since I found the knife.

"Yes. That is true. Oh, Ellie, you really need to do something. You can't ignore this."

"I know." I nodded, then asked, "And Dr Carson, did he help?"

"Yes, I think he did. I went to him for several sessions. Of course, it's very discreet, which is why no one had any idea. So I'm saying, why don't you try it, Ellie? What have you got to lose? And I was talking to him the other day, and this is interesting, he was actually telling me he's just finished writing a paper on nightmares and dream sequences."

"Really?"

"Of course I never mentioned you, but ..." he began and then changed tack. "So why is it you're so reluctant?"

"Oh, I don't know, I ... okay, to be honest ... I find him a bit creepy," I confessed. "And I know Penny does too."

James was amused, and he gave a small smile. "He's not weird. He's just a psychiatrist."

And I also smiled. "How well do you know him?"

"Not that well. He's not the type of person you'd go for a drink with. To be honest, I think he's a bit shy. He's not great outside of his work. Don't think he's married; he's never mentioned a partner. But anyway, next time I see him, I'll tell him you and Penny both think he's a bit creepy!"

"You dare!"

We both laughed before James said, "So promise you'll fix up an appointment to go and see him?"

I nodded. "Promise."

JAMES STAYED for another twenty minutes. We talked mostly about work, but he also opened up in more detail about his life since his wife died. To combat the grief, he'd immersed himself totally in his work, putting in as many shifts as health and safety would allow. But after around two months, he woke up one morning, his body as heavy as lead, his energy drained; it was a monumental effort to climb out of bed. He knew then he needed to address his grief. And that was when he went to see Dr Carson.

I wanted to comfort him, to go to him, give him a big hug. But I held back, worried that James might misinterpret the gesture.

However, as he was leaving, I did offer him a slightly awkward hug, and he squeezed me, smiled warmly down at me, kissed me briefly on the cheek, and said, "Thank you for listening." I shrugged, a gesture of "that's okay".

"See you Monday," he said over his shoulder as he walked towards his car. "And get Nick to contact the AA," he called out.

I waved him out of the drive, shut the door; then I rang Nick.

It went straight to his voicemail. He'd switched off his phone while he played golf. As a long shot, I decided to call Pete in case he'd left his phone on.

Pete answered after three rings. "Oh hi, Ellie, this is a surprise."

"Hi, Pete, can I just have a quick word with Nick, please?" I asked.

There was a moment's hesitation before Pete answered, "Er, sorry?"

"Nick. Can you pass the phone to him? Are you still on the golf course?"

"I'm sorry, Ellie," Pete said, sounding totally confused. "I've no idea what you're talking about."

"Are you not with Nick? When did you finish playing golf? Is he on his way home?"

There was a longer pause this time before Pete answered, "Ellie, I've not been playing golf with Nick. I'm at home. I've been home all day."

I let the phone drop to my lap. There was a sudden surge of panic in my chest, the realisation that Nick had been lying to me. I felt my face flushed pink with anger.

Then I heard Pete's distant voice. "Ellie, are you okay?"

I brought the phone to my ear, breathed in deeply before answering, "Yes. Sorry, Pete. My fault. I think it's one of his other colleagues he's playing golf with. Sorry to bother you. See you soon."

I slumped back into the armchair in the conservatory. I felt devastated, hurt, furious. Nick had lied to me. Why? Where was he – and who was he with?

CHAPTER FIFTEEN

I was pacing around the conservatory like a tiger caged in a zoo. My skull was throbbing, mind swirling, beads of sweat breaking out on my forehead.

I recalled the image of Nick and the attractive new employee as they chatted, heads close, her hands touching Nick as she spoke. Were they having an affair? Nick was not the flirty type. He wasn't Pete. But in all our time together, I had never seen Nick so animated in conversation with another woman.

My pacing took me into the kitchen. I pulled out a bottle of Bombay Sapphire and a small can of tonic. I sliced off a wedge of lemon, grabbed some ice from the freezer, chinked it into a tall tumbler, poured over a large measure of gin, then took my drink into the conservatory, where I collapsed back onto the sofa.

It was four o'clock, and I didn't move for the next two hours apart from to refill my glass. By six o'clock, the late evening sun was dipping down behind the leylandii at the bottom of the garden, casting dimpled shadows onto the lawn and filtering into the edges of the conservatory. My mind had played out every possible scenario.

The only truth I knew was that Nick had lied.

It was soon after six that I heard the garage's automatic door grinding open. I waited, very still, listened for the rollover door to shut before I heard Nick entering the hallway, the door shutting behind him.

"Ellie," he called.

I didn't answer. Nick entered the kitchen, saw me sitting quietly in the conservatory. "Oh hi, there you are," he said brightly. He came over, briefly kissed me on the cheek. "How was your day?" he asked.

I shrugged, not answering, but then asked coolly, my voice level, no hint of anger, "And how was golf?"

"Yeah, great," he answered. "Helped clear the head."

"And who won?" I asked, looking up at him for the first time, holding his gaze.

"Who d'you think? Pete. He's so competitive."

I'd been intending to keep my calm, not play all my cards, but I couldn't help it. I jumped off the sofa, my face fiery, screwed up in anger. "You liar!" I shouted. "You lying bastard!"

Nick staggered back, as if pushed by some invisible hand, his face startled, eyes wide, mouth slightly ajar. I didn't think he'd ever seen me like this. He managed to speak, but his words were floundering, incoherent. "Sorry ... what ... I ... sorry ... I don't ..."

I came right up to his face, and Nick must have felt the spray of spittle as I repeated, "You're a lying bastard, Nick! A lying bastard!" He took a rapid step back from me, his face confused, as I continued my rant. "You never went to golf with Pete. I rang him; he was at home. You never played golf with him, so where the hell were you?"

Suddenly he looked like a little boy caught in a shop for stealing sweets, a panicked face full of guilt and fear. "Oh. Right. Hmm, right, yeah ... sorry," he mumbled.

"So where've you been all afternoon?" I persisted. "Where the hell have you been and who with? Is it that woman from work, the one who was all over you last night ..."

"No," Nick managed to protest.

"Was it her, was it that woman?" I persisted, the anger exploding within me. "Eh? Was it, was it, was it?"

"No!" Nick replied more firmly. "You've got it all wrong."

And I paused, out of breath, my chest rising and falling. I tried to calm myself before continuing so my breathing levelled, and I managed to ask evenly, "Okay, Nick. If I've got it wrong, where've you been all afternoon, what have you been doing, and who've you been with?"

He nodded once, then paused. I wasn't sure whether he was taking his time to gather his thoughts or to find a lie that rang true.

Eventually he said, "Liverpool."

This was not the answer that I expected. "Liverpool?" I asked, incredulous.

He nodded.

"You went to Liverpool?"

He nodded again.

"Why?"

A moment before he answered, "You remember when we went to Liverpool a couple of months ago for the night?"

I nodded.

"And when we were shopping, we found that jeweller's that also made their own jewellery ...?"

"Wong's, yes."

"I've, er, I've been there," he told me.

I was thrown, totally confused. "Whatever for?"

"I ... well ... next month, it's your birthday. I wanted to have something made, something unique, a necklace, for you, so I went over today to choose and order it."

I couldn't answer at first. I was too shocked. Shocked and surprised. As long as I had known Nick, he had always been predictable. He wasn't hugely romantic or one for grand gestures. This was the first time ever.

But was he telling the truth?

He'd paused for long enough to think of an accomplished lie.

I felt a tinge of guilt for not trusting Nick, but I wasn't about to let him off the hook so easily. Over the years, the blackness inside my head had created an innate sense of survival and had instilled in me a cynicism that acted as a protective barrier. Nick had never really pierced it.

And maybe he never would.

"Okay, Nick. That's a lovely gesture, but please let me see the receipt." I held his gaze. "I don't want to spoil the surprise completely."

I could see the instant panic in Nick's eyes.

He is lying, I thought.

I held out my hand. "I don't need to see the price. Just a quick sneak at the receipt with the jeweller's heading."

"You think I'm lying?" he asked as if he was hurt.

"Just show me the receipt, Nick," I insisted.

"I ... I put in the order. I haven't paid for it yet. I have to pick it up in a week or two, so I haven't got a receipt," he stumbled.

I nodded. "Okay."

I turned and walked away.

"Ellie, please, I'm telling the truth."

I turned back.

"Please. Please believe me. I love you, Ellie. I wouldn't lie to you. I wouldn't do anything to hurt you."

Nick's eyes were clouded with desperation, the emotional pitch of his pleading was almost too much to take. But did I believe him? Could I believe him?

THAT NIGHT I had another nightmare. I dreamed I was in the city centre; I turned down a long, dark alley. It was ill lit with just one lamp covering the whole length of the alley. As I reached the lamppost, the bulb in it died. I stopped, and I became aware of footsteps behind me. I quickened my pace, and the footsteps quickened. I glanced over my shoulder. The alley was now only lit by a half-moon that suddenly disappeared behind a cloud, but I could just make out a dark figure in a large hoodie. I started to run. The figure started to run. The end of the alley did not seem to be getting any closer even when I ran as fast as I could. I could hear the sound of pounding feet behind me, and they were louder and louder as they closed on me. I took out my mobile, dialled Nick.

"Nick, Nick, are you there? I'm being followed, I'm being followed. Nick, Nick, pick up the phone ..."

And as I shouted desperately into the phone, the figure caught me up, and a hand grabbed my shoulder. I dropped my phone as the figure swung me round. The hooded face was grotesque: a twisted nose; dark, empty sockets where the eyes should have been. I caught the flash of steel with its distinctive mark of a unicorn.

When I woke up the next morning, the first thing I did was look under my pillow.

There was no unicorn knife.

CHAPTER SIXTEEN

It was Tuesday, three days later, and just before 8.30 p.m. when I drove into the hospital basement car park. I was meeting Dr Carson for my first session, and we'd agreed, for the sake of confidentiality, it would be best to meet out of office hours.

I'd talked it through with Penny the Sunday before. We'd met for a lunchtime drink in Didsbury Village at the Royal Oak. It was bustling inside, standing room only, but we managed to find a wooden bench table outside on the pavement area. There was a watery sun, a thin veil of cloud, but it was warm for late autumn.

We ordered two of the Oak's famous cheese and pâté plates that we'd first shared when we were students, and I filled Penny in with everything that had happened over the previous forty-eight hours.

Penny was rapt, her eyes wide in awe, as I held back nothing: Nick's office party, the taxi, the nightmares, the sleepwalking, my erroneous fear I'd been sexually attacked, my shopping trip, the two slashed tyres (Nick had arranged for his garage to go out and replace them), Good Samaritan James (Penny insisted James definitely fancied me), and, finally, my suspicion that Nick was having an affair.

I never mentioned the knife. Somehow it was that one detail that made me out to be genuinely crazy.

And Penny roared at the final piece of information. "Nick? You think Nick is having an affair?"

I nodded.

"Are you crazy?"

I jumped when Penny used the word "crazy", but she didn't pick up on it.

"He adores you, Ellie!"

I shrugged. "Does he though?"

"Yes. Definitely. The bigger question is whether you love him."

"You don't think I do?" I asked.

Penny gave me an enigmatic tilt of her head. "I'm not sure you even know the answer to that." And she stared at me, waiting for my reaction.

"Yes, of course I love him," I said a little too weakly.

Finally, I brought up James's opinion that I should set up some sessions with Dr Carson to discuss the nightmares. What did Penny think?

"I agree, he is creepy," she said. "But there again, if his recent research has been around nightmares, you never know, he might be able to help. What have you got to lose?"

So, on the Monday, I popped into Ben Carson's office, briefly described the stress caused by my nightmares, and Dr Carson nodded gently as I spoke, and when I'd finished, he said, "Dr Thompson, I'd be happy to start up some sessions. And I do think I may be able to help." And he actually smiled, though it looked like an effort, and the smile faded very quickly.

TODAY, the underground car park was totally empty. I parked in my designated space, stepped out of the car into an eerie quiet. As I walked towards the stair door – I knew the lift was out of order again – I heard the barrier rise on the ground-level parking area above, and the sound of a car entering. I stopped and listened. Could I have been followed? When I was driving to my appointment with Dr Carson, my head had been so filled with apprehension and angst that I hadn't been checking in my mirror.

I heard the car pull up, its engine killed, the echoed slam of its door, followed by the sound of heavy footsteps. Was the driver walking to the stairs? The footsteps stopped. I waited, listened intently. I was still nervous after my previous experiences, and, in fact, I'd bought myself a pepper spray off the internet. I started towards the door, felt in my handbag for assurance it was in there.

I paused to listen.

The footsteps on the ground level started up again. They sounded louder, closer. Then they were running. I looked across at the ramp, and in the dim light, the shadow of a tall figure appeared, running.

I quickly ducked inside the door. But I didn't run up the stairs to escape. Instead I pressed myself against the wall next to the door. I reached into my bag, grasped hold of the pepper spray, pulled it out and held it in front of me. My breathing was fast, my chest rising up and down, the adrenaline high in my bloodstream.

The door burst open, the figure appeared, and I held the spray at arm's length towards his face and pressed and kept on pressing.

The man screamed, his hands flying to cover his eyes. "You stupid bitch!" he shouted in pain.

And I recognised him.

CHAPTER SEVENTEEN

"Have you been following me?"

He couldn't answer. He took a grubby handkerchief out of his trouser pocket and started to rub his eyes.

"Did you slash two of my tyres on Saturday? Did you? Did you?" I demanded to know.

He still didn't answer.

"Have you got a white car? A Qashqai or a Kia Sportage? Have you?"

When he didn't answer again, I waited till he stopped wiping the tears from his eyes; then I spoke softly.

"I did everything I could to save your son."

He stared at me then, as his dark brown eyes continued to stream. When he spoke, his voice was slightly strangled. "You were negligent," he croaked.

"I was cleared," I answered evenly.

"Cover-up," he said, his voice hardly audible.

"You're harassing me, Mr Walker. I've already contacted the police about the incident the other week when a white car shunted into me," I lied. "If that was you, I could have you arrested."

He didn't respond, just stared at me blankly.

I held his stare and eventually told him, "I think you'd better go home."

I turned and started walking up the stairs. He didn't follow or call after me.

DR CARSON'S rotund frame was squashed into a black leather Chesterfield armchair, and his short, stubby legs only just touched the floor. He had a bald dome, as shiny as if he polished it every day, with a fringe of hair surrounding it. If he'd been wearing a monk's robe, he'd be a dead ringer for Friar Tuck. Instead, he was wearing a pair of grey slacks and a blue blazer, with a white shirt and red tie.

His office was expansive. An executive oak desk was positioned against one wall, its top uncluttered apart from a laptop and a tub of pens. On the wall behind the desk were half a dozen framed certificates and awards.

In the far corner was a Chesterfield sofa in black leather, matching the two winged armchairs that were positioned around a circular glass coffee table on which lay a notepad and pen.

When I entered his office, he stood up and gestured to the Chesterfield armchair directly opposite him.

"Sit down, Dr Thompson," he said and gave a little tight smile.

As I sat, I said, "Please call me Ellie; it feels less formal."

He nodded. "Of course." But I noticed he didn't make a similar offer to me.

I sat, crossed my legs and glanced up at him. I felt very ill at ease. He was staring at me, not speaking, and in the silence, I spoke defensively. "To be honest, I don't know what you can do for me. I've done loads of online research about nightmares and ... you know ... well, what can you do for me?"

He shrugged, gave another stiff smile, then asked, "Would you like to tell me about them ... when they started ... and describe them to me?"

And as I spoke, he didn't interrupt; he nodded encouragement, occasionally making notes in his pad. I told him how I'd had similar nightmares from my teens, but recently they had become more real.

"And were the nightmares triggered by any particular traumatic incidents in your life?" he asked.

I thought about it. "Well, my parents died tragically when I was quite young, so ..." I tailed off.

"And it was soon after that the first nightmares started?" he asked.

"I think it probably was, yes," I answered.

"And what about the other periods when they started up again?"

I realised now was the time I should tell him about my depression. I'd never told anyone.

But at this stage I didn't feel able to tell Dr Carson either.

Instead I answered, "I know you're suggesting that recurrent nightmares often indicate a problem in our waking life."

"They can do, yes."

"And I can understand that when my parents died ... but I've had no real major emotional problems since," I told him, which was a lie.

"Maybe none that you're consciously aware of?" he prompted.

"Possibly." I shrugged.

"Or maybe a problem you don't want to face up to?" he further suggested.

I wasn't sure how to answer. "I don't know. I don't think so." I paused before changing tack. "The last nightmare, I saw his face close up. He had no eyes. What d'you think that's about?"

Dr Carson paused thoughtfully before answering, "Oh. It could mean many things."

"Such as?"

"Well ... we always search for the truth in people's eyes, the eyes of a person tell us so much. If this ... figure in your nightmare has no eyes ... you can't see the truth." He paused for effect before adding, "Or you don't want to see it."

He looked at me for a response, but I simply shrugged.

Dr Carson stared down at his notepad, as if deep in thought. There was total silence in the room. I shifted my position in the chair. Finally he looked up and spoke. "The recurring theme of being chased or pursued by some kind of evil ... I don't know what you'd call it ... this could indicate some aspect of your emotional life you're trying to run away from."

I shrugged, noncommittal.

"Could be personal relationships, stress or work-related issues? But I won't know until we've had several sessions. Are you up for that?" he asked.

"Why not?" I said.

"In the meantime, I wonder whether you can control these nightmares."

I wasn't sure what he meant.

"I'm talking about lucid dreaming," he explained.

"You mean, am I aware that I'm in a dream ... nightmare?" I asked.

Dr Carson nodded.

"No," I answered. "I was. Early on. But not recently ... most of the time it's so real, like it's really happening, and that is freaky ... because it often mirrors exactly something I've done or said during the day ... and then it turns weird."

And I went on to explain how the nightmares are so real, so lifelike, it was almost impossible to differentiate between being awake or in the nightmare.

Dr Carson seemed to scribble furiously as I went into these details. When I stopped talking and he ceased making notes, he looked up.

"You've been under a lot of stress recently at work, haven't you?"

"Not particularly."

I felt uncomfortable at the direction this was moving in.

"Do you worry about making the wrong decision? The wrong diagnosis?" he asked.

And I immediately became defensive and threw back at him, "Do you?"

But he didn't answer, simply stared back at me.

I continued: "Are you referring to the complaint made against me?"

Dr Carson gestured a yes.

I spoke forcefully. "As you well know, Dr Carson, it was unfounded. Yes, a complaint is always stressful ... but I know I did everything I could."

Dr Carson paused, glanced down at his notes, and when he looked up, he said, "Do you want to meet the same time next week?"

I didn't like being put on the defensive regarding my work, and I was in two minds whether to continue the sessions, but eventually I nodded.

"Good."

And for the first time he smiled, a genuine warm smile, showing a set of uneven, slightly yellow teeth. He stood up, held out his hand. I took it. It was a little clammy. "Sorry if I made you feel uncomfortable," he said.

I shrugged an okay.

"But I should warn you, the deeper we dig and the more skins we peel off the onion—"

"I've never once been described as an onion," I interrupted.

He laughed, slightly forced. "There will be even more uncomfortable sessions, and I hope you're okay with that."

I nodded. "Bring it on."

"Next week, then," he said. "And if it's okay with you, once we start fully on the sessions, I usually record them."

"Fine." I shrugged, then paused at the door, turned. I should really tell him about the sleepwalking, about the knife and the broken glass.

"Is there something else?" Dr Carson asked, watching me closely as I opened the door.

"Er. No," I said. "I'll leave it for another time."

CHAPTER EIGHTEEN

I looked cautiously around me as I entered the underground car park. There was no sign of Rick Walker's father. However, I still nervously glanced over my shoulder as I hurried across to my car.

I jumped in, slammed the door and started it up. The engine turned over once, spluttered, died. I tried again. The same. Once more. Now it seemed completely dead. I cursed as I slammed my hand hard against the steering wheel.

I was meeting Nick in town in just over an hour. We'd arranged to go for supper together at Albert's Shed in Castlefield.

We hadn't spoken since the other evening, and he wanted to take me out to clear the air. I wasn't sure. In spite of his assurances that he wasn't unfaithful and Penny's unwavering belief that Nick adored me and would never stray, in my head a trust had been broken. I wondered whether the easy intimacy we'd had in the early days would ever return.

Did I want it to return? I'd hardly been working at it.

If we somehow did come through this, and I wasn't sure we could, I vowed to open up completely to Nick, including my past and my current fight against the dark forces within me. If I didn't feel able to, there would always been an emotional barrier between us. And therefore no future.

It was at that moment that my phone pinged. A text had come through. It was from Nick. He'd sent me a screenshot of an email from Wong's, the jewellery shop, confirming his order.

I felt absolutely terrible. I hadn't believed Nick's romantic gesture. It was against his natural character. Now it looked like he really had placed an order.

But then I studied the text more closely, zooming in on it. And my cynical side thought that Nick could have placed the order online without going into Liverpool.

I looked at the date of the email. The order had been confirmed on the Sunday, a day after the non-golf.

He was deceiving me. He was still lying.

But then, thinking it through logically, Nick could have gone to Liverpool on the Saturday, chosen a design, and Wong's had only confirmed the order the next day.

Good God, I thought, what was I turning into – this suspicious, paranoid woman who was starting to lose all objectivity? If I wasn't careful, I could topple over the edge again.

So what should I do about the car? I'd have to call the breakdown service – again. The breakdown contact number was in the glove compartment. I'd just opened it up when I heard the smash of the stair door.

I looked up quickly and caught a brief glimpse of a figure before it disappeared behind a pillar. Had Rick Walker's dad been waiting for me all this time? Did he still want revenge?

I twisted my head one way, then the other, a nervous panic building in my chest, but the figure had disappeared.

I kept bobbing my head, searching, when suddenly I realised the figure was standing by my door. I gasped, cried out.

A hand tapped on the window. I jumped. Then a face appeared.

"Bloody hell, James." I wound down my window. I was breathing fast. "What the hell are you doing? You scared the living daylights out of me!"

"Sorry, Ellie. I'd just popped back to my office for some papers I'd forgotten, saw your car parked up," he told me. "How did it go with Dr Creepy?"

I laughed, more out of a sense of relief. "Yeah, okay. It was just a preliminary meeting. I'm seeing him again next week for a fuller session."

"Oh good," he said, before asking, "Is there something wrong with your car again?"

"Yeah, it won't start," I told him. "I tried to switch on the engine again. It turned over but after that, nothing."

"I'd have a look under the bonnet for you, but I'm pretty hopeless with cars. I know my way around the inside of a body rather better than a car. Tell you what," he suggested. "Ring your breakdown company, find out how long they'll be; then we'll pop across to the Grafton and wait there. No use waiting here."

WE WERE ABOUT to cross the road to the Grafton when a car horn blasted. We both stepped back sharply onto the pavement.

A blue car swept by, its driver straining his neck to peer directly at me.

It was Rick Walker's father, Ray. But he definitely wasn't driving a white Sportage or a Qashqai. I tensed, and as James guided me across the road, with a loose arm around me, I knew he could feel the tension in my shoulders.

"Everything okay?" he asked.

I nodded. "Yeah, fine," I replied.

But my mind was spinning. If Ray Walker didn't own a white car, who was stalking me? Who rammed me? Who slashed my tyres? And why?

Was it Natasha? Maybe I'd been too quick to dismiss the idea of Natasha being my stalker. And yet, when I'd looked, she didn't have any damage to her car. It didn't make sense.

In the pub I rang Nick, but it went straight to his voicemail. He was working late, so he was probably still in a meeting. I left a message and told him I'd contact him once the car was sorted.

When the guy from the breakdown rang ten minutes later, James insisted on going across with me. "Just in case they can't get your car started and you need a lift," he told me.

And, in fact, the mechanic tried everything, but it wouldn't start. In the end he said, "I've no idea what's happened here. I'm going to have to call out a tow truck and get them to take you to the nearest garage," he told me.

"Shit," I said. "Can you take it to our own local garage in Didsbury?" I asked. "Leave it there, and I'll sort it out tomorrow?"

He agreed and very kindly said I didn't need to hang around.

In the end, I managed to speak to Nick. We agreed to

meet by the canal at Deansgate and walk along the towpath together to Albert's Shed.

As James's car filtered into the lane of traffic on to Deansgate, I said, "Here's just fine. Thank you."

"Are you sure?" he asked.

"Honestly. Nick'll be here any minute," I said.

As I was sliding out of the car, James stretched across and kissed me briefly on the cheek. "Take care."

"Thanks," I said with a warm smile.

He smiled back. "See you tomorrow."

I waved James off, crossed over Deansgate, dodging the traffic, then down some steps onto the towpath, where I expected Nick to be waiting.

He wasn't there. I rang him, and he picked up immediately. "Hi, Ellie, where are you now?"

"On the towpath, where are you?" I asked.

"I got out early, so I'm having a drink in Dukes 92. Shall I come to meet you?" he asked.

"No, it's okay," I replied, "You finish your drink. See you in a minute."

I set off briskly, it was quite chilly, and I buttoned up my coat and tied my scarf into a knot. It was quiet; there were no other people in sight along the towpath. I could hear the buzz of traffic noise above, and my heels echoed on the brick-laid path. Buildings from the far side of the canal were reflected in its dark waters. Large green-tinged slab stones, glistening with slime, edged the canal, and I kept well away, staying close to the safety of a warehouse wall.

I could see the end of the towpath where it broadened into Castlefield with its restaurants and bars, and I quickened my pace.

Suddenly my phone rang. The call came up as "private number".

"Hello?"

There was no answer. But I could hear breathing. Steady, even.

"Hello, who is this?"

Again there was no answer.

"Look, I can hear you," I insisted, rattled. "I know you're there; who is it?"

Then the caller replied in a robotic, metallic voice, "You're losing your mind, Ellie."

And the phone went dead.

I could hear my heart pounding. Was this real? Or was I in a nightmare? I didn't know. And that thought frightened me more than anything. I remembered what Dr Carson had said about lucid dreaming.

"Maybe I'm in a dream," I said to myself aloud. "Wake up," I told myself. "Wake up."

But nothing happened.

I picked up my pace, anxious to be off the towpath.

And as my shoes clattered on the brick paving, I heard behind me another set of footsteps. I glanced over my shoulder.

A dark figure, dressed all in black, hoodie up and wearing a balaclava, was about fifty metres behind me.

I started properly running. I could hear the figure behind me also start to run.

I took out my phone and pressed Nick's number. It went straight to his answering service. "Nick, Nick, where are you? I'm being followed!"

The call had slowed my pace, and the figure was now

only twenty metres behind. When I glanced over my shoulder, I saw a glint of steel from a knife in his hand.

I screamed. The faster I ran, the louder I screamed.

My head was exploding. "I'm in a dream. I'm in a dream. Wake up, please wake up. Wake up now!" My breathless voice screamed out, the words echoing in the stillness around me.

There was a tunnel ahead, above it the road, and beyond that, along the towpath, I could see lights from the pubs and bars.

Ahead of me a young couple turned onto the towpath. I ran towards them, screaming.

"Help! Help! I'm being followed."

The couple stopped, so surprised they seemed rooted to the spot. As I reached them, still screaming like some madwoman escaped from an asylum, I found I was so out of breath I could hardly speak.

The young man, I was guessing in his early twenties, looked both wary and shocked. "Are you okay?"

"No. No. I'm being chased!"

"You're being chased?"

"Yeah, he's just ..."

I turned to peer down the towpath. The figure had disappeared.

"There was someone," I gasped, confused. "He ... I don't know where he's gone. I ..."

And the man said, "You can get up to the road near the bridge. Maybe he saw us, escaped up the top."

And I could only nod, a little breathless, heart still pounding from the fear.

This was no nightmare. This was real.

CHAPTER NINETEEN

Nick and I were drinking gin and tonics, waiting for our starters to arrive. It was late, so the restaurant was quiet, just one other couple. I had relaxed now, nerves less jangled, but I still felt an undercurrent of anxiety.

I'd told Nick about the threatening phone call and being chased along the towpath. He seemed concerned though there was a hint of scepticism in his eyes that I picked up on, especially when he said, "But that couple, I'm not being funny, but ... they said they never saw anyone?"

Nick knew immediately this was the wrong thing to say.

"Are you saying you don't believe me?" I said, as my eyes flared.

"No," he replied unconvincingly, then in typical Nick fashion, "Let's just have a nice meal, shall we? Did you get my text, by the way?"

But I was not letting him off so lightly. "Nick, are you saying you don't believe me?"

"Ellie, I've said." He could see I wasn't convinced, so he

added, "Okay, I believe you. Was it this Walker fellah, Rick's dad?"

"I don't know."

"Did you check if he owns a white car similar to one that rammed you?"

I didn't answer. I looked away, picked up my gin and tonic and took a large sip.

"You didn't check, or no, he doesn't own a white car?" Nick persisted.

I eventually answered, my voice quiet. "No. He doesn't own a white car."

"Right." Nick nodded.

"But, Nick, I was being chased ..." I insisted.

"Okay ..."

"And what was so weird ... it was a bit like in my nightmares. And I thought I was actually in a nightmare, but I couldn't wake myself up. I'm not in a nightmare now, am I?"

And this threw Nick. He frowned, paused before answering, "Er, no."

"You're sure? You're sure it isn't a nightmare?"

"No, Ellie, it's not. Honestly."

"But how do I know? How do I really know?"

And realising how crazy that sounded, I added, "No. No, it's not a nightmare. I'm being silly. Forget what I said."

Nick nodded. But he looked wary.

He would have been even more wary if he'd known about the knife under the pillow. Again, I was glad I never told him.

"So could it have been that Walker guy?" Nick suggested after an awkward pause.

"Yeah. It could be, I suppose."

But I wasn't sure anymore. And then I added, "And what about the weird phone call? Someone is trying to scare me."

"Did you try ringing 141 to get the number?"

I shook my head.

"Try it now."

I pressed 141 on my phone, listened. I shook my head. "The number's been withheld."

Just then, my phone rang, startling me. I held it out, looked at the caller.

"Private caller." My voice was shaky. "I'll put it on speaker so you can listen in."

I answered, "Hello?"

It was an automated call. "Ever thought of insuring your life? You can never be too young or too old to die. It could happen anytime. So don't miss out on our unique insurance offer to cover all your funeral costs. Remember, we all have to die sometimes, and we never know what the future holds. Ring 0433 62799."

The message finished. Stunned, I couldn't speak at first.

"I did have a threatening call, Nick. You have to believe me, I did. He called me Ellie, used my name." I didn't add that the voice also said I was losing my mind. Instead I insisted, "And I was being chased."

Nick shrugged, a sceptical look briefly crossing his face.

"You don't believe me, do you?" I challenged.

"Yes," Nick replied unconvincingly. "I do believe you."

I had a sudden thought. "What if that automated message was set up? The fact it was about a funeral, whoever is doing this could have set it up!" I was talking animatedly. "Ring it. Ring that number back. See if it's genuine."

Nick shrugged, reluctant to make the call. I snatched the phone off him.

"Don't bother, I'll ring it!" I snapped.

I pressed to reply to the last number.

And I listened.

Nick watched my face closely. The call was answered, saying their office was closed until 9 a.m., but I could leave a message.

No doubt: it was genuine.

CHAPTER TWENTY

The sound of my screams brought Keith and Vicky running from the rectory. At first all they saw was me screaming and crying.

Keith put his arms around me, asking what was wrong, but then his wife saw Rachel lying in the pond, and she let out this high-pitched wail like an animal.

Keith's attention went from me to his wife to the pond. He called out something like, "Oh God, no, please God, no," and he jumped straight into the water, up to his waist and waded to Rachel. He grabbed her arm, pulled her up so her head was out of the water; then he lifted her into his arms, cradling her like she was a baby and he was christening her; then he struggled out of the pond and laid his daughter on the grass.

Vicky was still screaming, asking if Rachel was dead, and Keith, bending over her, looked like he was listening for her heartbeat, but he was not answering his wife. Then he shouted for her to call an ambulance.

Of course it was no good. Rachel was dead. They couldn't do anything for her. Was I upset? No. Of course not. Why would I be upset? But I do remember being afraid. I was afraid of being found out. I mean, I hadn't actually killed Rachel, but I could have rescued her; I could have screamed for help as soon as she fell in. But then I would have been in trouble for pushing her into the pond. And Rachel would have blamed me, and maybe then Keith and Vicky would no longer want me. So I did nothing. I watched. I watched Rachel die. But I didn't feel guilty, no. She tried to bully me. No one bullies me. It was her fault. She deserved to die. She was a horrible girl.

The local policeman took a statement from me later that day. He was kind and gentle, and when I told him I felt so guilty because I hadn't saved Rachel, he was sympathetic, and like Keith, he said there was nothing I could have done.

There had to be an inquest, but they didn't call me. The local police officer read out my statement. The coroner gave his verdict as "accidental death".

The funeral was horrendous for me because inside I was boiling over with anger, but all I could outwardly show was my grief. Rachel was a spoilt, nasty girl, yet the whole village crammed into the church to mourn her death; there were so many people that they overspilled from the church and had to listen to the service on speakers. Why was this mean girl so popular when I had always been regarded as an outcast? It wasn't fair.

Keith's grief was so overwhelming that he couldn't lead the service. A vicar from the next village was called in to conduct it. I sat on the front row between Keith and Vicky. Throughout the whole service there were moans and groans and sniffles of anguish and heartbreak from the congregation, especially when Keith stood up and spoke movingly about Rachel (even I was near to tears – for Keith not Rachel).

I knew I had to express my grief to the rest of the village and to my school, who were all in attendance. So I waited until there was a lull in the service, and then I suddenly let out this huge, ear-splitting cry, "No! No!" which I followed by loud wailing. I could hear people gasp out in sympathy, and Keith put his arm around me. I liked that.

I thought that now I was living alone with Keith and Vicky, they would make me feel special always. They had no one else. Only me. For the first time in my life I was going to be loved.

But it didn't quite work out like that.

I think they tried to love me. At least I know Keith did, and I think he was actually very fond of me. But Vicky, Vicky was too closed up with grief. And I knew even at eleven that the ghost of Rachel would always come between us. I could never replace Rachel.

Vicky could hardly speak to me. I once tried to call her "Mum" and give her a cuddle, but she snapped at me and told me she wasn't my mum. Keith took me out of the room and sat me down and tried to explain that Vicky was so racked with grief at the loss of Rachel that it would take time for her to return to how she was when they first took me in.

But six months later, she was no better. She couldn't show any warmth to me. She took little interest in me.

And one evening, I was in my room, putting on my pyjamas for bed. Then I went on to the landing to go to the toilet and clean my teeth, when downstairs I heard my name being mentioned. So I crept down the stairs and listened at the door. Vicky was talking. She said she couldn't do it anymore. She couldn't bring herself to love me. Keith tried to plead with her, for her to give me more time, but she wouldn't listen. And she said she didn't want me in the house any longer, and they had to get in touch with Social Services. They talked a lot more, saying things I couldn't hear properly, but in the end it was clear they'd decided they would contact Social Services.

It was the night before I was due to be picked up from the rectory that the tragedy happened in the village.

It was the evening of the school play in the village hall.

I'd told Keith I wouldn't go. I didn't want to go. I said that I'd be fine on my own. I was eleven years old, after all, and anyway, he was only a hundred metres away.

They never found out how the fire started. The investigators thought it was the electrics because they were so old and hadn't been updated for so many years; the fire was a tragedy waiting to happen. Three adults died in the fire, including Vicky and two children from the village.

But Keith was safe. I was relieved about that.

CHAPTER TWENTY-ONE

I had just finished the second session with Dr Carson. This time he had recorded it.

He had wanted me to talk about the death of my parents, but the subject matter was just too sensitive. I was evasive, blocking his questions or revealing false truths. I knew that in order for these sessions to be successful, I needed to be open, honest, expose my own vulnerabilities. Yet I was holding back.

In a doctor-patient relationship, trust is needed on both sides. If I didn't open up, it was a waste of my time and Dr Carson's. I might as well not bother going.

So I made the decision.

"There are more things I need to tell you, Dr Carson."

"Go on." He nodded.

And I told him about the sleepwalking, the glass in my foot; I told him about taking the kitchen knife, the same kitchen knife that was in my dreams, and placing it under my pillow.

And finally I told him about my nightmares coming alive.

He listened, nodding occasionally. And when I stopped, I confessed, "I'm frightened, Dr Carson, I'm really frightened. I don't know when I'm awake and when I'm in a nightmare, and I'm frightened that someone is doing this to me."

He nodded, looked sympathetic, and for the very first time he called me by my name. "Ellie, I can understand how you must be feeling and how frightening these events have been for you. Let's talk about them in some detail."

And now I opened the final emotional barrier.

"Dr Carson …"

"Please call me Ben."

"Yes. Ben. Something I haven't told anyone." I hesitated. "I suffer from regular bouts of depression."

He nodded. "And when did they start?"

"In my early teens. After my parents died. Obviously I didn't realise it was depression then. It was the fact that I was always unhappy, and I never knew why. Moments where I should have been happy, I couldn't enjoy them. I hid it. And outwardly I seemed happy. Of course, as I went from my teens into my early twenties, I started to understand what it was."

"Were there any triggers, or are there any triggers that start off a bout of depression?" he asked.

"Sometimes. If something went wrong in my life, it would trigger a depression. But the darkness could hit me any time. For no reason. And the only time I feel in control, the only time I'm really happy, is here, when I'm working and focusing on other people, when I feel I am doing good."

He nodded again. "And how has that affected your personal relationships in the past?"

"I've always found it difficult to sustain a relationship," I told him.

"Yet you've sustained a relationship with your husband?"

I shrugged, guarded.

"Have you told him about your depressions?"

"No." I shook my head.

"So how've you coped in the relationship when you've personally hit a bad patch? Has it affected your relationship?"

"I think so, yes."

Dr Carson paused then for what seemed minutes before asking the very delicate question, "And may I ask, do you love your husband?"

I SAT motionless in front of my dressing-table mirror, staring at my reflection and feeling completely remote from the woman who stared back at me. My auburn hair was tied up in a chignon style with a pretty silver brooch clipped to one side. It was not a style I had ever worn before, but this was a special day. It was my wedding day.

As I stared at my immaculate hair and my equally faultless make-up, I burst into tears.

I burst into tears, and I didn't know why. This was supposed to be one of the happiest days of my life. So why was I crying? I wasn't crying from happiness. It gushed out of me from the blackness inside. I should be happy, yet I wasn't. Why had this blackness returned on the very day I should be brimming with elation and delight?

My mascara was now running in streams down my face. I tugged out a tissue and swept the tears away, but the mascara smudged dark blotches of grey across my cheeks.

There was a knock on the door. "Ellie, are you nearly ready? The car's here."

It was Penny, my bridesmaid.

"Not quite," I called out, rubbing furiously at the smudged mascara.

The door opened, and Penny stepped inside. She also had her hair tied up, make-up flawless, a huge beaming smile lighting up her face.

Then she saw me, and her eyes darkened. "Ellie ... Ellie, are you okay?"

And she rushed towards me, kneeled by my side and placed an arm around my shoulder.

I shook my head.

"What is it? What's the matter?"

"I don't know," I replied, starting to cry again. "I don't know what's wrong with me."

"Pre-wedding nerves, that's all," Penny assured me kindly, though I could sense the unease in her voice.

I wiped away the last of my tears with the back of both hands and swivelled round to face her. "No. No, it isn't that." I hesitated. "I just ... I just wonder if I'm doing the right thing."

"Ellie, that *is* pre-wedding nerves."

"There are so many questions swirling around my head," I said quickly. "Am I doing the right thing? Do I love Nick? Do I really love Nick? And does he love me?"

I was about to continue before Penny interrupted. "Oh, Ellie, Nick is crazy about you."

"Is he?" I asked, needing confirmation.

"Totally crazy. You can see it in the way he looks at you."

"Can you?" I asked weakly.

"Yes. Absolutely."

And I replied, hardly stopping for breath, "Then maybe it's me. Perhaps I just think I love Nick, but I don't. I just like him cos he's the best and nicest guy I've met up to now because, let's face it, I've dated so many shitheads." I paused for breath before adding, "But that isn't love."

Penny didn't reply at first but shook her head slowly. "Oh, Ellie, I don't know. I can't answer those questions. All I know is that you seem perfect for each other."

I nodded once as if agreeing, but my head was in turmoil.

Penny continued, "Do you want to call off the wedding? Do you? If you do, I'll go along to the registry office and tell Nick. I'll sort everything out to cancel the reception. It's up to you, Ellie. Just tell me what to do."

And as the reality and implications of a cancelled wedding hit me, I shook my head. "No, you can't do that. No. What would that do to Nick? I couldn't do that. It isn't fair. It isn't right. Like you say, it's just nerves. I do love Nick. I do. I'm sure I do," I told her.

"Are you? Are you really sure? Because if you're not ...?"

"I am. I am."

But there was still a tiny voice inside my head giving much darker answers to my friend's questions.

BY THE TIME Penny had retouched my make-up, we were twenty minutes late arriving at the Manchester registry office.

We jumped out of the wedding car, pulled up our long

gowns (mine was cream; I refused to wear white), and inelegantly legged it up the steps.

As we entered the wedding room, breathless, my hair was now more a tumbling waterfall than a chignon. Nick was waiting nervously with his best man, Pete, and they both jumped up when they heard us make our dramatic entry.

"Sorry," I mouthed to Nick.

He smiled and kissed me on the cheek. "Thought you were having second thoughts."

I had insisted on keeping the wedding small. There were just the four of us for the wedding ceremony itself, but I'd arranged a reception in the evening to celebrate with a few colleagues and friends.

Nick had invited only Pete, no one from his office.

It did seem weird to me that Nick had invited Pete, my ex, as best man, but Nick explained that Pete was his closest friend, and anyway, as mature adults, we'd all moved on.

As we exited the registry office onto the street, I noticed an Asian man in his early seventies, small and frail, waiting near the entrance.

When Nick saw him, his body stiffened.

"You okay?" I asked.

Nick nodded, looking over at the man, "Excuse me a minute."

Nick went across and spoke a few inaudible words, they shook hands, and the man limped away. Nick returned to me, Penny and Pete.

"Sorry about that," he said.

"Who was it?" I asked.

"A long-time friend of my parents. Hadn't seen him for a while, so it was a bit of a shock."

Nick was an only child, and his parents had both died

within a year of each other from cancer when Nick was in his early twenties. He didn't like to talk about them, and I could certainly relate to that.

I WISHED I had never arranged a reception. Even though the guests were all my colleagues, I felt anxious and disconnected. My face was aching from permanent, forced smiling. My head was throbbing from a mixture of tension and too many glasses of fizz.

At one point Pete sauntered over to me and Nick and with a twinkle said, "Excuse me, I believe it's the best man's prerogative to dance with the bride?"

Nick laughed. "Go ahead," before adding, "If that's okay with you, Ellie?"

I shrugged a reluctant approval, and once we were on the dance floor, Pete nodded to the DJ, and he started playing Ed Sheeran's "Thinking Out Loud", a song Pete and I had danced to on our first date.

I stepped back. "No, Pete."

Pete ignored me and said, "Ellie, congratulations, I hope you'll both be very happy."

"Thanks."

I forced another smile before Pete pulled me in closer, moving against me in time with the song, and whispered in my ear, "Biggest mistake I ever made, letting you go."

"No, Pete," I answered quickly, "I let *you* go. Best decision I ever made." I pushed away from him, my cheeks burning with indignation.

By midnight, thankfully the guests were drifting away.

"I need my bed," I whispered to Nick.

"Count me in," Nick said, with a twinkle.

I leaned in to Nick, smiling, kissed him lightly on the lips. "Bit desperate for the loo."

"Don't be long; that bed is calling."

As I meandered my way to the far end of the room, away from the bar area, smiling and waving and thanking guests, I was about to enter the bathrooms when I saw James approaching, a warm, beaming smile lighting up his face.

"Ellie," he said expansively, "not had time to say ... well ... congratulations."

"Thank you, James. Hope you've had a nice time?" I asked.

"Yes, it's been lovely. Thank you so much." And he stepped in, curled both arms around me and gave me a gentle hug. As he pulled away, he kissed me on the cheek. "Good luck. I hope you'll be very happy, Ellie. You deserve it."

"Thank you, James," I said with genuine emotion. "And is ... is your wife here tonight?"

He turned. "Yes, she's over there."

We both looked across to the other side of the room.

Hilary looked older than James, maybe early forties, but very elegant and stylish.

As she noticed James and me look across at her, she raised her hand in a tiny wave.

And, afterwards, I couldn't help but think that it was as if she was waving goodbye.

In two months' time she was dead.

NICK and I spent our first night together as a married couple in my large, detached house. I was tipsy, but not too drunk to enjoy and remember that first night. Nick was loving and passionate, and afterwards we lay wrapped in each other's arms, and I felt warm and happy.

It felt so easy to dismiss my pre-wedding misgivings.

I slept soundly.

Until I was woken by a disturbing nightmare.

I was running away from Nick, but my legs wouldn't move fast enough, and no matter how quickly I tried to power away from him, Nick was always just one pace behind me.

"SO DO YOU LOVE YOUR HUSBAND?" Dr Carson repeated.

"We've only been … been married, well, just over a year, yet … I'm … I'm confused about myself … I don't know." I was clutching for the right words.

"Go on," Dr Carson encouraged.

"I question all the time whether I do love my husband. I question whether I did the right thing in marrying him. I keep pondering whether I should tell him my emotional problems, but I always shy away."

"And medications for your depression, Ellie? Have you been taking anything?"

"Since I trained, I've self-medicated on and off," I confessed.

He nodded; there was a silence in the room. Dr Carson's face was surprisingly warm and sympathetic.

He eventually said, "I think, for now, you need to be on regular medication to keep the clinical depression under control and not just when you feel you need it."

"Okay," I murmured, feeling an odd sense of relief as I listened to his instructions.

"So let's get on top of the depression first and take it from there. But to return to the nightmares and the somnambulism, I agree your experiences are very frightening, and we need to do something to help you."

"Any suggestions?" I asked.

He thought for a moment, staring into space, before looking directly at me.

"I take it you know what polysomnography is, Ellie?"

I nodded. "Sleep study, yes? Though I don't know much about it."

"Yes. It's a test to diagnose sleep disorders. It records your brain waves, the oxygen level in your blood, your heart rate and breathing as well as eye and leg movements. It helps diagnose sleep disorders, and it also gives me some idea of how to treat the sleep disorder."

I nodded, wanting him to continue.

"It's usually done at a sleep centre or within a hospital. Like the specialist unit we have here."

If this was what he was about to suggest, I wasn't keen and frowned at the thought of spending a night away from home in a wing of my own hospital.

Dr Carson picked up on this. "I understand you wouldn't want to do the study here, it's perfectly understandable, but I can arrange an overnight stay at Wythenshawe, who also have a unit?" He paused. "I take it you'd prefer that?"

"If I agree to do this study – if – then, yes. Definitely not here," I told him.

"That's fine. And I do think it's worth doing, Ellie. I really do."

"Give me some more background on dreaming. I mean, I've been looking it up, but I'd like your take before I make up my mind," I told him.

"Well, normally, people dream more than two hours a night, and a nightmare usually happens in the later hours of REM sleep. The dreamer often awakens from a nightmare with a good recollection of the imagery and content like you obviously do. However, if nightmares become frequent, such as in your case, frequent to the point of dysfunction, you may be suffering from nightmare disorder," he explained carefully.

"What's nightmare disorder exactly?"

"During sleep your body passes through different stages of sleep, as you know …"

"From light sleep to the deep sleep of REM," I continued.

"Exactly. REM sleep happens through signals from the pons, which is located—"

I interrupted him, pointing to the back of my head. "At the base of the brain."

Dr Carson smiled. "Sorry, Ellie. I hope I don't sound too condescending?"

"No, not at all." I was warming to Dr Carson. "Carry on."

"Okay. This is, in fact, where signals for REM sleep originate and where signals to the spinal cord shut off."

"Right. This is all new to me."

He continued, "It's why the body doesn't move during deep sleep. But if the pons does not shut down these signals, the individual may act out the dream physically – known as REM sleep behaviour disorder. So when you're being chased and you're running, you will literally start running."

"Which I do."

"It could also account for the somnambulism," he added.

I thought about it for only a second, then said, "Dr Carson, I'm up for the sleep study."

He smiled. "Oh, and Ellie, I just want to assure you that everything we've talked about today is totally confidential. You mustn't worry; no one at the hospital will know," he assured me.

"Thank you, Ben," I said, returning his smile.

I HAD JUST EMERGED from Ben's office when my phone rang. I didn't recognise the number. I wondered whether I should answer, but my curiosity was too great.

"Hello?" I asked cautiously.

"Dr Thompson?"

"Yes?"

"It's Liam at Didsbury Motors. About your car?" the male voice with its strong Mancunian accent said.

I felt a wave of relief. "Oh yes. Have you sorted it?"

"Yes and no," he answered. "We've located the problem."

"Oh yes, and what was it?"

Liam paused for a second before answering, "I'm afraid your car, Dr Thompson, has been vandalised."

"What d'you mean?"

"It took us a while to work out what the problem was," he continued. "Anyway, we've found out now. It seems a rubber ball or something similar was pushed up your exhaust, then hammered deep inside it. That was the cause of the starting problems. Sometimes, when you start a car with a blocked exhaust, it blows out the object, but this was so tight and so far up that it's stuck. In fact, we haven't been able to remove it, and it looks like you'll need a new exhaust."

It took a while for me to assimilate this information, and my heart started racing again. I told Liam to go ahead with a new exhaust, and I rang off.

I was definitely being targeted. My paranoia was real – the feeling of being followed, the white car that bumped me, my slashed tyres and now this. But who was doing this to me? Who had been chasing after me along the canal path? Were they responsible for these incidents too? My head was spinning.

But one thing I knew for certain. I was in danger, and I had a husband who didn't believe me.

CHAPTER TWENTY-TWO

It was 9 p.m., and I was stood at the reception desk of the Sleep Clinic. I placed my overnight canvas bag by my feet. It contained a change of clothing for the following day, a set of old-fashioned pyjamas that I hadn't worn since I shared a room while at uni (traditional cotton flannel), and a bag of toiletries.

I was a little tense and anxious.

The young woman at reception was scrolling on her phone as I approached. She looked up when she heard the door swing to, stuffed her phone under the desk, and her face broke into a work smile, fixed with eyes unsmiling.

I had been expected at 9 p.m., so the woman said, "Dr Thompson?"

"Yes."

"Welcome to the Sleep Clinic."

She smiled again, showing a perfect set of very white teeth. Her hair was fiery red, pulled back off her pretty, pale face in a ponytail.

"If you'd like to take a seat, Anne will be with you in a

minute, and she will take you through to your room," she told me.

There were half a dozen chairs in the reception area, and I chose an end one. The receptionist had spoken as if Anne were my personal friend, and when Anne entered a few minutes later, she was indeed very friendly. In her forties and wearing the uniform of a staff nurse, her round, beaming face matched her equally round body and sturdy legs.

"Dr Thompson," she radiated, arm extended, and I shook her cool, firm hand. "How lovely to meet you. If you'd like to follow me, I'll settle you in your room and take you through all the procedures."

I stood up and followed Anne into a corridor with a row of doors either side. "You're our only 'guest' tonight. We try to keep it to urgent cases on a Saturday, and Dr Carson fast-tracked you," she explained as we entered the first room on the left.

The room was like a side ward in a hospital except it was less cold and impersonal. Small touches had been added, like fresh flowers on a coffee table, and bright, sunflower-patterned curtains. The walls were painted a restful light taupe, and on each wall hung pictures of beautiful sunsets, one over a beach, one rural over rolling hills. The bed, too, was not standard hospital issue; it was a pine rather than on wheels with metal sides. I found out later that the mattress was not standard hospital issue either – hard and firm and covered in plastic so the sheets slid and puckered up. Instead, it was very comfortable memory foam.

"As you can see," Anne said, "we try to make the room as comfortable and homely as possible. You have your en suite here too."

I pushed open the door. The en suite consisted of a toilet

and basin, adapted for patients with disabilities with a wet room shower.

"You have a bathroom robe in there as well and, of course, towels," she said, indicating.

She saw me glancing at the apparatus lying on the bed. "Yes, these are what we call our 'instruments of torture'," she joked, with a little giggly laugh. I smiled.

Anne then asked me to change into my pyjamas, which I did in the en suite, and next she conducted a general health check: temperature, pulse, blood pressure. She ascertained I didn't have any current infections before talking me through each of the assessment tests they would be doing.

Electrode sensors were placed on my chest to monitor heart activity. Less comfortable were the sensors near each eyelid to measure which stage of sleep I was in.

"REM or non-REM," Anne explained, and I nodded.

Next came the sensors on my head to measure electrical signals from my brain, then sensors fixed on each leg to assess muscle activity; bands around my chest and stomach for my breathing; a nasal cannula – the two plastic prongs up my nose to monitor my breathing – and finally an oximeter on my finger to record oxygen levels.

"I know people worry they'll never get to sleep being 'wired up' like this," Anne said, doing finger quote marks, "but you'll be surprised. There's a button here next to your bed in case you need us urgently. I'm here all night, so don't worry. And finally ..." She pointed to a camera in a corner that was angled towards the bed. "Are you okay for this to be filmed?" she asked.

"So long as it doesn't appear on YouTube," I joked.

Anne gave a huge belly laugh that my joke didn't deserve. When she stopped laughing, she continued, "Anyway, I'll leave you to it. Make yourself comfortable. And when you're ready to sleep, just switch out the light. There's a small nightlight in this corner here so there's just enough light to film, but hopefully it won't keep you awake. And if you're not tired, you can watch television."

She pointed to a TV positioned on the wall.

With that, Anne turned and left me to it.

I emptied the rest of my things from my overnight bag, hung them up in the pine wardrobe, went to the toilet, cleaned my teeth, switched out the light and climbed into bed.

The glow from the small light in the top corner shed an eerie shadow across the room, and I was sure I wouldn't sleep.

But by eleven after turning over, this way and that, sitting up, lying down, on my back, on my side, I finally slipped into sleep.

I WOKE up when my phone started buzzing on the bedside cabinet. I was still half asleep as I sat up, fumbled for the phone, grasped hold of it and pressed the green answer button.

"Yes?" I asked sleepily. There was no answer. "Hello?" Still no answer. "Hello? Who's that?"

And then I heard the same metallic voice as before. "Hi, Ellie, you lost your mind yet? Cos I'm outside."

I almost shrieked with fright. The phone went dead as the caller rang off.

Was he really outside? Where was Nick? I was alone in the bed. Where was he? Maybe he was downstairs?

"Nick," I shouted. "Nick!" But there was silence.

Then it hit me. Aren't I in the Sleep Clinic and not in my bed? No. This was my bed and my bedroom. The Sleep Clinic was the previous night. Saturday night. Tonight is Sunday.

So where was Nick?

Suddenly the doorbell rang and let out a tight scream.

I grabbed my phone, dialled 999, but nothing happened. The call wasn't going through. I tried again. But my screen went black. My phone had died. But how could that be? I thought. I had only charged it before I came to bed.

The doorbell rang again. Constantly now, like the caller had left his finger pressed hard on the bell.

I jumped out of bed, wrapped a dressing gown around me, switched on the bedroom light, went onto the landing, switched that light on and then systematically entered every room in the house, switching on the lights until the whole house was illuminated. All the time the doorbell rang and rang and only stopped when I switched on the external light that overhung the front door.

I was panicking, but I fought to stay in control. I refused to be intimidated. I would fight back. But my chest felt tight, and my heart was pumping.

I hurried into the kitchen and withdrew the unicorn knife from its block. And as I walked from the kitchen into the hall, I held the knife in front of me at arm's length. I wasn't sure what I was going to do, but I edged slowly towards the front door, small, cautious step by small, cautious step. Just as was within striking distance of the door, all the lights went out, and the house was plunged into total darkness.

I gasped and dropped the knife. It clattered onto the

parquet floor, breaking the silence. I stood very still, frozen, listening. No sound from outside the front door.

My iPhone was in my hand, and I lifted it to my face and pressed on the torch icon. I flashed it around the floor in a looping arc until I saw the knife, grabbed it, before shining the torch at the front entrance.

Through the frosted glass, I could see the shadowy outline of a tall, stooped figure. I jumped as the door handle suddenly started rattling, moving up and down, as if testing to see if it was open. The rattling stopped as the figure now put his shoulder against the door.

It was then that I realised the door wasn't double locked, nor bolted. Panicking, I ran to the door, reached up to the top bolt, but before I could slide it across, the glass splintered, a gloved hand was thrust through the shattered glass, and the knife it was holding sliced into my throat.

I SAT up in bed screaming, clutching at my throat. I was gasping, my chest rising up and down, heart racing.

I peered around, confused by the unfamiliar surroundings. My head felt strange, and I put my hand to it, touched the sensors and the nasal cannula before realising where I was. The Sleep Clinic.

It had been a nightmare. I lay back on my pillow, a sense of relief flooding over me.

I was about to nestle down back under the covers when I caught a glimpse of movement out of the corner of my eye. It was to my left next to the door. I squinted in the gloomy light.

A figure was standing there, very still, hood over his face, a knife in his right hand.

I shot upright, screaming, as the figure moved slowly towards me.

"Who are you? Help!" I screamed. "Please, someone, help me!"

Where was Anne? Surely she could hear my screams. Why hadn't she come in?

I scrambled for the emergency button, but the figure pulled my arm away.

And at the same time, he raised his knife.

CHAPTER TWENTY-THREE

I wasn't sure how long I'd slept, but when I woke, a sliver of light was edging its way between the curtains.

As I sat up, it all came flooding back. Waking from my nightmare. Only to find the hooded figure in my room.

Did an intruder really enter my room? Or was it a nightmare? If it wasn't, if it was real, why didn't the intruder kill me? And how did he get into the Sleep Clinic and to my room? What did he want? And why?

I thought it through logically and concluded that the whole idea of an intruder was utterly ridiculous. My reasoning helped lift the tension that was pulsating in waves of stress through my entire body.

I badly needed a cup of tea, so I reached across to press the button to call Anne. As I did so, I glanced at the pad by my bedside cabinet.

There was something scribbled on it. I picked it up, read it.

"You've lost your mind, Ellie."

I screamed.

"DR THOMPSON, I am positive no one could have got in your room," Anne assured me.

"How can you be certain?" I asked.

"I was on duty all night at reception," she explained.

"And you never left the reception, either to go to the toilet or to make yourself a drink?" I persisted.

In reply, Anne looked down, giving me her answer.

"So someone could have crept into my room? You weren't there all night, were you?"

"I think it's highly unlikely anyone entered your room," Anne said.

"Well, it's not. How do you explain the note? I didn't write it. It's not in my handwriting, so how can you explain that?"

Anne couldn't. She simply shrugged, lost for words.

I stood up from where I was sitting on the edge of the bed. I was still in my pyjamas. I started pulling all the sensors off my face, the two belts from round my body; then I ripped the oximeter off my finger.

"An intruder came into my room last night," I continued to insist. "I know it. This message proves it. I need to see the video footage," I said, pointing to the camera in the corner. "That will show you I'm telling the truth, and then we can pass it on to the police."

Anne didn't reply at first.

"Well?" I pressed.

"I'm sorry, Dr Thompson, I'm not authorised to give it to you or for you to look at the recording."

"Then who is?" I asked. "Authorised to view it?"

"The recording could be emailed over the weekend to Dr

Carson in light of the circumstances," Anne said as she shrugged an apology.

I nodded. It would have to do.

THE REST OF THE WEEKEND, my head was in turmoil.

I rang Dr Carson, and without going into detail, I explained an emergency had arisen at the Sleep Clinic, and they were sending over the recording, and could I call in early on Monday morning to view it together. He wanted more information, but I didn't want to go into a long explanation over the phone. However, Dr Carson was intrigued and agreed to see me before we both started work.

Nick wanted all the details about my night at the Sleep Clinic, but I told him only the bare basics, not mentioning the frightening incident with the intruder for a reason I couldn't quite articulate. Somehow I didn't quite trust his reaction. Although he would strenuously deny it, I still suspected a sense of scepticism from him regarding my nightmares and the possibility of a stalker.

And niggling at the back of my head were the continued doubts over Nick's fidelity. They hadn't gone away, but we'd never talked about it since that day when he wasn't at the golf.

In truth, all weekend I had also questioned myself, questioned my sanity. Was I wrong? Was there really someone in my room? Was it a nightmare, or was it real?

But I had been stalked; that wasn't in my head. My damaged car was real. The phone calls, the message written on the pad, they were all real.

So the more I thought about it, the more frightening it

became. Even at the Sleep Clinic I was not safe from this stalker. And if I wasn't safe in that environment, where was I safe? Not at home. Not at work. Nowhere.

Once I had the recording – the proof – I would go to the police. I had prevaricated long enough. And the police could check my phone for the anonymous calls I'd been receiving, and maybe they could track the caller.

This whole situation was ruining both my personal and professional life.

I needed to bring it to a full stop.

CHAPTER TWENTY-FOUR

I had arranged to meet Dr Carson in his office at 7 a.m., so the rush-hour traffic along Wilmslow Road and then Oxford Road was light, as it was still so early.

I drove down into the underground car park. There were a few cars dotted around belonging to those night-shift staff who were due to finish at 7 a.m. I still felt uneasy as I parked up and walked swiftly towards the lift.

Thankfully it was now working.

"Come in," Dr Carson called when I knocked on his door.

He was sitting behind his desk as I entered, his open laptop in front of him. He smiled, his lips not parting. He stood up, came round the desk and shook my hand. It still felt clammy, but he seemed taller than at our last interview. I'd guessed he was around five feet five to my five feet seven, but he was now at eye level with me. It was only when I casually glanced down that I noticed he was wearing shiny black boots with evident lifts.

"So tell me, Ellie," he said, in a very friendly tone. "How

did it go on Saturday? And why are you so desperate to see that recording of the night?"

We sat down opposite each other in the Chesterfield armchairs, and I described in detail the nightmare where I thought I was at home before I woke up to find a hooded stranger in my room.

I told him the figure at the Sleep Clinic resembled the person who was repeatedly in my dreams and was the same familiar figure who had followed and chased me along the canal towpath in Castlefield. I told him, too, about the anonymous threatening phone calls with the same message that I'd seen written on the bedside notepad, suggesting I was losing my mind.

Dr Carson let me talk uninterrupted, occasionally nodding his head. When I finished, he stood up without commenting. "The link to the recording has arrived. Shall we take a look at it?"

I nodded, but at the same time a surge of nerves flooded over me, an almost overwhelming sense of anxiety at the thought of seeing this intruder stooped over my bed.

But, I told myself sternly, it had to be done.

We moved across to his desk, sat opposite each other, and he angled the laptop so we could both see the screen. He clicked on the downloaded link. "I've fast-forwarded to just after you fell into sleep," he told me as the footage started playing.

And suddenly I felt vulnerable, with an edge of embarrassment, that Dr Carson must have been watching me in my pyjamas, as I went to the en suite, then climbed into bed.

The image of me in bed now filled the screen. I was asleep but restless. My legs were moving under the duvet, tiny groans coming from me.

"I'm going to forward it slowly to the point where you wake up with the nightmare," he said.

We both leaned forward nearer the screen as he forwarded the recording, not too fast, but enough to recognise any changes. His finger was poised over his laptop. "I know this is slow and tiresome, but we don't know the exact time you were woken by the nightmare, and we don't want to miss it. So bear with me."

I nodded. My eyes didn't leave the screen.

We sat like this, motionless as statues, eyes fixed to the screen, for what felt like hours until suddenly the image of me blurred as I shot bolt upright.

Immediately Dr Carson paused the screen.

In the frozen image, my eyes were wide and staring, filled with utter fear. Dr Carson had paused the screen at the moment where I was holding my throat, as if trying to stem the flow of blood.

Dr Carson looked across the desk at me and asked, genuinely concerned, "Are you okay?"

I nodded, but in fact my hands were shaking, and I had to place them on my thighs to steady them. My chest felt so tight like a metal band was constricting my breathing.

"I'm going to start the recording again. And from what you've told me, once you realise where you are, you should then see a figure in the room who comes towards you, and we should pick him up on the camera. Are you sure you're ready for this, Ellie?"

I nodded without taking my eyes off the screen.

"Okay," Dr Carson said.

He pressed play, and on the screen I came alive. I looked disorientated. I rubbed my eyes, peering around in the gloom, squinting, before my face registered where I was.

There was a relaxing of muscle tension in my face, and it appeared that I was about to snuggle back down in the bed, when my eye caught sight of something off camera. I sat quickly up again, and the fear suddenly reappeared in my eyes, and my whole body tensed stiff.

I started to scream hysterically, eyes bulging, mouth open wide, a classic expression of anguish and trauma like that captured in Edvard Munch's *The Scream*.

It was like watching myself in a horror movie.

"This is where he comes towards me! It's here! It's here! He's coming now," I said urgently.

And on the screen my eyes peered up as if at the approaching figure, in total fear, my mouth still opened in a scream.

And it seemed I was looking directly up at him from my bed, like he was looming over me.

Except the figure didn't appear.

"Where is he? Where is he?" I shouted. "He should be there. Where is he?"

In the recording I slumped back down onto the bed with my eyes shut, and I stayed there completely motionless.

"What's going on? I don't understand," I said, full of anxiety.

"Let's just keep playing it and see what happens next," Dr Carson suggested softly.

He let the recording run. And run.

No hooded figure appeared.

I watched, stunned, while my sleeping self lay motionless in bed, almost peaceful. When my eyes shot open again, I looked dazed as if half awake.

I slowly sat up, my eyes vacant and glazed.

"I don't understand this," I said. "I don't understand what's happening."

Very slowly, from the bedside table, I picked up the pen. I leaned across, and I started writing on the pad.

I wrote only a short sentence before I dropped back down again. I stayed very still, stretched out under the duvet, and within seconds I was snoring.

I was so shocked I couldn't speak. I fell back in my chair, casting a look of bewilderment towards Dr Carson. He was staring at me, his face impassive.

"I didn't write that note. That note was not my handwriting."

On the laptop the recording continued to run.

No intruder appeared. There was no intruder.

CHAPTER TWENTY-FIVE

"It's called a false awakening."

Dr Carson and I were in the cafeteria. It was still early and very quiet. We sat at a corner table.

"A false awakening is a vivid and convincing dream about awakening from sleep while the dreamer in reality continues to sleep," Dr Carson explained.

I tried to take this in. "So when I woke up in the hospital and saw that figure, I was still in a dream?" I asked.

"Yes. That's what false awakening is. It's like a double dream or a dream within a dream."

"So that figure, that figure in the room, he was never there; he was part of my dream within a dream?"

"Exactly."

"So how do you explain the note? Me waking up and writing a note that wasn't even in my own handwriting?"

Dr Carson didn't answer at first. "I haven't got an easy answer for that. But this is what I suspect happened. When you woke up suddenly the second time, you were still having a false awakening, you were still in a dream within a dream

…" He paused. "And all I can surmise is that in that one moment you took on the role of the intruder, your pursuer, so when you wrote the note, without realising it, the handwriting was his and not yours," he said, watching me closely for my reaction once he'd stopped talking.

I shook my head, slumped back in my chair. "That is too scary."

We didn't talk for a minute or two. I was deep in thought, taking it all in, yet hardly able to believe it.

Finally, Dr Carson spoke, his voice a little hesitant. "I think … Ellie, I think … we need to consider that you may be suffering from PTSD."

I shot him a look, leaned forward across the table. "No …" I said, unable to countenance the possibility.

"Listen, please, Ellie. You might not like to admit this, you may not even realise it, but you have been under a lot of stress at work. We're understaffed, the working hours are ridiculous, and those conditions added to … and I know you were cleared of all negligence, and rightly so, but it has been a very stressful time for you … and on top of that, your depression … so maybe, just maybe you are suffering from PTSD."

He stopped, nervously looking across at me again for my reaction.

This time I didn't react aggressively, so he continued, "I don't know whether you're aware of this, Ellie, when you researched about nightmares, but PTSD can also cause hallucinations."

He knew this was delicate, and he was treading barefoot on eggshells. My body stiffened. He saw my response and lifted both hands in defence. "I know, but it's something we shouldn't completely dismiss."

"I'm sorry, but that's ridiculous," I said, ignoring Dr Carson's advice and immediately dismissing his tentative suggestion. "Hallucinations refer to something that isn't really there," I continued.

He nodded.

"An auditory hallucination is where you hear voices that aren't there, yes?"

He nodded again before picking up on my theme. "While visual hallucinations involve seeing something that isn't there."

"And that's what you're suggesting, Dr Carson? That I'm suffering from visual hallucinations. So that the man who followed me wasn't really there. The car that followed me and rammed my vehicle didn't really exist. In fact, it's an hallucination, it's all in my head!" I raised my voice, growing more agitated with each sentence.

"All I'm saying—"

"Is that you think I'm crazy," I interrupted.

"No, that's not what I'm saying. But I think it's an area we should explore," he added a little weakly.

"The dent in my car was real; how do you explain that?" I snapped.

"Maybe someone did run into the back of you ... accidentally," he suggested with a shrug.

"No! I was rammed. I was followed," I insisted.

"Let us just assume for one minute that you are suffering from a mild form of hallucinations ..."

"NO!"

"We have to look at that possibility, Ellie. And maybe, just maybe, what is happening in your dreams plus possibly some form of PTSD, maybe that is causing the hallucinations, and the reality is that maybe you had an accident, backed into a wall or something, I don't know, but in your hallucination you blocked that out, and it then becomes part of your nightmare."

I jumped up. "This is drivel. Pure drivel. I opened myself up to you, told you personal things, and you come up with this total, total ... shit!"

Dr Carson was clearly embarrassed. He glanced around the cafeteria, but no one was paying us any attention.

He also stood up, tried to calm me. "Ellie, please listen. I think you definitely need to take time off work."

I scoffed. "I'm not doing that! I don't need time off, and what's more, there's no way I can take time off."

I started to walk away. Dr Carson called after me, "Ellie, please, you need to take some leave. I will have to recommend you take sickness leave."

I didn't turn round, but I was aware of Dr Carson watching me weave my way between the mostly empty tables.

"I am not crazy," I mumbled to myself. "I am *not* crazy."

CHAPTER TWENTY-SIX

I liked my room in the Children's Home. It was small but cosy. And I loved my little desk where I could read and do my homework in peace without being bothered by all the other kids.

Because as a child I was left so much on my own, I'd taught myself to read by the time I was four, and I devoured books from our school library once I went to school at five. I'd read them in bed with a torch under the blankets after my parents switched out my light.

It was one of the reasons the other kids called me weird because my head was always in a book when they couldn't even read or they were still at the stage of learning simple words and sentences.

So once I arrived at the home, I was happy to shut myself off in my own private room as often as the staff would allow.

As for the house itself ... God, I remember every inch of it so well ...

No one walking past the large Edwardian house could

have possibly suspected that inside were eight unwanted, damaged kids, aged ten to fifteen. But step inside and it was like the Tardis.

On the ground floor there were three single bedrooms off the hallway, then towards the rear of the house was a huge kitchen and off that an equally big dining room with a long trestle table large enough for the eight kids, the two managers, Gavin and Joyce, and, I think, about three other care officers.

The basement had been converted into a massive playroom. At the nearest end was a vast TV mounted on the wall, tatty worn sofas in a semicircle around it. At the far end was the games area – table tennis, a mini billiard table, stacks of board games, though I never bothered playing any of them.

The first floor had been converted into five more bedrooms, four single and a shared bedroom. My bedroom was one of the two that looked down onto the garden at the back.

I'd met the rest of the kids at dinner on my first evening. Joyce came to collect me from my room, and I followed her downstairs into the dining room, where all the kids were sat round the table.

Gavin stood up, introduced me to all these kids, and then we went round the table with each one telling me their names. The youngest was Katie, ten, very shy, head down as she spoke into her chest, and I could hardly hear her mumbled name. One girl, Teresa, about the same age as me, never spoke. Ever.

The eldest was Andy, who was fourteen. He was a big lad, overweight but tall. He was the only one to stand up, announcing his name in a loud voice.

I knew he'd be trouble, and I was right, but I didn't realise how soon.

It was only my first night. We had to be in our rooms by

8.30 p.m., lights out at 9 p.m., which was fine by me. I preferred my own company. We shared a bathroom on our floor, and I had just cleaned my teeth, returned to my room, changed into my pyjamas, when suddenly my door was pushed open, and there was Andy. I asked him what he thought he was doing and told him to get out. But he took no notice, stepped inside and shoved the door to. I told him again to get out, but he said I'd been given the best room in the house, and he wanted it. I told him to get lost. So he then came up close so his face was almost touching mine, and he said he was going to make my life endlessly, utterly miserable, day and night, and before he left, he told me I'd got an enemy now, and I'd better watch my back.

I was furious. He wasn't going to get away with threatening me like that. I decided I wouldn't report him. I'd deal with it in my own way.

I couldn't get to sleep, wondering what I could do. I waited, and I listened until there was no sound in the house. I heard Gavin and Joyce climbing the stairs up to their attic room, waited another half hour till I was sure they were asleep. I crept downstairs to the kitchen, boiled up a kettle and filled a large mug with the steaming hot water.

I carried it carefully back up the stairs. I thought I knew which was Andy's room, and very quietly I opened his door. The landing light had been left on, so as I entered, I could see him in his bed. He was fast asleep, snoring. Fortunately he was lying on his back.

I slowly pulled back the duvet, and he didn't move.

He was quite still – until I poured the boiling hot water over his penis.

I just had time to run out of the bedroom, dart across the

landing and into my room and shut the door behind me before I heard his screams of pure agony.

He guessed it was me, even accused me, but nobody could prove it. He never bothered me again. And I was able to keep myself to myself for the rest of my time there.

CHAPTER TWENTY-SEVEN

In many ways, I knew Dr Carson was right. I was in no fit mental state to act in the best interests of my patients.

And what if I was suffering from hallucinations? The image of me in the Sleep Clinic as I scribbled the note continued to haunt me. I couldn't forget it. Maybe every incident up to now really had been a hallucination.

It had truly scared me when I'd discovered the knife under my pillow, but now what had happened in the Sleep Clinic felt even scarier. Was I close to a breakdown? I was constantly tired with the broken sleep; my depression seemed to hang over me, darker than ever; my stress levels were out of control.

So I did seriously consider taking time off, but I told myself it wasn't fair on our already understaffed medical team. I didn't want Dr Carson to report our sessions or his concerns to Mr Ahmed, the consultant and head of our team. But just to cover myself, I told Dr Carson I would ask Mr Ahmed's advice. That seemed to satisfy him.

In the end I didn't go to see Mr Ahmed because what I

really needed was a series of nights with uninterrupted sleep, so I self-prescribed myself some sleeping pills.

On the first night I slept right through, no significant nightmares, and in the morning I felt slightly drowsy, but after breakfast I was far more refreshed than I'd been for months.

The rest of the week I coped well at work. I received no more anonymous calls. Neither was I followed, not on foot nor in my car.

Unless, of course, I had never been followed at all. Unless, of course, it was all inside my head. I mustn't think like that; I mustn't go there.

King Lear's words popped into my head, "Oh, that way madness lies."

I wasn't mad. I wasn't crazy.

Don't even think about it, I told myself.

I had only one nightmare that week. It was an anxiety nightmare. The previous evening I'd taken Samson for a walk in the park. I'd let him off his lead, and he ran off and disappeared into the bushes. I called for him, but he didn't come. I started to panic and kept calling his name urgently. Finally he appeared, running towards me and jumping up to lick my face. I was so relieved I stood there with him in my arms, petting him for a good five minutes.

I told Nick about it. "For a minute I really thought I'd lost him, and I was so panicked because he never runs off like that."

"Samson would never run off; he loves you to bits," he said.

However, that night, I dreamed I was in the city centre, and I'd lost Samson, and I was running along the empty streets, calling his name more and more urgently, when suddenly the hooded figure appeared round the corner, pulling Samson along on his lead.

"Hey, that's my dog!" I shouted.

And as the figure picked Samson up, I ran towards him, shouting to put him down. But the figure produced a knife. He held it towards Samson ...

And I woke myself up, crying and screaming.

Nick was comforting me. "Ellie, Ellie, it's okay."

I told him the nightmare.

"That's just anxiety from when you thought you'd lost Samson in the park," he said.

"I know, I know, but it was still scary." I couldn't stop shaking. "It felt so real," I sobbed.

AS THE WEEKEND LOOMED CLOSER, I had one serious concern that left me feeling edgy.

From Friday, Nick was away for two nights on a course in Birmingham. He'd offered to postpone it, but I insisted, "No, you go. I'll be fine."

"I could cancel," he suggested.

"It's too late, Nick. Honestly I'll be fine."

"I don't like leaving you when ..." He tailed off.

I felt myself become a little prickly. "When what?"

"When ... you know, when you're ..." he said cautiously.

"Having these delusions?"

"No. When you're, you know, like, on edge," he said tentatively.

"Nick, I'm not on edge," I lied. "I've been fine all week. I'm dealing with it."

If only I were.

"Ellie, you could always ask Penny to stay over."

"Honestly, Nick, no babysitter required." I smiled as brightly as I could. "No need for anyone to stay over."

IT WAS FRIDAY, 7 p.m., Penny, James and I had just finished in surgery for the weekend. I felt exhausted from the effort of keeping up the outward pretence that I was in control; I knew I was smiling too much when inside my guts were churning.

Penny and I were tucked in a corner of the bustling Lower Turk's Head while James was at the bar, buying the drinks. It was noisy and buzzing, and we had to raise our voices over the bursts of laughter and lively music.

"So what are your plans this weekend?" I asked.

Penny's face brightened into a deep smile. "Tom's wife is away for the weekend – so he's coming to stay with me."

I shot her a disapproving look. "Right."

"Yes, I know you don't approve, and I understand why ... but I can't help myself, Ellie," she explained.

I replied, a little curt, "Okay." Then I added coolly, "You know how I feel, so ... let's hope it works out for you."

"I think this time it will." Penny smiled. "Anyway, why did you ask?"

"Doesn't matter," I said.

"Ellie, what was it?" she insisted.

As I started to explain, James arrived with our three drinks clasped between his hands – two white wines and a pint. "It was just ... with Nick being away, I thought we could go out."

"Thanks, James," Penny said as we all picked up our

drinks and chorused a "cheers". Then Penny asked, "Not worried about being on your own?"

"Course not!"

"I could cancel Tom, stay over with you instead," she suggested.

"No way. You enjoy yourself," I said with just a hint of sarcasm.

Penny glanced at James and asked mischievously, a twinkle in her eye, "You got any plans this weekend, James?"

"Not really. Very boring, I'm afraid."

"Really? Ellie's all on her own."

Penny's lips twitched, holding back a smile as I shot daggers at her.

Then her phone rang in her handbag. She pulled it out, glanced at the caller.

"Ooo – it's Tom. Excuse me. I'll take it outside; too noisy in here."

We watched as she threaded her way between the groups of drinkers, answering her call.

"Penny's going to get hurt," I said to James.

"You're probably right." He took a large sip of his pint, placed it back on the table, looked over at me. "Ellie, if you do have a really bad night ... while Nick's away, give me a ring, and we'll talk things through," he offered.

"I couldn't do that!"

"Why not?"

"It's not fair on you. And anyway, it'll be the middle of the night."

"I really don't mind," he said.

"That's kind, but Nick said I could call him on his mobile if I have a really bad one. But it's nice of you to offer." I smiled at him. "Thank you."

"I mean it," James reiterated. "If you can't get hold of Nick, call me." And he fished in his jacket pocket, producing his card. "Take this anyway, it's got my numbers on, and if it's an emergency, use it. Please," he insisted.

I smiled a thank you, took his card, and James held my gaze that little bit longer than was necessary. I realised my cheeks were burning.

CHAPTER TWENTY-EIGHT

I arrived home just after nine. I didn't fancy cooking for one, so I stopped off in Rusholme and picked up a takeaway – chicken dhansak with pilau rice.

As I parked up in the garage, I could hear Samson in the hall whining and scratching at the door. Nick had popped back from work to let him out before driving off to Birmingham. When I opened the door into the house, he was jumping up at me, tail wagging faster than windscreen wipers.

"Hello, Samson." I kneeled, stroked him, and he rolled on his belly for me to scratch his tummy. Then he was up, sniffing at my plastic bag of curry.

"Not for you, Samson," I told him. "Come on. I'll feed you."

He trotted after me into the dining kitchen.

As Samson licked at his food, I sat on a high stool at the island, relishing my curry washed down with a large glass of Australian Shiraz, left open from mid-week.

I thought about watching some trashy TV, but I was

exhausted and decided to have an early night. I let Samson out into the garden; then he followed me up the stairs. I contemplated whether to take a sleeping pill but decided against it. If I had a disturbed night, I could lie in all Saturday morning.

I was about to undress when my mobile, lying on the bed, rang. It surprised me, but I assumed it was Nick making sure I was okay.

It wasn't. And I didn't recognise the number.

"Hello?" I answered cautiously. I could hear breathing but no voice. "Okay, who is this?" I asked more assertively than I felt, sensing the tension rising in me.

"Ellie." I recognised the voice, but it was drunken, slurred. "It's Pete."

"Pete? What are you doing ringing at this time?"

I relaxed, but I was angry.

"I know Nick's away," he said, the words sliding into one another. "And I was just in Didsbury having a drink ..."

"*A* drink? You sound pissed, Pete," I told him.

"Yeah, I am. A bit. But I've been thinking about you."

"I'm very flattered," I said sarcastically.

"Oh good. Well, I'm outside now, and I thought I could pop in for a drink or ... you know ... or something?"

He was outside? Shit. I went to my window, pulled the curtains wide enough to peep through, and there he was, on the road, standing outside the gate. He caught a glimpse of me and waved.

"Pete, you're pestering me. You're like a bloody stalker," I told him sharply, tugging the curtains to.

"Aww, don't say that. You see, Ellie, there's, you know, stuff ... things ... I want to say to you. About me and you cos I still feel—"

"Pete, piss off." And he never finished his sentence as I ended the call.

Once in bed, with my head now full of Pete, I took a while to fall asleep. It must have been midnight by the time I nodded off.

I SHOT BOLT UPRIGHT, screaming, gasping for air, covered in sweat, my chest rising up and down. I leaned across to switch on my bedside light, sat up very still until my breathing evened out.

I'd had the same recurring dream as in the Sleep Centre. The one where I had the phone call saying my nightmare figure was outside and where it finished when the intruder pushed a knife through the window of my front door and stabbed me.

Samson, fast asleep at the bottom of the bed, now woke up and yawned.

I glanced across at my bedside clock. It was only just before midnight. Not 2.09 as in my nightmare.

I felt a desperate need to talk through the nightmare with Nick. I knew at this time he would still be awake, probably in the bar, so I grabbed my phone from my bedside, punched in his number.

It went straight to his voicemail.

I thought of ringing James, but waking him at midnight to talk about a nightmare seemed so trivial. Instead I decided I'd make myself a warm glass of milk, especially as I now felt fully awake.

I had just thrown back the duvet, swung my legs off the bed when my phone rang. I was relieved; Nick must have seen my missed call. I pressed the green answer icon, not glancing at the caller.

"Hi, Nick. Thanks for ringing back."

But there was no answer.

"Nick? Nick?"

Then I heard the breathing. "Who is it?" I demanded. "Who is it?"

A pause, then a tinny, robotic voice. "You know who it is."

I gasped, closed the call down, panic rising inside my chest, heart thumping again, hands shaking.

Maybe I was still in a dream. A dream within a dream.

But how could I tell?

"I don't like this," I said to myself. "Wake up, Ellie. Please wake up. This is a nightmare."

But nothing happened.

I didn't want to be on my own, and I thought about James again.

My handbag was on the dressing-table stool, covered by my crumpled clothes I'd thrown off. I went across to the bag; the leather handle was peeping out from under the heap of clothes; I tugged at it with shaking hands, my clothes toppling on the floor; then I opened the bag up and in the inside zip compartment found James's card with his numbers.

This is real, I told myself. *He gave me his card; this is real. I'm not in a nightmare.*

I paused, hesitating, before making the decision to ring him.

James's phone rang three times before he answered in a slightly sleepy voice, "Hello?"

"James, it's Ellie. I'm so sorry to bother you," I began.

I could hear the rustle of bedclothes as James sat up, his voice now alert as he replied, "Ellie. It's okay. It's okay. You've had another nightmare?"

"Yes," I answered. "And another of those weird phone calls," I told him.

"Right," he said firmly, and I could hear the effort in his voice as he jumped out of bed. "I'm coming round now."

"No, really, James, there's no need. I just wanted a chat," I assured him.

"Honestly, Ellie, you don't want to be on your own when you're getting threatening calls. Give me half an hour."

"If you're sure."

"I'll get dressed; I'll be round as soon as I can."

"Thank you so much, James."

Once the call ended, I pondered whether to change into my clothes or simply drag on my kimono before James arrived. Clothes, I thought. It would be less awkward.

Back in the bedroom I was just about to start changing when my mobile rang again. I looked at the caller. Number withheld.

Should I ignore it? I let it ring and ring, and just before it went to voicemail, I thought, if this is no dream, then I won't be terrorised by this total weirdo, so when I answered, it was in a very sweet, gentle voice. "Hello, Ellie here; is that my nightmare calling?"

My tone obviously took the caller by surprise, so I continued, "Lost for words ... DICKHEAD!"

I was about to hang up when he answered, "Hello, Ellie, yes, it is indeed me – and I'm outside your house. I've come for you."

My phone went dead as he rang off.

It shook me for only a second before I decided the caller

was bluffing. He'd been thrown by my initially cool response, so he'd notched up the fear, but I wouldn't fall for it.

He wasn't outside, he couldn't be outside, and anyway James was on his way. I was safe. As I left the bedroom, Samson trotting after me, I did, however, switch on all the lights as I shuffled in my slippers on to the landing, down the stairs, into the hall, checking the top and bottom bolts were in place on the front door, and then through into the kitchen.

I was just filling the kettle when my doorbell rang.

How could James have made it round to my place so quickly? I moved cautiously into the hall, switched on the outside porch light, and through the frosted diamond-shaped glass, I could see the outline of a shadowy figure. He didn't seem tall enough for James.

I approached the door warily, calling out, "Is that you, James?"

In answer the figure started pulling on the door handle and pushing his weight against the door.

I jumped back with a strangled cry, running into the kitchen. Samson started barking and followed me.

I was about to take out the unicorn knife from the block when I paused.

Don't repeat what you did in your nightmare. And again the thought struck me – what if this really was still a nightmare? What if it wasn't real? A false awakening, a dream within a dream? How could I prove it?

Wake up, I told myself again. *Please wake up. For God's sake, Ellie, wake up!*

But nothing happened.

I was aware my hand was still glued tense round the handle of the unicorn knife. I'd just let it go when there was a loud tap on the window behind the sink.

I shrieked as an illuminated face appeared at the window, and my shriek grew into a loud scream. The face was shrouded in a balaclava with night-vision goggles strapped over the eyes, and a torch was pointing up over the face, making it look ghostly and contorted. Then, next to the face, a gloved hand appeared, grasping a long, broad knife.

CHAPTER TWENTY-NINE

I snatched up my phone from the breakfast bar. "I'm ringing the police! I'm ringing the police, you fucking weirdo!" I screamed.

The face ducked away as I tapped in 999.

It was answered immediately.

"Hello, what service do you require?" a female voice asked.

"Police. I need the police; someone's trying to break into my house!" I spoke fast.

"Putting you through now," she answered, and the phone went dead for only a second before another female voice said, "Greater Manchester Police."

"I have someone outside my house trying to break in! He has a knife!" I said, a desperate urgency underpinning each word.

"Could I have your name and address, please?"

"My name's Dr Ellie Thompson, and I live in The Gables, Moorland Road, Didsbury."

"Okay, Dr Thompson. I'll get the nearest patrol car in the region to you right away," she answered.

"Yes. But please hurry."

I was still in my pyjamas, my silk kimono wrapped around me. I shot up the stairs, changed quickly into the same clothes as the previous evening, jeans and sweater, and ran back downstairs to wait for the police.

As I waited impatiently, anxiously, I paced around the kitchen, now and again glancing at each of the four windows. I didn't go into the conservatory, as I knew it would leave me feeling too vulnerable and exposed because of the large expanse of windows.

And I listened to every sound, every rattle or tap or knock.

But there was nothing.

My phone never rang again.

And all the time, as I paced, waiting, I wondered if I was about to wake up.

But I didn't.

Within five minutes I was relieved to hear the police siren, distant, breaking through the hum of traffic along Wilmslow Road, rising in volume as it turned up my road, the headlights flooding through into the kitchen as tyres screeched onto my drive and the vehicle parked up.

I peeped through the kitchen window to see two uniformed officers climbing out of the panda, one a huge, broad PC in his forties, his size a very comforting sight, and accompanied by a petite, younger PC in her early twenties.

I ran to the door, flung it open, feeling enveloped by a huge sense of relief.

PC GRIFFITHS WAS TAKING notes as I briefly described events of the last hour while PC Garner searched around my garden in case the intruder was still hiding. When PC Garner returned, he said, "No sign of him. Maybe he scarpered when he heard us coming."

"I did shout to tell him I was calling you," I explained.

"That's probably it, then," he said.

We all looked around when we heard another car entering the drive. I wondered if it was James, but PC Garner said, "This'll be DS Williams. I'll just let him in."

DS Williams was in his thirties, tall and broad with a gruff Welsh accent. He asked for a quick update from PC Griffiths, listened quietly, nodding, and when she'd finished, he asked, "And you've checked outside the house?"

"I had a quick look around but didn't see anyone," PC Garner answered.

DS Williams asked me, "Do you have outside lights you can put on?"

"Er, yes, front and back," I answered.

"Can you switch them all on, please. PC Garner, can you take a closer look round the gardens and check for footprints around the front door and the kitchen window and for any signs of attempted break-in."

After I had illuminated the whole rear garden and the front of the house, we sat down at the dining table, Samson perched on my knee, PC Griffiths taking notes as the detective asked me questions.

"So you just heard the burglar, you didn't see him …?" he kicked off.

"Well, he was at the front door trying to get in. I saw his shadow. Then in the kitchen, like I said, his face at the window, and he was wearing a balaclava and something over his eyes like goggles – but he wasn't a burglar," I explained.

"Sorry?" DS Williams looked confused.

"It was to threaten me ... scare me ... I know this sounds crazy, but, well, it was like ... very similar to a nightmare I've had," I explained tentatively, but as soon as I saw the police's reactions, I immediately regretted connecting the attempted break-in to my nightmare. I quickly added, "Like I say, it sounds crazy. But the recurring nightmare I've recently had, it was like it was suddenly happening to me in real life."

And this only made things worse. I caught the quick glance between the two officers, their faces sceptical, incredulous, and I knew instantly I needed to pull back. I sounded like a woman on the edge of a breakdown, making no logical sense. So I changed tack. "I've also been getting these weird threatening calls where the caller says he's coming for me, stuff like that."

"Really?" DS Williams said. "You say 'calls', how many exactly?"

"Hmm, several." I picked up my phone, which was resting on the table. "I've still got them on here, though he didn't leave a message. And he withheld his number."

"Right." DS Williams seemed unsure of how to continue, as DC Garner returned.

"No sign of attempted forced entry," he told them. "I've checked the grounds. No footprints, no signs of any disturbance."

DS Williams asked, "Have you got any CCTV outside the house?"

I shook my head, immediately thinking I'd have some installed first thing on Monday.

DS Williams stood up. "Well, it looks to me, Dr Thompson, that the burglar was just trying his luck."

"I've told you it wasn't a burglar …" I insisted.

But DS Williams ignored my interruption and continued, "And as soon as you woke, switched on all the lights and your dog started barking, you scared him off. I think it's unlikely he'll be back."

"I've just said it wasn't—"

DS Williams cut me off again. "We'll check any local CCTV cameras to see if there were any suspicious cars or individuals in the area …"

"And the weird phone calls, d'you want my phone, d'you want to check my phone to see if you can track the caller?" I asked, offering it to him.

"Not at this stage, Dr Thompson. We'll see where our enquiries take us first."

He was already halfway out of the dining room, his two officers following, the young PC last out, pausing and nodding a thank you.

As the three of them walked into the hall and DS Williams opened the front door, he glanced at the other two and raised his eyebrows as if to say, "That was a waste of time."

As they walked towards their cars, the two men laughed loudly, while PC Griffiths didn't respond but turned back and waved at me as I stood, cross-armed, at the door.

They weren't taking me seriously.

They thought I was crazy.

The two police cars were about to pull out of the drive as James's car drove in. PC Griffiths unwound her window, poked her head out, looking over at me.

"It's okay, thanks," I called out. "It's a colleague. I rang him earlier."

As James climbed out of his car and waved, I wondered if, when he heard my story, he would also think I was crazy.

Maybe I was.

Maybe Ben Carson was right.

Maybe it was all a hallucination.

CHAPTER THIRTY

James and I were sitting on stools at the island. We'd agreed tea and coffee were off the menu, and something stronger was needed, especially as we weren't on call the next day. In fact, James had brought over a bottle of Jameson's Irish whiskey. "Named after me," he joked.

He poured two generous measures into tumblers, we chinked glasses, and James said, "So tell me all about it."

I described the initial nightmare, waking up distressed, how reality was mirroring the nightmare. How I wondered if I was in a dream within a dream, and then finished with an angry and frustrated tirade against the dismissive police response.

"I mean, I tried to explain how what happened was just like in my nightmare, and they looked at me like … like I was crazy," I said.

And James's lips twitched just a fraction, and I caught a hint of a twinkle in his eyes.

"Yeah, just like that," I said.

"Sorry. I'm here to support you not to belittle what

you're saying," he apologised, holding both hands up in contrition.

"Okay, okay. No. I don't blame you." I shrugged. "Suppose I don't even blame the police. I mean, come on, why should anyone believe me? I wouldn't. Nightmares coming alive? Yeah, right!"

And suddenly I felt totally overwhelmed. My face broke, like the build-up of stress had just taken hold of me; I couldn't keep it in any longer, and the dam burst, tears flooding, one hand covering my eyes, as if trying to hide my face or to stem the flow of tears.

"Hey, hey, come on." James comforted me and slid an arm gently round my shoulders. I leaned my head on him as he continued to softly whisper consoling words. "It's okay, Ellie, it's okay. You've been through a lot. It's okay."

And we stayed like that for a minute or so until I lifted my head from his shoulder, smiled, nodded a thank you. "Okay now?" he murmured, and I nodded again.

Then I said, "Ben Carson suggested I could be suffering from PTSD."

"Oh, I don't know, Ellie. Suppose it's possible, but ..." he finished uncertainly.

"He said hallucinations are a symptom of PTSD and that possibly some of the incidents I told him about never actually happened," I confessed.

James looked astounded. "Really? How did you react to that?"

"I said it was drivel, total drivel!"

James laughed. "I'm with you."

"Though later, when I was on my own, I tried ... tried not to dismiss it out of hand, but then I thought ... I am being stalked. Someone did ram me ..."

"And I can testify your tyres were slashed," James added. "And remember what the garage said about your car."

"Exactly. And tonight. Tonight happened. But of course the police would say there was no evidence of an intruder. What if I'd made it up ... in my head?"

"Oh come on, Ellie, don't go there."

I shrugged. "And you, you're real, aren't you?" I poked him on the arm with my forefinger.

"Yes, I'm definitely real." He laughed. "You are not in another dream." He paused, held a stare.

"What?" I asked.

"Okay. Let's look at the idea that these nightmares *are* coming alive ..."

I was about to protest.

"No, no, let me finish. You had a dream about being chased; then you were chased, right?"

I nodded.

"You've had dreams about someone breaking in here; someone tried to break in tonight, okay?"

"So what are you saying, James?" I asked.

"If your dreams are being recreated in your waking life, who's doing it?"

"Good question."

"But a better question is ... doesn't it have to be someone who knows your nightmares? Someone you've described your dreams to?"

I pondered for a second, nodded. "Have to say that crossed my mind. And I thought about it and ... well, the thing is ... whoever's doing it has to have a grudge against me. You know, a huge grudge. As far as I'm aware, the only person who has such a grudge is Rick Walker's dad – but he doesn't know anything about my nightmares."

"Okay, so who does know?" James asked.

"Well ... Nick obviously. Penny ..."

"Me," James added.

I laughed. "Yes, you. But you see what I mean. Nick, you, Penny, three of the people I'm closest to."

"And who else?" James asked.

I had to think, then said, "Obviously Ben Carson, but I mean, come on ... Then ... oh yes, Pete."

"Who's Pete?" James asked.

"He's an ex of mine, works with Nick. He actually rang me tonight. He was standing outside my house, drunk, wanting to come in," I told him.

"Really?" James raised his eyebrows. "Has this guy got a grudge against you?"

"Hmm ... not a grudge exactly, but I finished with him, and even after well over a year, he tries to flirt with me behind Nick's back. But I don't think he's vindictive."

"Well, I wouldn't dismiss him," James said. "Any others?"

"Yes. An ex-girlfriend of Nick's, Natasha," I told him.

"Why her?"

"She was obsessed with Nick, stalked him and possibly me during the early days of our relationship."

"Has that continued over the last year?"

"I thought it had stopped. But after Nick's office party, I saw her parked outside his office block."

"Really?"

"We saw each other just as my taxi was pulling away. Anyway, I decided to go and visit her. Especially as she's got a white car, a Kia Sportage. But when I drove round there, I checked out her car, and this was a day after I'd been shunted, but there was no damage. So she couldn't have been the one who shunted me."

"But could she still be stalking you both?"

"Yes, she could. I was walking away from her car, and she came out of her block of flats."

"Wow. That must have been awkward," James said.

"Just a bit. Anyway, we talked about the previous evening, and she said she'd been waiting for her boyfriend cos he works in the same office block. But I thought after, this was ten o'clock at night. He wouldn't be working at ten on a Friday night. Anyway, I was about to walk away from Natasha, and she said something weird ..."

"What?"

"She asked how my nightmares were."

"You're kidding."

"I had talked about them when we were ... well, not friends exactly ... and she'd said she also had bad nightmares. But it came out of nowhere, so I was a bit spooked."

"Bet you were."

"I suppose she could still have a grudge against me because I married Nick. Or against Nick himself. But the thing is, she can't know the details about my current nightmares."

There was silence in the room as we both pondered all the implications.

It was a comfortable silence, and I decided I felt relaxed enough to completely unburden myself.

I looked across at James and said tentatively, "James ..."

"Yes?"

"Something I've not even told Nick."

James's eyebrows lifted, waiting for me to continue.

"Ever since my parents died, I've been suffering from bouts of depression."

"Oh, Ellie, I'm sorry. I had no idea. I could never have guessed."

"No. I hide it well." I gave a small smile. "Ben Carson's prescribed me fluoxetine, but I'm trying to cope without medication at the moment, so I've not started on them. However, the depression mixed with the nightmares, the somnambulism, and possible PTSD – well, it's not a great mix for my mental stability."

"Ellie, honestly, no one at work would know; you've been absolutely on top of everything, you really have."

"I appreciate that, James," I murmured.

We sat, thinking it through, the house deathly quiet.

Eventually James broke the silence as he was about to fill up my glass. "You're definitely not on the fluoxetine?"

"No. Definitely not."

"Right. Then I'll top you up!"

We raised glasses again, chinked "cheers"; then James paused, looked intently at me. "Ellie, d'you want me to stay till daybreak?"

"I can't ask you to do that!" I protested, thrown by the offer.

"Or if you want to go back to bed, I'm happy to crash down here, and if you do have another nightmare ..."

"James, that's really nice of you but ..." I considered for a second before adding, "You sure?"

"Positive. Or ... if you want to join me, we could just stay up all night ... morning, whatever ... talking, sharing that bottle. Tempted?"

He smiled at me, a warm gleam in his copper-brown

eyes, his crow's feet creasing the edges as he waited for my reaction.

"Sounds good." I returned the smile. "Don't think I've done that since my student days."

WE WERE SITTING in the conservatory. I was sprawled lengthways along the biscuit-coloured rattan sofa with pale cream cushions, the type you only buy if you have no children. An oblong rattan coffee table separated me from James, who was slouched deep in the matching armchair, his long legs stretched out, his shoes discarded by the side of his chair.

An empty bottle and two glasses lay on the coffee table. Outside, a band of light was broadening slowly above the regimental rows of leylandii at the bottom of the lawned stretch of garden.

"How you feeling now?" James asked, gently slurring his words.

"Pissed. Very, very pissed. And tired," I answered, my lips moving imperceptibly like a bad ventriloquist.

I wasn't sure where the last five or six hours had gone. By our second glass of whiskey, we'd settled into the more comfortable conservatory and hadn't moved since – apart from a couple of visits to the loo. Our conversation was relaxed, flowing; no awkward, embarrassing pauses except for reflection on what the other person had said. We'd talked about our student days, past relationships, the current state of the NHS, which led on to politics, and James talked at length and fondly of his late wife. He talked about his childhood, his upbringing, how happy it was, his two brothers and one sister, all very bright, university-educated in good jobs, and the four of them still close to their parents, while I skated over mine as best I could. Nor did I talk in any depth about Nick, only in the broadest strokes, how we met but not the current state of our marriage. I told the story of Natasha and the dinner party, the knife in the cheeseboard, the engagement ring, the threat of suicide as Natasha balanced precariously on the balcony ledge.

"Oh my God!" James said. "Unhinged or what. Definitely keep her on your list of suspects!"

"Yeah, but you know, I think she actually liked me," I reflected. "But Natasha's definitely an eccentric, a one-off."

Now here we were, morning light drifting in shadows through the large windows and both of us very tired.

"Relaxed?" James asked.

"Relaxed? I'm like a wobbly jelly!" And I flopped back in the sofa like I had no control of my muscles. James laughed. "Bit decadent, mind you. Pissed at six a.m.," I said.

"Got all day to sleep and sober up."

"Feel a bit guilty, though."

"Why?"

"There's Nick, slaving away at some conference … having an early night … and here I am …"

James sat up slowly in his armchair, groaning as if each small movement was an effort, which it was. "Early night? Come on, Ellie, you've been to conferences … who has … who has early nights? He'll be having, he'll be having a great time," he managed, struggling with each sentence.

My body stiffened a little, and James picked up on it. "What is it?"

I shook my head.

"Something to do with Nick?"

"No," I replied unconvincingly.

"Come on, Ellie, I'm not stupid, even though I'm very drunk. Don't you trust him? Is that it?" he asked.

I immediately rose to Nick's defence, sitting up. "Yes! Of course I do!"

But I could see from James's reaction that my face told a different story. James could see I was upset. But he said nothing, waited for me to speak. Eventually, I continued, "He said he'd leave his mobile on all night. He hasn't."

"So maybe he forgot," James suggested.

I shook my head before confessing bitterly, "I think the bastard's seeing someone from work."

And although I was trying to keep a lid on the tears, I welled up. I hated crying, it was weak, and I wasn't weak; I'd always been so strong, but with a heady mix of too much alcohol and my life under constant pressure, I succumbed to sobs.

James jumped out of his chair, wobbling slightly, steadying himself on the coffee table, weaved across to me, banging his toe, crying out and then collapsing onto the sofa next to me, where he placed a reassuring arm around my shoulder.

"Hey, hey, come on, Ellie. You're gonna be fine ... you are, you're gonna be fine. Stop crying." He wiped away a single tear from my cheek. "That's it, stop crying."

And his cheek was very close to mine, and he pulled away slightly, aware that his stubble, unshaved since the previous morning twenty-four hours ago, was as prickly as a hedgehog.

"Okay?" he asked softly.

And I nodded.

Eventually, he said cautiously, "You don't think ..."

I looked up at him. "What?"

He shook his head. "No, forget it."

"No, go on, what?" I insisted.

"What we were talking about earlier, you know, all the possible suspects who could be doing this to you ..." He stopped again, reluctant to continue.

"Yes, what about it? Have you got another idea who it could be?" I asked.

"Well, it's just ... if what you say is true ... if Nick really is having an affair ..." and he didn't finish the sentence, let it just hang there and shrugged instead.

"That it could be ... it could be Nick?"

He gave a non-committal shrug before adding, "You seem ... you seem like you don't, like you don't trust him ... has he been unfaithful before?"

I simply shrugged once more. "I don't think so. But I think he's having an affair now. I just don't know who with."

"Oh, Ellie, I'm so sorry." And James pulled his arm tighter round me, leaned in and kissed me gently on the cheek. "I'm really sorry."

I thought it was a comforting kiss, a supportive kiss from a friend.

But then he stared into my eyes.

And we both held the gaze.

He leaned in closer. I didn't pull away. I realised I wanted him to kiss me. And I didn't feel guilt. I was just taking in the moment; no thought of consequences passed through my mind.

So I didn't stop him. And we started to kiss. Slowly at first, gently. It was like a plane, ready to take off, taxiing steadily, then the pause before the final surge and lift-off into the air.

CHAPTER THIRTY-ONE

My phone was ringing on my bedside table. I moaned and turned over.

The phone finished ringing.

I nestled deep into the bed. But one minute later the phone rang again.

I groaned, a long moaning growl like an animal cornered. My arm slid from under the duvet; I grasped the phone, pressed answer and put it to my ear, all without opening my eyes.

"Yes?" I answered, voice gravelly, tongue dry, mouth dehydrated.

"Did you ring me last night?"

It was Nick. My eyes popped open; I propped herself up on one elbow. I realised my head was throbbing, the beating thud of a drum knocking against the insides of my skull.

"Oh hello, Nick. Yes," I managed, trying to add an edge of enthusiasm to my voice but failing badly. "Yeah. Why didn't you answer?"

"Sorry. My battery was flat," he explained. "Are you okay? You sound a bit—"

"Yeah, I know," I interrupted as I glanced at the clock. It was almost midday! "I was having a lie-down, had a bad night, just woke up when you rang."

"Another nightmare?" he asked.

"Yeah. Didn't sleep at all last night. Terrible nightmare. It's why I rang you; I wanted to talk." And I managed just a hint of an accusing undertone to my voice.

"Sorry, sweetheart. But you're okay now?"

"Yeah."

"Sure?"

"Yeah. Just tired."

"I'll let you go, then, sweetheart. I'll ring you tonight, yeah?"

"Something else ..." I said before he rang off.

"What?"

But I didn't reply at first.

"What, sweetheart?"

"The nightmare ... the one where someone was trying to break in ..."

"You had that again?"

"Yeah." I paused, not sure whether to tell him. "It happened for real."

"What you mean?" Nick asked anxiously. "We had burglars?"

"No. Whoever's stalking me ... doing this to my head ... it was them," I told him, my voice hoarse, and I could feel the bile of stale whiskey at the back of my throat.

Nick was quiet on the other end.

"Nick?" I asked.

"Yeah. You called the police?" he answered.

"Yeah."

I was too weary to go into the details, and I sensed Nick's scepticism even over the phone, so my responses became monosyllabic.

"And?"

"And what?"

"They came? The police came?"

"Yeah."

"And what happened? What they say?"

"I'll tell you when you get home," I said, wanting to cut the conversation short.

"But you're okay? Cos you don't sound it," he said.

"No, I'm fine," I said. "Honestly."

"You want me to come home tonight?" he offered.

"No. I'll be okay. But thanks, I'll see you tomorrow."

"Hey, and I'm missing you," Nick added quickly.

"And you," I managed to squeeze out. "Bye."

And I finished the call.

I threw my phone onto the bed and snuggled back down under the duvet, facing the clock on the bedside cabinet. *Another hour*, I thought.

"So you're awake, then. Was that Nick?"

I shot bolt upright, mouth open, eyes wide, throbbing head forgotten and horror plastered all over my face. Oh my God! James! How could I have forgotten?

And there he was, stepping out of the en suite, hair wet and spiky, a far-too-small towel wrapped around his waist.

"Oh God ... sorry ... I ... oh ... oh God," I spluttered.

"You okay?" James asked casually.

"Did we ...? Of course we did, stupid question," I stumbled as my face coloured, and I looked away, embarrassed.

I jumped out of bed. I was naked. Fortunately my

kimono lay on the end of the bed, and I grabbed it, pulled it on and wrapped it tight around me.

"This is all wrong, James," I said. "I shouldn't have done this."

James shrugged, answering coolly, "Okay."

"But it's not okay. I don't feel it's okay at all. I mean, we shouldn't have ... I shouldn't have ... James, I'm sorry, but ..."

"You want me to go?" he offered.

"Please. I'm sorry. I'm really sorry, it's just ... sorry, sorry," I kept repeating inadequately.

"Don't worry. It's fine; you don't need to apologise."

It didn't feel fine to me. I was mortified.

He moved to the other side of the bed, his back to me as he dropped the towel, and I sneaked a glance as he sat on the edge of the bed, bent over to pull on his grey marl Calvin Klein underpants and started to tug up his jeans. Both had been discarded in a hurry only a few hours earlier.

Flashes came back to me. I remembered how we'd staggered up the stairs, lips locked, hands everywhere, stumbled into the bedroom, fumbled with zips and buttons, then, naked, toppled on to the bed. I remembered the feel of James's body against me, lean, muscled, and I couldn't help but compare it to Nick's growing flab.

And that was all I could remember. Did I enjoy it? I presumed I must have, though not necessarily. Did I have an orgasm? If I did, what a shame I couldn't remember it.

Now James finished dressing as he pulled his sweatshirt over his head, then stood and came round the bed to me. I noticed he was wearing only one sock. He flashed me his doctor's sympathetic, bedside-manner look, warm, comforting, assuring, as he said, "Look, Ellie, you really don't need to apologise; it's my fault. I shouldn't have let this happen. You were vulnerable. I took advantage—"

I interrupted him. "No, it wasn't like that—"

"I was out of order. I initiated it," he said.

"Did you? I can't remember. I thought I did. I mean, it doesn't matter. Fact is, we drank too much."

"Yes. Yes, we did. And I'm sorry if you feel bad, and I can understand why, but *I* don't regret it. It was one of the best nights ... or mornings of my life. So thank you."

He smiled at me, that lovely, charming smile, where the edges of his eyes wrinkled, full of warmth.

Then he added, "By the way, have you seen my other sock?"

And that broke the tension, and I had to laugh.

We looked everywhere and eventually found it under the duvet at the bottom of the bed. "Oh my god," he said, in mock embarrassment. "I must have jumped into bed naked but wearing one sock!"

We laughed again, and I went to him, kissed him briefly on the cheek and said, "Honestly, James ... I had a really lovely night ... or as you said, morning ... I had a lovely morning, but it can't happen again ..."

James nodded. "I understand. It's no problem. But hey, is it okay to get a coffee before I leave?"

"Of course, don't be silly," I said.

"Okay, I'll go and make it. I'm having black this morning. Same for you?"

"Please."

As James left the bedroom, I had a sudden thought.

I peered under my pillow. No knife.

CHAPTER THIRTY-TWO

After James left, I went straight back to bed. I was totally exhausted and still suffering from a throbbing hangover.

As the sun was streaming into my room, I pulled the curtains tight shut and flopped into the bed.

I was just drifting, on the edge of sleep, when Samson popped into my head. Had I fed him earlier? Had I let him out into the garden? Had I even seen him? I drifted deeper into sleep, and the questions remained unanswered.

I WOKE up screaming around an hour later.

The nightmare was more disturbing than any I had ever experienced.

It was a replay of the one I'd had the previous week where Samson had been taken by the hooded figure.

I was walking along the same deserted city centre street, searching for Samson and calling his name, becoming ever more frantic, and then ahead of me the hooded, shadowy figure turned a corner, and he was pulling Samson on a lead.

I stopped. I told myself I had to rescue Samson from this man before he killed him. I decided to face my fear, so I slowly walked towards him.

"That's my dog," I called. "You dare hurt my dog, and I will kill you."

In the nightmare I was carrying a knife.

"Hurt my dog, and I will kill you," I repeated my threat.

Then slowly the man bent down and eased Samson off the lead.

As soon as Samson was free, he ran to me.

But as he closed in, I saw my dog's eyes were fierce red, and his teeth were bared.

"Samson. Samson, are you okay?"

Samson reached me and leaped at me as if flying through the air, and his paws landed on my chest, catching me off balance so I fell to the ground. Samson was on top of me, growling, and suddenly his bared teeth sank into my neck, and I started screaming as he bit deeper and deeper, and blood was spurting from my neck as if Samson had cut into my jugular.

Out of desperation, I raised the knife that was still in my hand, and I stabbed and stabbed it into Samson until he whimpered and then fell off me, eyes no longer red but lifeless.

I STOPPED SCREAMING, but I was still gasping for breath.

And then panic hit me. Where was Samson?

I jumped out of bed.

"Samson," I called as I ran down the stairs.

No answer. Samson usually came bounding up to me.

I ran into the kitchen. He wasn't curled up on his bed.

So where was he?

Then I noticed that the conservatory door was slightly ajar. I had a vague memory that James and I had opened it the previous night to let in some fresh air. Surely it hadn't been left open since then?

I wasn't sure.

Maybe I'd let Samson out earlier in the morning and left the door open, but my brain was so frazzled with stale alcohol I couldn't be sure.

I went across to the conservatory and slid the door wide, stepped out onto the paved patio, then onto the grass, all the time calling Samson's name.

No sign of him.

This was not like Samson. He never strayed far. He wouldn't have run off.

And the thought struck me; someone had taken him.

Although there was still the possibility that Samson had squeezed through the hedge into one of the next-door neighbours' gardens. Maybe he'd seen a cat and chased after it.

I searched round the whole garden. Nothing.

No sign of him.

I decided to first call round to the neighbours to my left who owned a cat. They were an old, retired couple, and they'd lived in their detached house from when it was first built, and although they talked about downsizing, they had brought their three children up there, and it held too many good memories.

Their blue Mini was in the drive, so I knew they were at home.

They liked me. The wife, Maria, opened the door, a tiny woman, her face as wrinkled as a prune, but she was still bursting with energy. She greeted me with a big smile.

"Ellie, how lovely, how are you? Haven't seen you around; do come in," she said.

I smiled. "No, it's okay, Maria, thanks, just popped round because Samson's gone missing," I told her.

"Oh dear, no," she replied, full of genuine sympathy. "When was this?" she asked.

"Not long ago. I wondered whether he got through into your garden," I said.

"Well, we haven't seen him, Ellie, but if you'd like to come in, we'll have a good look round."

Maria's husband, Anthony, used to be an avid gardener until he developed arthritis in his hands and knees. His once immaculate garden had become a little overgrown and wild at the edges, so it was possible Samson could be hiding in bushes or behind the shed at the bottom of the garden, which was covered in vines and needed cutting back.

I followed Maria into the hall and through the kitchen, unchanged since the 1980s with heavy wood units and yellow tiles, then through into the original conservatory. Maria's tabby cat was curled up on a battered sofa.

In the garden, we both called Samson's name, and I carried out a thorough search, peeping into the bushes on either side of the lawn and exploring the undergrowth.

But no Samson.

"I'm sorry," Maria said, "I do hope you find him."

I called on the neighbours the other side of our house, but there was no answer. They were a middle-aged couple with two teenage sons, who'd only moved in a couple of months earlier, and Nick and I hadn't really connected with them. But it was unlikely Samson could have escaped into their garden, as there was a strong, high fence between us.

I went home. I searched on my laptop for a good photo of Samson; then I made a "LOST" poster with my mobile number, asking people to call if they found him.

Even as the printer churned out a few copies, I thought it was a forlorn exercise. I genuinely believed Samson's disappearance was no coincidence. It was part of a campaign of intimidation and harassment being waged against me.

But no matter how much I racked my brain and narrowed down the number of people it could be, like I'd said to James the previous evening, the only one who made logical sense was Rick Walker's father. And really, would he go to such lengths to persecute me?

I felt I had to do something positive to find Samson. Maybe a passer-by had seen someone carrying or dragging a reluctant Samson away, or possibly noticed a barking, stressed dog at the rear window of a car. So I spent the next two hours sticking up my posters on lampposts, bus shelters, shop windows and pubs and bars in Didsbury.

I thought about ringing Nick and telling him about Samson's disappearance, but his afternoon conference session would have started. Anyway, what could he do to help?

When I arrived home, it was late afternoon. I flopped into the conservatory sofa, exhausted, drained, the alcohol and lack of sleep playing hell with my body. I'm definitely never drinking to that excess again. This raised a smile. The number of times I'd said that to myself as a student after waking with an earth-size hangover. And this current hangover was the first since those student days.

The thought of ringing Nick reminded me of the conversation I'd had with James. Could Nick really be behind all the intimidation? The more I thought about it, the more ridiculous and outrageous it sounded. And it couldn't have been Nick last night because he was at the conference ninety miles away.

But maybe he wasn't at a conference in Birmingham after all. Maybe he was with his new girlfriend.

I remembered my accusation a few weeks ago when Nick had lied about playing golf with Pete. I still didn't know if he'd been telling me the truth, about driving to Liverpool to order a necklace from Wong's.

I had an idea.

I googled Wong's, found their website and pressed "call".

"Good afternoon, Wong's; how may I help you?" a woman's voice answered, with just a hint of Scouse.

"Oh hi, my husband came in three weeks ago, Saturday twentieth, and placed an order; we wondered when it might be ready to pick up?" I asked.

"What was the name of the order, please?"

"It would be under Nick Matthews, The Gables, Moorland Road in Manchester," I told her.

"If you could bear with me, I'll just check on the computer."

"Okay, thanks."

I stood up, paced the conservatory nervously, glancing out through the windows in case Samson was there.

It was a few minutes before the woman returned to the phone. "Yes, I've found the name."

I felt a huge surge of relief mixed with guilt for not

trusting Nick. "Oh good. Oh, that's great. Thank you so much," I gushed. "Can you tell me, did he come in on Saturday twentieth himself and place the order?"

A moment while the woman checked.

"Oh, no. It was ordered entirely online on Sunday twenty-first." She paused. "We will email when it's ready."

I was stunned. "Right. Okay," I mumbled, feeling like I might vomit.

I sagged back down onto the sofa, then spoke quietly, "Thank you," and finished the call.

Nick had lied to me. He'd only ordered the necklace *after* he'd been cornered in his lies. I'd suspected as much when he sent me that screenshot. But this was now proof.

What a bastard! What a conniving bastard! I could kill him!

I was about to ring him when I thought: no, slow down, it would be better to confront him face to face, to look into his eyes, to watch him squirm. Think this through first. Think of the implications.

In a way, I was relieved I knew the truth. It focused my mind, away from the disturbing, petrifying thought that everything that had been happening to me was a hallucination. I felt more in control. My life wasn't spiralling wildly away into some sort of manic oblivion. My suspicions were real and couldn't be used against me. Nick's infidelity was real. It wasn't in my head. It was no hallucination.

It should have been devastating news to me that my husband was a liar, an unfaithful, deceitful manipulator – but, bizarrely, instead it was a comfort.

Suddenly my phone rang. It was Penny.

I'd had a huge urge to speak to her, if only to release the pressure building inside my loaded head, but I hadn't rung her because I knew she'd be too wrapped up with Tom.

"Penny, how are you? Hope you and Tom are having a great weekend," I said, mustering up as much enthusiasm as possible.

"Oh yes, it's been brilliant, Ellie, and how are you? How's your weekend going?" she asked.

I didn't answer at first, and Penny picked up on it.

"Ellie, what is it?"

"Someone's taken Samson," I told her, on the edge of tears.

"What? Someone's taken Samson. You mean stolen him?"

"Yes. But I've had the most awful nightmares, and the worst one was Samson being stabbed …"

I couldn't tell Penny that I was the one doing the stabbing.

"Oh, Ellie, you poor thing," Penny commiserated.

And once I'd opened up, the verbal dam burst, words crashing into each other as I described the nightmares, the phone call, the intruder, the police, and the whole story was interrupted and littered with Penny's repeated responses: "Oh my God, no," "Good God, no," "Fuck!" and "Oh fucking hell!"

"And I thought I was going crazy, Penny. I genuinely thought if some of these things that have happened to me are indeed hallucinations, it's like … well, it's like one step towards insanity."

"Oh, Ellie."

"But, Penny, I know I'm not crazy. I know now someone is doing this to me." I spoke with total conviction. "And I think it's Nick."

I could hear Penny gasp at the other end of the phone. "Nick?!"

"Yes. Because I'm absolutely sure Nick's having an affair."

For a second there was no answer from Penny, she was so stunned.

"Penny?" I queried.

"Sorry, you just said you think Nick's been doing this ... this stuff to you cos he's having an affair?" she asked, incredulous.

"Yes, I do," I replied. "I know it sounds crazy—"

"Ellie, it sounds totally crazy! I know you said you suspected him of having an affair, but ... wow ... I mean, so why are you now sure? What have you found out?"

I explained the lies Nick had told about buying a necklace in Liverpool to cover his tracks when he hadn't actually been there at all.

"Wow. I get you. So who you think he's having an affair with?" Penny asked.

"Someone from work. I think it's this woman who's recently joined the company, she was all over him at that last party we went to, and Nick was loving it," I explained. "And I wouldn't be surprised if they've been together all this weekend, either at this conference or not, if there really is a conference."

Penny paused before answering, "Well, if you're that sure, yes, you should check it out. And will you confront him when he gets home?"

"Too bloody right I will!"

"And are you going to be okay tonight after what happened last night?" she asked.

"Yeah, yeah, I'll be fine," I answered hesitantly, thinking

about James and knowing I couldn't even begin to tell her about that as well.

"I can come over and stay the night with you," Penny offered.

"No, I really don't want to spoil your weekend." I was adamant.

"Look, ring me any time," Penny said. "I don't care if it's the middle of the night, just ring me."

"Thanks, love. Appreciate it. See you Monday."

"Yeah, see you Monday. And fingers crossed Samson's just lost and he turns up really soon."

CHAPTER THIRTY-THREE

After the call, I felt so much better, energised by the relief of unburdening myself. I would be positive and proactive. Samson nagged away at the back of my head, and I felt helpless about it, but the rest I'd cope with. Earlier in the day I'd felt I was up to my neck in quicksand, slipping slowly under with no branch to grasp hold of.

But now I tried to keep my positivity going into the evening, holding down tight on any fragile emotion that surfaced. Maybe I should start the Prozac just to keep on top of everything, I thought. The medication might help to push aside the doubts that had been lurking inside my head, the doubts about my own sanity.

No, I won't go there, I told myself. *I'll stay in control.*

I fancied going out to eat. I didn't mind sitting in a restaurant on my own, surrounded by chatty couples or noisy families. The glances and discreet nods towards the solo female customer, the poor, sad figure alone on a Saturday night, didn't trouble me. Sometimes I liked the solitary comfort of not having to chat.

Because I was an only child, you'd think as I got older, I'd crave the company of other people. Especially once my parents died. You'd think I'd be needy. Desperate not to be left alone. But it wasn't like that. It was the reverse. I enjoyed being solitary. It wasn't that I was a loner or that I didn't have friends when I was younger. But I had no one close. I supposed Penny was the closest I'd come to having a best friend, but I sometimes felt I didn't really know her. Nor her me.

It was the same with boyfriends. I'd never craved them. I'd never worked at chasing them. Any relationships I had just seemed to happen. And with most of them I lost interest after a very short time. Pete just about summed up the type of men who went for me. Thinking me a challenge. I always got bored. And maybe that was what'd been happening with Nick. Maybe he sensed it – my distance. I wasn't making excuses for him. I didn't like being lied to, and I wouldn't let myself get hurt.

I liked the idea of a robust plate of pasta, so I booked a table for 7 p.m. at Casa Italia. I thought about walking to the restaurant, but physically I still felt a little drained, so I drove the short distance into the Village, finding a parking spot up a side road.

The restaurant was heaving, all tables full, bristling with noise; and a young, smiling Italian, his accent underscored with a hint of guttural Mancunian, showed me to a far corner table squeezed against the wall but by the window. I ordered a lasagne, a salad and one bottle of still water. My stomach wasn't ready to accept any alcohol just yet.

MY MEAL HAD JUST ARRIVED, and I picked up my knife and fork to prod the lasagne and release some of the hot steam from it. I was about to take a mouthful of salad while the lasagne cooled when my phone rang. I jumped, but my immediate thought was Nick, checking on how I was before going down to dinner. I couldn't speak to him, but as I picked up the phone, I saw it was a number I didn't recognise.

I was relieved it wasn't the withheld number, but even so I answered cautiously. "Yes?"

There was silence the other end.

"Yes? Who's that?"

Still no answer.

"I said who's that?"

"It's Natasha."

I was taken by surprise. "Natasha? What are you ringing for?"

"I should have told you when I saw you outside my flat," she said.

"Told me what?" I asked.

"About Nick."

"What about him?"

Natasha hesitated a fraction before answering, "He's having an affair."

"How would you know?"

"I saw him. I saw him in town. With this other woman. They were all over each other."

I couldn't answer at first.

"Ellie, I warned you what he was like—"

"And did you know this woman?" I asked.

"No. But I took a photo."

A moment as I thought about this. I believed Natasha.

"Can you send me the photo?"

"And I've got photos of someone who's stalking you," she continued.

"Who?" I asked anxiously. "Who is it?"

"Someone we both know," Natasha answered enigmatically.

"Who? Tell me who it is."

Natasha didn't answer at first.

"He followed you into the restaurant."

"How do you know?" I asked, totally confused.

"Because I'm parked outside," she told me.

"What?!"

I glanced out the window. I saw the Sportage and Natasha's face staring across at me. She smiled, gave me a little wave.

"I want to see you. I want to talk face to face, and I'll show you the photos."

"And how did you get the photos?"

There was no reply.

"You've been stalking us, haven't you, Natasha?" I accused.

"I'll be in touch again soon, and we'll arrange to meet up."

And the phone went dead.

I looked out the window again, but the Sportage had already driven off.

I pushed my plate away. I'd suddenly lost my appetite.

I NEEDED A LONG SLEEP, a full eight hours undisturbed. But I knew Natasha's news about Nick, about some stalker and Samson's disappearance would all keep me awake. I believed Natasha about Nick. But the stalker? And why did she want to meet me? She was always unstable. Scary. If I met her, it had to be in public.

I decided to take another sleeping pill. But before I went to bed, I switched on every outside light, front and back and in the porch. I flooded the inside of the house with lights – in the conservatory, the hall and the dining kitchen. I felt safer.

In bed at eleven, by eleven thirty I was fast asleep.

But not for long.

CHAPTER THIRTY-FOUR

I shot up in bed, gulping for air, tears streaming down my face, woken by the same nightmare of Samson attacking me and then me stabbing Samson.

I waited for my breathing to ease before switching on the bedside light, expecting Samson to be lying at the foot of the bed, but he wasn't there.

And that was when it came back to me.

I felt an overpowering sense of relief that Samson wasn't dead. He had simply gone missing, and he would turn up.

I stared at Nick's empty space next to me. Even though I had the whole bed to myself, I still slept on my side of it, not sprawled and spread out in the middle. I wondered if Nick was still in bed, sleeping next to ... who?

After an hour of calming myself, pushing thoughts of the alleged stalker and Nick's infidelity to the back of my mind, I eventually fell asleep.

I woke up just after eight. I sat up, my thoughts starting to hop around over the disturbing events of the weekend, and I climbed out of bed, showered, dressed: a casual pair of jeans, and a long-sleeved designer T-shirt that I'd picked up cheap from TK Maxx.

When I entered the kitchen, the first thing I did was check the block of knives after my nightmare about killing Samson. It was a huge relief to find there were none missing.

I made myself a quick breakfast of orange juice, scrambled eggs on toast and fresh coffee.

And I thought about Nick.

What was I going to say to him? I thought maybe I'd say nothing but just watch him. I also needed to find out whom Nick was actually seeing.

I washed up the breakfast dishes rather than slot them into the dishwasher, slipped on my trainers and was about to leave when I noticed the kitchen bin was overstuffed and bulging. I tugged out the liner, tied the ends into a knot and carried it towards the front door. I flung open the door, cursing as I dropped the heavy, awkward bag, but fortunately it didn't split. I picked it up, carried it towards the wheelie bin by the side of the house. I was about to open the bin lid when my eyes were drawn to something small lying next to it.

I bent down, peered at it and immediately reared back in shock.

It was a dog's collar. In fact, it looked very like Samson's bright red collar. Delicately I picked it up with two fingers and noticed the metal tag dangling from it with Samson's name and my phone number printed on it.

But then, as I brought it closer up to my face, I noticed the inside of the collar was covered in blood.

I WAS CRYING, as if in pain, sobbing like a baby. I dropped the collar, stepped away from it without taking my eyes off it. My chest was rising up and down, fast, my head pulsing.

What did it mean? Was Samson dead?

Was he in the bin? Had some sick bastard killed him and placed him in the wheelie bin?

I didn't want to look, yet I knew I had to.

Slowly, very slowly, I lifted up the lid. The wheelie bin had been emptied just before the weekend, so if Samson was inside, he would be lying in the bottom.

My shaking hands held on to the bin edge as I stretched on tiptoes to peer inside.

The bin was completely empty.

I let out a huge sigh of relief. I grabbed the bin bag, hauled it into the bin, dropped the lid.

I peered down at Samson's collar before picking it up carefully; then I ran back into the house, slamming the door.

In the kitchen I placed the collar on Samson's bed.

I was pacing the kitchen, crying again, wiping the tears from my cheeks with the back of my hand, my eyes drawn constantly towards the bloody collar.

I was confused. What should I do? I walked round and round the island in circles. My head was pounding, my heart hammering; I was hardly able to breathe.

Samson must be dead. He must be. How did the collar get there? Who could have left it? And why?

My mind was bouncing around, one thought tumbling over another.

Or maybe Samson wasn't dead. Could it be someone trying to frighten me? The deranged freak who'd been ringing me up. The stalker. Who was it? It must be someone I knew, but who? And why?

I thought about James. Apart from me, he was the last person to see Samson alive. Could he have done this?

Don't be ridiculous, I thought. *You're losing any objectivity. It's preposterous. How could you even think like that?*

James was lovely. He had no motive. How could I even contemplate such a thought? A case of extreme circumstances sending logic out the window, I decided. And that made me feel guilty. I was so fond of James. When we were emptying the bottle of whiskey, sitting opposite, talking easily, laughing, thoughts had flashed through my head – if only I could have this rapport with Nick. If only I were single again. And now I was slotting James into the role of a psychotic dog killer. I half laughed, which spluttered into the flow of more tears.

Rick Walker's father still seemed the only possibility. But I didn't really believe he would go to such lengths for revenge. And I'd more or less disregarded him once I found out he didn't own a white Kia Sportage or a white Qashqai.

Then a terrible thought hit me. A devastating thought.

What if I had killed Samson? What if I had sleepwalked when I had the nightmare? What if, while stabbing Samson in my nightmare, I was actually stabbing him for real, and I just couldn't remember? The thought made me shudder.

It had happened to me before. I didn't remember taking the knife up to my bedroom and placing it under my pillow. I didn't remember breaking a glass and cutting my foot on it.

If I had done it, if I had killed Samson, how did the collar get there? And if I had dropped the collar, I must have been outside with Samson. But he wasn't in the wheelie bin, so where was he?

I ran across to the block of knives on the kitchen island and frantically pulled each of them out of the block and inspected them for blood, Samson's blood. No sign. But that meant nothing. I could have washed the knife clean before placing it back in the block.

I ran to the toilet, kneeled and threw up in a series of huge retches, again and again, until my stomach was empty and there was nothing left.

I stood, grabbed some toilet roll and wiped the sick from around my mouth, then rinsed my entire face with cold water. Should I call the police? But what if my worst fears were right? What if I had, in fact, killed Samson while sleepwalking? I shuddered and felt the bile scorch my throat once more.

Suddenly the front door rang.

I started. I wasn't expecting anyone. My hopes rose. Maybe someone had found Samson and was returning him.

I ran to the door and flung it open.

CHAPTER THIRTY-FIVE

"James, what ...?"

His face screwed into an apologetic frown. "Sorry, Ellie, for calling round unannounced, but ... I've left my phone here ..."

"Really?"

"Yes. I realised I'd lost it when I got home yesterday, and I looked all over for it but couldn't find it, so I checked 'find my phone', and it's somewhere here." He shrugged another apology.

I opened the door wider. "Okay. Right, you'd better come in."

James stepped inside and closed the door behind him. "I'll look on the sofa in the conservatory; it might have dropped down the side ... is that okay?" he asked awkwardly.

"Of course."

James followed me into the kitchen, but as soon as I passed Samson's bed and glanced down at the bloodied collar, I stopped dead in my tracks.

"What is it?" And he looked down at the bloodied collar. "Is that … Samson's?"

I nodded before it all came bursting out – my nightmare about killing Samson, his bloodied collar left by the wheelie bin and my terrible fear that I had killed him while sleepwalking.

James was too stunned to answer at first. He sat me down on a stool at the island, put his hands on both my shoulders, looked closely into my eyes and spoke softly. "Ellie, you haven't killed Samson. I'm sure of it—"

"But what about …?" I interrupted.

"If you'd sleepwalked and killed Samson … where's the evidence? Where is Samson's body? There would be blood everywhere. Have you seen any blood around the house or on you or your clothes?"

I shook my head.

"There you go."

But James's question, "Where is Samson's body?" didn't reassure me, it made me more anxious. If I had killed Samson, where had I put him? Had I buried him? I must have buried him. There was no other explanation. If I'd buried him, he would be in our back garden. I needed to find out. But James was also right, there would be blood – all over my clothes – and if I was sleepwalking when I killed him, it would be over my pyjamas.

I now wanted James out of the house as quickly as possible. "I'm being silly," I said.

"You're not being silly …"

"So let's move on. I just needed your logical reassurance, so thank you, James." I paused before changing tack. "Right, let's find that phone of yours. I'll try ringing it."

"It's probably dead."

My call went straight to his answering service.

"Think you're right."

I moved across to the conservatory.

"Let's check where you were sitting," I said as if I had suddenly returned to normality and the previous Samson conversation had never happened.

James frowned, watched as I started searching for his phone down the back of the sofa.

"Ellie ..."

I ignored him. "Doesn't seem to be here." I bent down to peer under the sofa. "James, it's here!"

I reached under the sofa, and as I stood, I somehow managed a big smile. It was a smile I'd practised all my adult life.

I held the phone out to James, who took it, nodded a thank you without taking his eyes off me. "Ellie, are you going to be—"

"I'm fine. Yes, I'm going to be fine," I finished. I forced my lips into a broad smile again. "Honestly."

"Are you sure? I mean, d'you want me to stay because—"

"No," I interrupted firmly. "Thank you, James, but I think I need to be on my own now."

"Okay. If you're sure. But ring me ... as you know ... any time."

We were talking as if last night had never happened.

"Thank you, James," I said, that permanent false smile now fixed on my face.

I saw James out of the house, and as soon as I heard his car drive off, I ran upstairs two at a time, into my bedroom, and went to the corner where my wicker wash basket stood. I dragged out all the dirty clothes lying on the top. Nothing. There must have been two weeks' washing in there. I dug deeper. Maybe I'd hidden the bloodied pyjamas at the bottom. So I tugged everything out until I found a pair of my cotton pyjamas patterned with pink flamingos. No blood on them. Not a speck.

It was a relief. But I wouldn't be convinced until I'd searched for any newly dug earth in the garden.

I ran down into the hallway to the connecting door into the garage. I was looking for the spade. I pushed open the door, scanned the room, and I saw it standing in the far corner next to the rake and lawnmower.

I picked up the spade and carried it out of the garage, into the kitchen and through the conservatory into the garden.

I looked around the borders for any freshly dug earth. I didn't see any at first but then I noticed a patch that was broken up, in between some dying brown ferns.

I started digging. There had been rain overnight, and the earth was soft and easy to break into. I started slowly but then became more frantic as I dug deeper, throwing the loose earth over the ferns.

I was about to give up when the spade struck something. It wasn't a stone. It was softer.

My head was throbbing with tension and fear. I pushed the earth away gently with the end of the spade, eased it around the edge of whatever lay there.

And then I saw it.

I could just make out the little body and the head. I started crying, howling out sobs of anguish at what I must have done.

I dug the spade around the side of the body to ease it up out of the earth. And as I did, I gasped. It was a gasp of relief rather than shock.

This was not Samson.

And then I remembered. Earlier in the year, around July, me and Nick had woken one morning to find a dead fox lying on our lawn, which Nick had buried. I'd forgotten all about it.

I threw the earth back over the fox's remains until it was fully covered. But then I started digging indiscriminately. I must have looked wild and demented as I dug one hole before moving on to another and then another and another until after an hour, I sank, exhausted, onto the damp grass.

I didn't move for several minutes.

What did it mean? If I had killed Samson, where had I put him? I'd had no time to take him anywhere except in the house or garden.

"Ellie, Ellie, what are you doing?"

CHAPTER THIRTY-SIX

Penny was staring at me as I slumped on the grass, surrounded by mounds of soil and scattered large holes dotted along the borders.

"Ellie, are you okay?" Penny asked, coming over to me, kneeling and placing a concerned arm around me. "I've been ringing your door for ages. What's going on?"

I couldn't stop shaking, shivering as if I were standing naked outside in a snowstorm.

Penny squeezed me tighter as she beckoned towards the holes. "Ellie, what are you doing?"

"I'm ... I'm trying to find Samson," I answered.

"Sorry?"

"I thought ... I thought ... no, I think maybe I've killed him ... during one of my nightmares ... so I was looking for him," I stuttered as I started sobbing. "Penny, I think I'm going mad."

"Oh, Ellie. Come on." Penny squeezed me really tight, and we stayed like that for some time before she stood and helped me up. "Let's go inside."

I nodded like an obedient child, and together we walked back silently through the conservatory doors.

"I'VE BEEN WORRIED about you all weekend."

Penny was talking as we sat at the dining table, sipping on strong tea.

"I rang you earlier but got no answer, so I decided to come round to check on you ..." she continued.

"I left my phone in the house while I was ... searching for Samson." And the mention of his name brought prickly tears to my eyes. "I really think I am going crazy, Penny. Not just about Samson ... about everything."

"Ellie, you are not going mad," she assured me.

"But I feel like my life's out of control. The nightmare at the Sleep Centre where I wrote the message myself, I mean that really spooked me out. Then thinking I'm being followed ... or not being followed. I'm beginning to think that Ben Carson was right," I said.

"In what way?" Penny asked.

"He said there was a possibility that I could have PTSD."

Penny shook her head.

"No, listen. He said one of the symptoms of PTSD could be hallucinations—"

"No way," Penny cut me off, threw me a disparaging look.

"But what if he's right?"

"No, no way."

"What if, for example, I never received those threatening phone messages—"

"Have the police checked the phone calls?" she asked.

"No. They didn't seem interested."

"You should take your phone to them and insist they do something about it," Penny urged.

"You're right. Yes, you're right. That's something positive I can do," I said, momentarily feeling better.

"How many calls did he make?" she asked.

I picked up my phone, which was lying next to her on the table. "Hmm … quite a few."

I opened my phone on recent calls and scrolled through the list, slowly at first, then more rapidly.

I started to feel more and more frantic.

"What is it?" Penny asked.

"I can't find them! They're not here," I answered, my voice desperate.

"They must be."

"They're not. They're not here!" I was close to hysteria. "They're not on my phone! Why are they not on my phone? Oh my God, Penny. What if they're not on my phone because they never happened? I never had the calls. They were all in my head! Or on Friday night, no one was breaking in, either it was a hallucination, or possibly I could still have been dreaming. Penny, I AM going mad!"

CHAPTER THIRTY-SEVEN

Penny had stayed for another hour, trying to reassure me I wasn't going crazy, comforting me.

But it hadn't worked.

Nick was due back very soon, and I had to clear my head and act as stable as possible. It wasn't going to be easy.

I had decided I wasn't going to confront Nick about his possible affair with Clarissa. I wouldn't make an accusation, maybe just drop in a few gentle probing questions about his weekend.

I didn't feel on strong moral grounds to accuse him because nagging away in my mind was a tinge of guilt, a recognition of my own hypocrisy.

Yes, I was fuming with Nick for having an affair, his apparent layer upon layer of deceit; yet this weekend I'd slept with another man. Not only that, I'd had disloyal fantasies about leaving Nick and being with James instead. I tried to rationalise it, to find excuses in order to absolve myself from the responsibility of my own infidelity. But I couldn't.

Was I no better than Nick?

I wasn't calculating and deceitful like he had been. It was a drunken impulse, and although this didn't excuse me, it was a one-off that I'd immediately regretted the following morning.

But did I genuinely regret it? And was I secretly hoping it wasn't a one-off?

I was emotionally confused. Anyway, instead of confronting Nick, I would watch him carefully.

And I would contact Natasha again on Monday. I needed to see those incriminating photos – if they existed.

I also wouldn't mention my horrific fear that I could have killed Samson while sleepwalking. In the same way, I couldn't tell Nick about the knife under my pillow. Nor the threatening phone calls that had never existed.

He would think I was crazy. And I knew now that maybe I was.

IT WAS AROUND HALF four when I heard Nick's car pull into the drive, followed by the grating sound of the garage door. I was waiting in the conservatory, and I stood and walked into the kitchen. I heard Nick entering the house, and he called, "Ellie?"

And I replied, "In the kitchen."

He entered, placed his small suitcase next to the door and smiled across at me. "How are you, sweetheart?"

I eked out a tiny smile, moved across and pecked him on the cheek.

"I'm fine," I said before adding, "Well, I'm not actually, Nick. Samson's gone missing."

"Samson? What d'you mean he's gone missing?"
"Someone took him."
"Someone's stolen him? Are you serious?"
"Yes. I've looked everywhere for him, put posters up around Didsbury. Nothing."
"Well, I suppose it's only a day. I bet he'll turn up," Nick said, not sounding too worried.

I didn't agree with him, but it was easier to change the subject. "How was the conference?"

"Oh, you know, okay. Bit boring."

"Who went? I know Pete didn't."

"No, he didn't. As head of sales, he wasn't required to be there, but how did you know?"

I decided to feed Nick just a titbit of information. "He rang me on Friday night, drunk, wanting to come round."

"You're kidding!"

"No."

"He was pestering you?"

"I told him to piss off."

"Bloody hell. I'll definitely have a word with him."

"So who else was at the conference from the office?" I asked casually.

"Oh, all the sales team. The ones you know, Jim, Terry, Ursula ..."

"Clarissa?" I asked casually.

"Of course Clarissa was there. Craig was leading a session, and as Clarissa's having an affair with him, he wouldn't leave her off the list."

"She's having an affair with Craig?" I asked, astonished.

"Yeah." Nick raised his eyebrows. "In fact, he's left his wife for her, and they're moving in together."

"Good God."

"I know." Nick came in close to me, placed both arms around me and said, "I've missed you."

I smiled at him. He leaned in and kissed me briefly on the lips. "I'm going to unpack; then we'll have a drink."

As Nick turned, picked up his case and disappeared out of the kitchen, my mind was in overdrive.

If Nick wasn't having an affair with Clarissa, just who was he having an affair with?

I WAS TOTALLY EXHAUSTED, and my head was teeming with distressing images that flashed across my brain, a kaleidoscope of Samson, James, the police, Natasha, Nick, Clarissa ... all of them fighting for space inside my head.

I was in bed by half nine, apologising to Nick for being so weary.

But I couldn't sleep.

Nick slid in next to me around an hour later. He spooned his body next to mine.

"You awake?" he whispered.

"Yes," I answered softly.

"I do love you, Ellie. And I know you think I've been having an affair. But promise, I've not."

I didn't answer.

He started kissing the back of my neck, and his arm sneaked round me and cupped my breasts.

"Nick, I'm so sorry, I'm totally exhausted," I whispered.

"It's okay. Hey, and if you're worried about Samson, we will find him," he assured me.

But then the image of a lifeless Samson as I stabbed him again and again flashed into my head.

No, we won't, I thought.

He's dead. Samson's dead.

And I killed him.

CHAPTER THIRTY-EIGHT

I woke around 2.30 a.m. I put a hand out to touch Nick, but his side of the bed was empty, the duvet thrown back.

There was no light on in the en suite, so I wondered where he was. Maybe he'd gone downstairs for a glass of water.

It was just then that my eyes adjusted to the dark, and I saw the outline of a figure standing just inside the door.

"Nick? Nick, what are you doing?"

But as the figure moved closer and the outline became more distinct, I realised this wasn't Nick.

I screamed. "Nick!" I called out. "Nick! Nick, where are you?"

Now the figure walked slowly round to my side of the bed. I scrambled across to Nick's side and jumped out.

I ran to the door, threw it open. As I entered the landing, I snapped on two switches that lit up the upstairs landing and the downstairs hall.

As I ran down the stairs two at a time, the figure was out of the bedroom and following me.

Now the house was flooded with light, I could see it was the same scary figure that had inhabited all my nightmares: long trench coat, hoodie, eyes black.

Was I in a nightmare now? Or was this real?

If it was real, how did he enter the house, and where was Nick?

I reached the hall, dashed into the kitchen, banged on the lights.

As I ran to the island, I grabbed the unicorn knife from its block, and as I swung round to face my attacker, he entered the kitchen.

He stopped.

"Don't come any closer. Just get out of my fucking house right now."

He didn't answer but took a step closer.

"Who are you? Who the fuck are you? I want you out of my house and out of my head."

Then slowly the figure pulled back the hoodie.

I screamed, "No! No! It can't be!"

The eyes were black, but there was no mistake.

I was staring at my own face.

I thrust the knife outwards towards my own throat.

I WAS WOKEN up by Nick's screams.

"What the fuck, get off me, get the fuck off me, Ellie!" he was shouting in panic.

And as my eyes flashed open, I realised I was sitting astride Nick. The unicorn knife was pressed against Nick's neck, and he had both hands grasping my hand, trying desperately to push the knife away from his body.

As soon as I realised what was happening, I cried out, threw the knife on the floor as if it was burning my hand and started to cry.

"I'm sorry. I'm sorry, Nick, it was a nightmare. Oh God, Nick, I'm so sorry. I could have killed you; oh God. Oh God, what did I nearly do?"

"What the fuck, Ellie," Nick shouted as he switched on his bedside light, his face screwed up in disbelief and his chest rising rapidly.

"It was so real. He'd come into my room, you weren't there, and I escaped down into the kitchen, and as he came for me, I grabbed the knife and stabbed at him," I gabbled, my voice hysterical.

But however distressed I was, I knew I'd never told Nick that I'd recognised the face.

And when I stopped, Nick nodded, regaining his breath, his composure. "Okay. Okay, Ellie. That was so scary."

"I know, I know, I'm sorry," I gulped as I continued to cry.

Nick eased himself out of bed, bent down and picked up the knife.

"Let's get rid of this," he said. "And I think you and I need to talk. What just happened there ... wow, Ellie, what is happening to you?"

And this set off me again. "I know, I know I need help!"

THE REALITY of what I'd done was still too much to comprehend. As I drank a cup of hot chocolate, my hand was shaking.

My voice, too, was shaky, trembling on each word as I

said, "I ... I must have ... I must have been, well, I must have been acting out my nightmare. I must have, I must have come downstairs, got the knife, to ... to defend myself, then, somehow ... must have ... still asleep ... must have gone back upstairs, got back in bed and ..."

When I stopped, I was crying again, and Nick closed an arm around my shoulders. "It's okay, Ellie."

"No, it's not okay. Not okay at all. I could have killed you."

"Well, you didn't."

"What's happening to me, Nick? It's like I'm, like I'm losing control. Over my life."

My shoulders were heaving, and then I started speaking quickly, and it all poured out, everything that had happened over the whole, horrifying weekend. I held nothing back (apart from James): Samson's collar, my fear that I'd killed our dog when I was either sleepwalking or hallucinating, digging for Samson, everything, including the incident at the Sleep Clinic.

And Nick let me speak, never interrupted, and his face was aghast, his mouth drooped open.

When I eventually stopped, he just said, "Christ."

"Nick, I ... I don't know what's real anymore and what isn't, and I'm, I'm scared. I'm scared of what I've done, and I'm scared what I might do."

Nick simply kissed me on the top of the head.

"And I'm scared to go to sleep. What if I attack you again, or I hurt myself like with the broken glass?"

Eventually he spoke. "I think ... I think you need to go back and talk to Dr Carson; tell him everything. Like you say, Ellie, you need help. You can't carry on like this. We can't."

"Yes. I will. I promise. First thing tomorrow."

"And maybe you should take time off work?" Nick suggested.

"Yes," I agreed. "I'm in no fit state to ... to attend to my patients."

"Ring in sick tomorrow, take the day off, and I'll take the day off too, yes?"

"I'm not sure ..." I wavered.

"I'm insisting, Ellie. And tomorrow maybe Dr Carson can fit you in some time?" he suggested.

I nodded in agreement, then paused for a moment before adding, "I think I'd better sleep in the guest room tonight. And I think you should lock the bedroom door."

"Christ, Ellie."

"For your safety. So I can't get to you. Yeah?"

And, reluctantly, he nodded.

We went upstairs together, Nick taking my hand. I kissed him briefly before he entered the bedroom; then I waited until I could hear him the lock the door before I went across the hall and into the guest bedroom.

But I couldn't sleep. I was too afraid to sleep.

CHAPTER THIRTY-NINE

Soon after eight I rang in sick and apologised to Mr Ahmed, my consultant surgeon. I told him I would like to have a chat. We arranged to meet later that morning. I liked him, and he respected me, so I knew he'd understand.

Then I rang Dr Carson.

He answered after the first ring. "How are you, Ellie?" he asked, his voice soft.

"I need to see you. I really need to see you." I knew I sounded desperate, and I could feel my eyes filling up. "I've had such a bad weekend, Ben. I really need to talk. Things ... things have happened, and I'm out of control, and I'm sorry what I said last time we spoke; it was rude, and I was out of order and—"

Ben Carson's voice was gentle and reassuring as he interrupted me. "Ellie, don't worry about that. I'll fit you in and see you any time you can make it today, and we'll take it from there."

"Thank you. Thank you, Ben. I've decided to take some leave like you suggested," I told him.

"Good. I'm pleased about that. I think you've made the right decision."

"And I'm seeing Mr Ahmed at eleven a.m., so if I could come over to you after, I'd appreciate that."

"Yes, of course, Ellie. I'll look forward to seeing you."

AS I PARKED up at the Royal, I saw James's car was already in its bay, and the thought of seeing him raised a feeling less of excitement, more of apprehension.

My meeting with my consultant surgeon was fine. He'd actually recommended I should take time off after the Rick Walker case, but I'd dug in my heels, so now that I was asking for two weeks' leave, he agreed it was a good idea.

Next, I bumped into James on a corridor by the lift as I made my way to see Ben Carson.

"Did Samson turn up?" he asked hopefully.

I shook my head. "James, I still think I may have killed Samson."

James could see I was welling up as I talked about Samson, and at one point he edged towards me as if to give me a hug, before leaning back.

"But, James, last night. Last night I sleepwalked in my nightmare, and I finished on top of Nick, a knife at his throat."

As I spoke, I burst into tears.

"I don't know what's happening to me," I cried.

This time he did move in, and his arms encircled me, and he held me.

I needed it. I needed a hug.

"Oh, you poor thing. I can't imagine how ... what you're going through. If there's anything I can do. Anything ..."

I nodded a thank you as I pulled away from him.

"I'm on my way to see Ben Carson," I told him, wiping the tears from my face.

"Okay. Well, let me know how it goes with him and keep in touch over the next two weeks while you're on leave. You can ring me any time. Any time, Ellie. I'll come round."

And he looked deep into my eyes as he said it.

"Promise you'll call if you need me?"

"I promise," I replied.

"You're so loved here at the Royal, Ellie, remember that. And you'll get through this, I know you will."

He leaned forward, kissed me on the cheek. Then he pulled away, and I watched him as he continued along the corridor. But as he reached the corner, he stopped, glanced back and smiled.

I TOLD Ben Carson everything that had happened to me over the weekend – but obviously not about James. I finished by describing the events of my nightmare the previous evening.

"And when the hoodie was pushed back, I recognised the figure." I paused as if it was too difficult to carry on. "Ben, it was me. It was my face. And I stabbed the knife in the neck, and that's when I was woken by Nick's screams. I was on top of Nick, pushing the knife at his throat."

As I paused, I couldn't stop the tears flowing, and Ben Carson pulled a couple of tissues from a box on his side table and passed them to me.

I wiped my eyes, blew my nose. "Sorry," I whispered.

"Don't be, Ellie. I'm very sorry you've had such a tough weekend."

"What d'you think it means, Ben? That figure being me. Has it been me all the time? And that's why there was no listed phone calls, because it was all going on just in my head?"

Ben Carson was chewing on the end of his pen, deep in thought, a slight frown across his forehead. He let his head fall back, as if looking up at the ceiling, closed his eyes for just a few seconds before opening them and looking across at me.

"Can I ask you, Ellie ... regarding the nightmare where you woke up trying to kill your husband ... how is your relationship with him at the moment?"

I took time to answer.

Eventually, choosing my words carefully, I said, "It's not great. We've only been married just over a year, and we haven't got the closeness we had in the early days. A lot of that is my fault because, as I've said, I've been down quite a lot."

I paused before I continued, "But I've caught him out in one or two lies recently. I think he's having an affair. He denies it, but I'm almost certain he is. I've also had a call from someone who says she's seen Nick with another woman."

I stopped, looked across at Ben, who nodded. He seemed to nod a lot.

"But what about the figure being me? What does it mean? And d'you think the person chasing me in my nightmares has always been me? And if so, why?"

"First, let's take the incident with your husband and the

knife ... possibly, because you've been troubled by the state of your marriage and a loss of trust in your husband, it could be manifesting itself in your dreams. The need to hurt your husband in return for his ... his possible infidelity. You're angry with him."

I nodded as Ben continued, "Have you spoken to your husband, confronted him about your suspicions?"

"Not directly, no. But he knows I suspect him. You think I should challenge him?"

"Challenge is maybe the wrong word. I think it needs to be brought out in the open. Maybe even with a marriage guidance counsellor."

"And the nightmare attacker being me?" I pressed. "What does that mean?"

Ben took some time to answer, pondering different possibilities. He chewed on the end of his pencil again before finally speaking. "I think, Ellie, you're carrying an awful lot of guilt around with you. Your depression is at the core of this guilt, and you've never confronted it till now. How it's affected your relationship with people over the years. So the figure ... you ... who is chasing you and trying to kill you ... it's a way if punishing yourself."

He paused for me to take this in.

"So how do I stop this? How do I control these nightmares?" I asked.

"Well, it's also possible, now you've identified your attacker as yourself, that they may stop. I can't guarantee that, but it is a possibility."

"Okay. But what if ... if all these things that have been happening to me ... they haven't really been happening, they are just hallucinations like you suggested? That is scary, Ben. I feel so out of control."

I was near to tears again.

"Are you taking the fluoxetine?"

As an answer, I looked down. Ben didn't rebuke me.

"Now I'm taking two weeks off. I'll start taking them today."

Ben again did his impression of a nodding dog in the rear window of a car. "I'm still hopeful the antidepressants will help with the nightmares and the somnambulism. So please do start taking them, Ellie."

"I promise. And the results from the Sleep Clinic?" I asked.

He had my file in front of him, and he opened the report. "I've studied the recorded data. It doesn't tell me very much, I'm afraid. On a scale of sleep apnoea severity, yours was normal, your AHI is five per hour, and your oxygen desaturation number was also normal, stayed above ninety-five per cent. There was an excessive amount of leg movement, probably during your nightmare. But overall, nothing conclusive."

I looked at Ben; neither of us seemed terribly reassured.

WHEN I ARRIVED HOME, Nick had left me a note. He apologised, but he'd had a call from work, and they needed him in. He'd be back early evening.

It was around half six when I heard Nick's car pull into the garage.

The first thing he asked when he entered the kitchen was, "How are you, Ellie?"

I shrugged.

"How did it go with Dr Carson?"

"Okay." I shrugged again, uncommunicative.

"Did you tell Dr Carson everything?" Nick persisted.

"More or less, yes."

"And did he have any answers?"

"Not many. But he thinks some of it is to do with our marriage."

"You're kidding me. He said that?"

"And maybe we need to see a marriage guidance counsellor."

"I'm not doing that. There's nothing wrong with our marriage." He paused. "We're just going through a bit of a bad patch."

I looked at him closely. "Are we? Are we really? Is that what it is? Nothing you want to tell me?"

Nick looked perturbed, frowned. "No. I don't know what you're talking about. We've talked about it before, Ellie. I'm not having an affair, if that's what you're implying."

I simply shook my head, turned.

"I'm tired. I need to lie down," I said to Nick over my shoulder. "Sorry. Can you get your own dinner?"

I'd felt lethargic all day since I'd arrived home from the Royal; maybe it was the effect of the antidepressants I was now taking.

I lay on top of my bed, and within five minutes I'd dozed off.

THAT NIGHT, I slept in the guest room again and insisted that Nick lock his door, just to be on the safe side.

I actually slept really well. No nightmares. No stranger pursuing me. No stranger who looked like me.

But the truth was, my real nightmares were about to return.

CHAPTER FORTY

I spent the morning pottering around. I went outside with the spade and filled in all the holes I'd manically dug up. It looked as if a mole had invaded the garden. I tidied the kitchen, which I'd neglected over the weekend. The food bin, stored under the sink unit, needed replacing, so I dragged out the small bag, struggled to tie the bag in a knot as it was so full, and carried it out the front door.

The small food recycling bin was left near the wheelie bin along with the containers for plastics and bottles.

As I opened the lid to drop in the bag, I let out a huge gasp that led to a piercing scream.

The inside of the bin was splattered and streaked with blood.

At the bottom of the bin, lying in a shallow pool of blood, was a bunch of Samson's fur. I reeled back screaming in shock. I could hardly breathe.

I started crying hysterically, my chest heaving.

I must have killed Samson in my sleep, during my nightmare with the figure holding Samson on his lead.

What had I done? Where had I put his body?

And then the awful truth hit me as I stared down at the bin.

There had been a collection the morning after my nightmare. I must have stabbed Samson in the small bin and then thrown him into the wheelie bin. He'd been taken away, discarded like a stinking pile of garbage.

I ran back into the house, howling.

I ran upstairs, threw myself on the bed, and the howl shifted to a whimper.

"No! No! NO!" I kept crying out. "This is a nightmare. I'm in a nightmare. This isn't happening. I'm going to wake up. Wake up! Please wake up."

But it was no nightmare.

I had killed my own dog.

I had stabbed Samson to death.

If I had killed my own dog and I couldn't remember, what was I capable of?

Who was safe from me? No one.

My head was bursting, fear fighting inside my skull, the implications for my life overwhelming. I was unstable. I was crazy.

How could I maintain a relationship? I had no chance.

And what of my work? In my current state of constant paranoia, there was no way I could return to the Royal. It wasn't safe. It wasn't safe for me. It wasn't safe for my patients.

Would I ever be able to go back? My work was my whole life. If I couldn't work, I had nothing. What was the point of living if I couldn't follow the career I loved and had worked so desperately hard for?

And if I died, who would miss me? Nick was having an

affair, I was sure of that. He wouldn't miss me. James maybe. Penny.

But who else?

My bottle of fluoxetine was on my bedside table. It would be so easy to take them all. To close my eyes, sleep, just slip away. I was so exhausted. The thought felt almost comforting, rational.

I opened the bottle, spilled them all over the bed. I looked at them. Should I do it? Should I take them all? I was too exhausted to fight anymore. I'd fought the darkness inside me for most of my life. There was no more fight within me. It would be easier to give in. To drift away.

There was an empty glass on my bedside table. I picked it up, eased off the bed. My legs felt leaden. I made it into the bathroom, filled the glass with water, returned to the bed, lay down.

I would do this. I needed to. I saw no use to my life anymore. It felt pointless.

I placed three of the pills in the palm of my hand. I stared down at them, paused, uncertain, and then threw them into my mouth. I was about to wash them down with the water when I paused.

What was I doing! Think. What the fuck was I doing? This wasn't me. This was not me. I spat them out onto the bed.

The phone started ringing. But I let it ring. I didn't want to talk to anyone. Then the answerphone clicked in.

"Hello there. My name's Amelia Pace, and I live at the end of Moorland Avenue, and I've just seen your poster about your missing dog, Samson ..."

I jerked upright and snatched up the phone.

"Hi, it's Ellie here; you have some news about my dog?"

"Oh hi, Ellie. Yes. I think I saw him on Saturday afternoon around three o'clock. He was being pulled along Moreland Road towards Wilmslow Road like he didn't want to go. I didn't think much of it at the time but—"

"Who was it pulling him?" I interrupted anxiously.

"Couldn't be too sure. I'd just glanced out my front window. Someone in a baseball cap, a hoodie, jeans, trainers …"

"Man or a woman?" I asked.

"Difficult to tell. Sorry. Not very helpful."

"No. It is. Thank you so much. You just saved my live!"

"Sorry?"

"Thank you. I owe you."

And I finished the call.

Yes, maybe Samson wasn't dead. Someone had taken him, and that someone wanted to drive me over the edge and into insanity.

And they'd almost succeeded.

CHAPTER FORTY-ONE

How low had I sunk that I could even entertain the thought of taking my own life? I felt ashamed and embarrassed. It would be a secret that I would never reveal to anyone. Even through my darkest periods of depression, I had never once contemplated suicide.

Although still emotionally fragile, I knew I had to fight back.

First I would secure the house. I had to feel safe.

Once I'd done that, I could focus my mind on finding the truth. Who'd been stalking me? Who'd killed Samson? Who was playing with my head?

Whom could I trust?

And whom should I fear?

Maybe, I thought, *when I find the truth, the nightmares will disappear and the sleepwalking cease.*

SAM HARRIS WAS a burly man with a cheery round face. I was watching him, my arms folded, as he stood on the top rung of his ladder.

"Okay, that should do it," he called down to me.

He'd just finished fitting sensor lights and security cameras at the front and rear of the house.

He gingerly stepped down the ladder one rung at a time. Once he'd reached the safety of the drive, he turned, beaming at me.

"Right, I'll show you how you can access the CCTV footage on your laptop; then you said you wanted some hidden security cameras inside the house, yeah?"

"Yes."

I had found Sam's company online, a local family firm. I'd rung Sam, explained exactly what I required, and he said he couldn't do it for a couple of days. I offered to pay double his labour costs, and he arrived within the hour.

I was determined to feel safe in my own house.

And who knew what the security cameras might pick up?

Retrieving the CCTV footage on my laptop was simple.

"Got that?" he asked after he'd taken me through it.

"No problem."

"Now as regards the hidden security cameras …"

He opened his large black toolbox, bent down into it; his head disappeared for a second; then he reappeared with both hands clasped in front of him.

"These are perfect," he said.

He opened both palms, rather like a magician performing a trick, and lying in each palm was what looked like black buttons, with a camera eye at the centre.

"These are wireless security cameras, which also pick up sound, and I can place them discreetly" – and he emphasised the word "discreetly" – "anywhere in the house."

I nodded. I felt deceitful placing hidden cameras in the house – I didn't intend to tell Nick – but I'd decided I would trust no one but myself from now on.

He hid the tiny cameras in three rooms: the kitchen/dining room, on top of the kitchen units, the eye panning the whole of the kitchen and stretching beyond the dining area into the conservatory; in the TV lounge, where he perched one on top of a picture frame; and in our bedroom, where he placed it "discreetly" on my dressing table, invisible among the cluttered contents of make-up, moisturisers, hairspray, antiperspirant and bundles of jewellery.

Once they were all in place, Sam explained, "You can also access the footage from your iPhone as well as your laptop. So you don't even need to be home to check it."

"Thank you, that's great."

"Any questions?"

"No, I don't think so; you've been very helpful."

"Any problems, just give me a call. You've got a two-year guarantee for everything."

"Thank you. And I'll make the transfer today."

"Perfect. Have a good day, Dr Thompson."

As I waved goodbye to Sam, my mobile rang.

I recognised the number.

"Hello, Natasha," I answered.

"Hi, Ellie, how are you?"

"Err, I've been better," I said before continuing, "Okay, Natasha, what have you got to tell me?"

"Are you free tomorrow night? Come over to my place

tomorrow evening around five, and I'll show you everything I've got."

"Can't I come over tonight?"

"No. I've another meeting. Tomorrow at five."

"But what can you tell me now? I need more information, Natasha. Please?"

A pause before she answered, "Okay. Like I've said, Nick is not who you think he is. He's got form. He lies. He finds it hard to stay faithful. He has a temper that he controls most of the time but not always. I did warn you when you started seeing him. You can never trust him." She spoke calmly, unemotionally. "Has he ever spoken about his past to you?"

"Not really," I answered.

"Well, he did to me. Once. When he got drunk. He's got stuff in the past ..."

"What sort of stuff?"

Natasha didn't answer directly. "Look, after what happened at your apartment, you probably think I'm crazy."

I agreed with that assessment but thought it best to stay silent.

"Well, I'm not. I really liked you, Ellie. I'd hoped we could still be friends ... but ... once you started dating Nick, it became impossible."

"I understand that."

"I've got on with my own life. I've got a decent job. I've been seeing a nice guy for six months now, and he's asked me to marry him." I wasn't sure I believed that last bit. "It's just, like I told you, I saw Nick in town with this woman, they were all over each other, so I took a photo. I thought you needed to know."

"That's very kind of you," I said with a hint of sarcasm.

"And you mentioned another person ... someone who was stalking me? Who was it?"

"I'll tell you tomorrow face to face."

"No, Natasha, you'll tell me now," I insisted.

Natasha hesitated before replying, "I saw him. On Saturday night. In Didsbury. When you were in that Italian. I was parked up waiting for my boyfriend."

"Did you recognise who it was?" I asked, my voice now slightly anxious.

"Yes. It was that ex of yours, Pete. I never liked him. Too smarmy."

And Natasha could hear my sharp intake of breath. She continued, "He followed you inside the restaurant. At one point you got up, he went over to your table where you'd left your phone, and he picked it up. I don't know what he did. He glanced out the window, and I think he might have seen me in the car."

This completely threw me, and my heart surged. I couldn't answer at first; finally I asked, softly, "Okay? What time did you say tomorrow?"

"Five. But something else, Ellie. I have other photos. Of someone else. Not Pete. I really think you're in danger."

"Who? Who is it?" I asked, my anxiety skyrocketing.

"I don't know. But you might." She hesitated. "Really looking forward to seeing you, Ellie. I'll give you a big hug!"

I pulled a face as I hung up; I wasn't sure about the hug.

I felt a surge of tension inside me.

Tomorrow I would find out whom Nick was having an affair with.

And what of Pete? Why did he want my phone? Had he really been stalking me?

And who was this other person? Natasha's words echoed in my ears:

I really think you're in danger.

CHAPTER FORTY-TWO

Nick rang me at around five o'clock.

"Sorry it's late notice, Ellie, but the boss wants to take some of the team for a meal tonight."

"That's okay," I answered coolly, not believing a word he said. "Probably be in bed when you get in. I've had a tough day."

"Why, what's happened?" Nick asked, a hint of concern in his voice.

"I'll tell you tomorrow."

There was a pause from Nick's end before he spoke again. "Ellie, there's ... there's something else ..."

For a second I thought he was about to confess to having an affair. "What?"

I was in for a shock.

"Ellie, are you having an affair with Pete?"

"What? What did you say?"

"I'm trying not to get angry. I just want the truth. Are you having an affair with Pete?"

"Are you kidding me? You know I can't stand the guy.

Pete? What the hell makes you think that?" My voice was a mixture of confusion and anger.

"Okay. I went to have a word with Pete after what you told me about him going round on Friday when I was away. Anyway, he wasn't in, but he'd left his phone on his desk, and I noticed his home screen photo. It was of you."

"What?" I was incredulous. "Bloody hell, Nick. He's made it plain he still fancies me, but that is obsessive."

"The thing is, Ellie, the photo, it wasn't one from when you were going out with him; it was a photo I took of you only a few weeks ago ... in our garden, and you liked it so much I sent it to you."

I was stunned. I remembered the photo. It was early autumn; the sun was streaming into the garden through the trees, casting dappled shadows across my face.

Eventually I answered, "Well, he couldn't have got it from my phone, so he must have got it from yours at work."

But Natasha's call about seeing Pete in the Italian restaurant flashed into my head.

"Believe me, Nick," I continued, "I'm not having an affair with Pete. The thought of it ... Christ no ..."

"Okay, okay. I believe you." He hesitated before asking, "Will you be sleeping in the guest room again tonight when I get in?"

"Hmm, I think so. Just to be on the safe side. For now."

"Okay. I understand."

And he rang off.

In fact, I was using the somnambulism as an excuse not to share a bed with Nick.

As soon as the call finished, I checked my phone. I went on to my texts, and there it was.

Two recent photos of me, including the one in the

garden, had been sent from my phone to Pete. That was what he had been doing when Natasha saw him through the restaurant window.

I deleted them both in case Nick asked to check my phone.

But a more chilling thought hit me. Maybe Pete had also deleted the "nightmare" phone calls. How else could they have disappeared? There could be no other explanation.

If so, Pete was my stalker. Pete knew all about my nightmares.

But why was he doing it? It wouldn't drive me back to him.

Maybe he just wanted revenge. Maybe he'd never accepted our break-up and never accepted my marriage to Nick.

And did he take Samson?

If so, then Pete was the crazy one. Not me.

I DIDN'T HEAR Nick arrive home that night. But when I woke up the following morning after a solid eight hours' sleep, with no dreams or nightmares that I remembered, I could hear sounds downstairs in the kitchen.

Nick was pouring out a mug of fresh coffee as I entered.

"Hi," I said, forcing my lips into a false smile.

"Just in time. Want a cup?" he asked.

"Please."

I sat down at the island, and as he placed a large cup of fresh coffee and a small jug of milk in front of me, he asked, "How did you sleep?"

"Fine, actually, yeah."

"Good." He took a sip of his coffee. "And what's with the Blackpool illuminations? I arrived home, and as I drew up, the whole place flooded with light. And are those cameras on the front?"

"Yes. I need to feel safe in my own home, Nick. So I got a local guy to install them yesterday."

I wasn't going to tell him about the hidden cameras.

He sat down next to me, sipped his coffee before asking, "And yesterday, you said you needed to tell me something?"

My heart surged. I needed to tell Nick about Samson. My grief had been temporarily eclipsed by Natasha's phone call, the implications of which filled every inch of my head.

Nick picked up on my alarmed expression.

"What is it?" he asked.

I took a moment to answer. How best to tell him? I decided to hold back the information that I knew someone had taken Samson. Instead I'd lead him to think that I had killed him.

"Nick, Samson is ... Samson ..."

And I couldn't continue as the mock grief overwhelmed me, and I started sobbing.

"Ellie, Ellie, what is it? What's the matter, tell me?"

Nick came over, draped a gentle arm over my shoulders.

And slowly, I fed him the story of how I had found Samson's blood and fur in the recycling box and that I thought I had killed him and put him in the wheelie bin, which the bin men had taken away. And as I spoke, I never took my eyes off Nick, watching his every minute reaction.

And this time Nick did look genuinely shocked.

But I never mentioned why I suspected Pete. And I never mentioned Natasha.

ONCE NICK LEFT FOR WORK, I made up my bed in the guest room before popping into the bedroom we usually shared.

Nick had just dragged the duvet back. As I went to tidy it up, I instinctively picked up his pillow and inhaled.

It didn't smell of Nick's aftershave. It smelled of perfume, a kind I couldn't quite place. But it wasn't my perfume.

It belonged to the woman Nick was having an affair with.

I had all day to fill before I would find out the truth from Natasha.

CHAPTER FORTY-THREE

I was fifteen when Steve arrived at the home. He was not only the same age but, like me, also a survivor. There the similarities ended. He had a big cheeky smile, black, scarecrow hair permanently ruffled, and a huge laugh so loud he could wake the dead. He looked so cool, with his scuffed leather biker jacket, which was never off his back, a faded Green Day T-shirt and his tight jeans tucked into black boots. (I found out later his hairstyle was copied from Green Day's lead singer, Billie Joe Armstrong.)

From the moment he entered the home, everyone loved him.

I was now the eldest in the home. All the kids respected me, and yet ... and yet somehow they didn't actually "love" me. They liked me, I think, but they were wary of me, in awe, a little scared.

Of course, if they really knew me, they'd be more than a little scared.

The moment Steve entered the home, he was the magnet

that drew everyone to him. So I had every reason to dislike and resent him. He wasn't clever like me, but he had ... charisma. It was a word I'd come across when reading about iconic actors or musicians, and as soon as I met Steve, I could see he had it in bucket-loads.

I also knew he was a survivor because Gavin and Joyce had told me a little about him before he arrived, and they were asking me to keep an eye on him and help him to settle in.

He didn't need my help.

Steve's mother had been a single parent, a drug addict. I found out much later on that he didn't know his father. Steve was taken into care when he was only five years old. His mum had died of an overdose when he was six, so he couldn't remember much about her.

He was a disruptive child both at home and at school. He was always being moved on. Then by the time he reached secondary school, he constantly bunked off. It was only his natural charm and megawatt smile that saved him.

He joined me at my school, but I only saw him at break times and dinner. I was in all the top classes while Steve had been placed in the lower ones. I did notice that his popularity peaked very quickly, particularly with the girls from my year. By the second week, several girls were vying for his attention. I could see he loved it.

From when he arrived at the home, it took him three months to win me over. I stayed aloof. I'd never met anyone like him before, and he did fascinate me. I could see from the first day that he was equally fascinated by me.

Finally, I was reading in a corner of the garden, and he sauntered over and sat next to me on the bench. And I remember this conversation so clearly, word for word.

He didn't say anything at first as I continued to ignore him; then he said, "I won't bite, you know."

I shot back without looking from my book, To Kill A Mockingbird, "No, but I will."

And he roared with laughter. When he stopped, he said, "You like reading, don't you?"

Still not looking up, but not seeing the words on my page, I answered, "Yeah, do you?"

"Yeah, course," he said, with mock confidence. "Love reading. I read all the time."

I rested the book on my knee, glanced across at him and asked, "What's your favourite book, then?"

He shrugged. "Loads. I like loads o' books."

"Thomas the Tank Engine, I bet that's your favourite," I said, sneering.

He didn't laugh. "You're funny, aren't you?"

"Funnier than you."

And he stood up and walked off, head bowed.

Later that week, I was sitting on the same bench, and he walked across to me, less confident than previously. He was holding a book in his hand, and as he sat down, he handed it to me.

He said, "I saw you reading about mockingbirds, so I got you this one."

I took it, glanced at the cover. The Guide to British Birds.

I could have torn him apart. I could have destroyed him and made him the laughingstock of both the home and the school. But somehow, I found it sweet and endearing, so I just smiled at him and said simply, "Thanks."

Much later he told me he'd nicked it from a bookshop in Stockport town centre.

I found out he could hardly read, and once we started going out together, I gave him secret lessons. He was too proud to let anyone know.

I realised as we spent more and more time together that Steve was extremely bright. He'd not been interested and so had wasted his educational chances, but he had a sharp mind and could pick up things quickly if he chose. He was reading fluently within a couple of months. I told him that with his personality and sharp brain, he could do anything with his life, and it still wasn't too late. But he just laughed at me.

When he eventually plucked up the courage to ask me out, he'd suggested we go to the movies. I said yes, so long as I could choose the film. He agreed, so I took him to see Harry Potter and the Sorcerer's Stone *though he wanted to see the latest* Fast and Furious.

He really enjoyed it, and he started reading all the books. In the cinema, he slipped his hand into mine, and we both smiled at each other. Now we were fifteen, we were allowed out until 9 p.m., so we caught an early showing, and when we walked home from the cinema, he slipped his arm round my shoulder.

On the doorstep before we entered the home, he paused, turned me round to face him, and we kissed, and he asked if I'd be his girlfriend.

"No," I said.

He looked hurt and asked, "Why not?"

"But I will let you be my *boyfriend."*

And he looked puzzled.

I'd always regarded myself as emotionally tough and aloof, but suddenly that all changed. For a time I became one of those girls at school whom I despised, the "girly girls". Okay, I didn't dress like they did, pinks and pastels, but in the rest of my behaviour I aped them because I became besotted by Steve. And he was besotted by me. We lost all objectivity. I knew he wasn't good for me, but I didn't care.

We both got off on danger.

And it was a danger that would shape the rest of our lives.

CHAPTER FORTY-FOUR

I was driving to Natasha's flat. As I prepared for the meeting, all sorts of questions buzzed around my head.

Could I trust Natasha?

Or was I in danger?

Was Natasha unhinged? She didn't sound unhinged on the phone; she sounded very rational. But how had she acquired all these photos if she wasn't stalking me and Nick?

I turned into Alexandra Road South. Three hundred metres up on my left was Natasha's block of flats.

My nerves cranked up a touch.

I was only fifty metres away when I saw, parked up on the road ahead, an ambulance and a police car.

I drew up not far behind the police car, climbed out. Ahead of me I could see a cluster of about eight or nine people gathered on the pavement outside the flats. I strolled up to them, and I spoke to a man with a small white poodle standing on the edge of the group. "What's going on?" I asked.

"Dunno," he said. "I was just walking past, wondered what was going on meself."

Then a woman in her forties, standing at the head of the group, overhearing the query, looked round over her shoulder and said, "It's one of my neighbours."

I squeezed between a couple of older women with identical grey bobbed hair until I was at the front next to the neighbour, whose hair was in bog foam curlers, and she was still wearing her pyjamas under a grubby grey dressing gown, even though it was almost 5 p.m.

"Excuse me, I'm supposed to be meeting a neighbour of yours at number eight."

The woman's head swung round. "Natasha?"

"You know her?"

"I live across from her. You a friend?"

"Err ..." I wasn't sure how to answer. "Er, yeah, sort of."

"Well, I'm sorry to tell you, that's why the ambulance and police are here."

"Why?"

"She's committed suicide."

"What? She's dead? No ..."

"Sorry. She is. I found her," she told me.

"You found her?"

"Yeah. We have a key for each other's flats, just in case, you know. Anyway, I hadn't seen her all day, and I had a funny feeling, you know. She usually goes for a jog round the park, so I knocked on her door just to say hello, didn't get an answer, so I went in." She paused. "She was in the bath. She'd cut her wrists."

"Oh my God!" I couldn't believe it. "I only spoke to her yesterday; she seemed fine; she didn't sound ..."

"I know. I saw her yesterday an' all. But I tell you, biggest shock o' my life finding her in that bath."

"Yeah, must've been awful," I agreed and then asked, "How well did you know her?"

"Well, we didn't go out for a drink together, nothing like that. I mean, to be honest, we hadn't got a lot in common, but we'd pop in and out of each other's flats for a cuppa, you know."

"She ... she told me she'd been seeing some guy for a couple of months, and it was good," I said.

"Yeah, he seems a nice guy. He's going to be devastated." She paused, in thought, before continuing, "Seeing her like that in the bath, it'll stay with me for the rest o' me life. And she'd seemed so happy. I don't understand it."

My head was spinning, my thoughts in complete turmoil. Natasha's death was too much of a coincidence. Why would she arrange for me to go round and then kill herself? And she seemed to have got her life together: a job, a boyfriend. It didn't make sense.

Someone must have killed her.

Then a thought struck me.

Could it be Pete? If he'd seen Natasha watching him in the Italian restaurant, maybe he'd gone round to confront her.

Or what if it was Nick? Nick and his girlfriend – whoever she was.

As casually as possible, I asked the neighbour, "As far as you know, did she have any visitors today or last night?"

She thought about it. "Er, not today but I remember hearing voices in her flat last night. And it didn't sound like her boyfriend."

I was about to ask a couple more questions when the

doors swung open. Two paramedics appeared pushing a gurney with Natasha's body wrapped in a zipped-up body bag.

The neighbour started sobbing, and everyone watched in horrified fascination as they pushed the gurney along the path, out the gate, with the crowd separating to let the paramedics through as they called, "Excuse us, out of the way, please."

Then two police officers emerged from the front entrance, and I immediately recognised PC Griffiths, who was the slightly more sympathetic officer when I'd reported the attempted break-in. She was with another female officer, who looked no more than twenty.

As they came along the path, PC Griffiths broke away from her partner and came across towards us. I thought I'd been noticed, but she went directly to the neighbour. "Mrs Bowden, would it be possible to take a statement from you?"

"Yeah, sure."

"My colleague will take the statement inside your flat if that's okay?"

The neighbour nodded, and PC Griffiths was about to spin away when she noticed me and turned back. "Er, Dr Thompson?" she said, surprised.

I nodded. "PC Griffiths."

"What are you doing here?"

PC GRIFFITHS and I were sitting in her white Hyundai police car, and I was telling her the full background story.

"I'm convinced Natasha's death was no suicide," I said. "If you check on Natasha's phone, I think you'll find a photo of my husband with another woman and a photo of an ex of mine who's been stalking me. And Natasha told me about someone else she thought was a danger to me."

I paused, looked at PC Griffiths and finished with, "I really need to be taken seriously this time. You all thought I was crazy, and I thought I was too."

PC Griffiths took her time to reply before nodding. "Thank you for this, Dr Thompson. And we will take it seriously. We take all deaths seriously. I'll pass this on to my boss …"

"Not that sergeant who came out with you on Friday night?" I asked anxiously.

A wry smile played on PC Griffiths's lips before she added, "No. It'll be a detective inspector. We'll carry out an autopsy in the next few days to find the cause of death, and that will indicate any suspicious circumstances around Natasha's death. I'll be asking my boss to get forensics into the apartment tomorrow. I didn't see a phone, but we didn't search the apartment, so …"

A thought struck me. "If someone did this because of incriminating photos on the phone, maybe the phone won't be there; maybe they took it?"

"We'll see." PC Griffiths nodded, then shot a genuine smile at me. "Thank you, Dr Thompson, you have been very helpful."

As I opened the car door, I pulled out my card from my handbag. "If you find the phone and the photos, please ring me."

"I will. Promise."

BY THE TIME I arrived home, it was turned 6 p.m., and Nick's car was already parked up in the garage. I pondered how much I should tell him about Natasha. She was his ex, after all, but in the end I decided to hold back until I heard from the police.

I needed to lay out my thoughts in a regimented line, analysing and deciphering truths and theories.

At the moment my thoughts were a confused, jumbled mess, like tangled threads of wool impossible to separate.

Who could it be? Pete? Nick and this other woman? And who the hell was the *third* person Natasha mentioned?

Or, I thought, maybe it was none of them. Maybe Natasha was still as crazy as she'd always been. Maybe there were no photos.

But if there were no photos, why was she killed?

Just after ten, Nick popped his head in the lounge, where I was watching the news.

"I'm off to bed," he said.

"Okay," I replied. "I'm off to bed soon as well."

"Guest room?" he asked.

I nodded, and Nick didn't pursue it.

IT WAS AROUND 11 a.m. the next day that PC Griffiths drew up into my drive.

As I opened the front door, I immediately asked, "Some news?"

"Yes. We've still not ascertained Natasha's cause of death, so that's ongoing. However, we've had forensics going through the house. And, Dr Thompson, we haven't been able to find Natasha's phone," she told me.

The news neither surprised nor upset me. Except it confirmed the existence of incriminating photos on Natasha's phone.

"We also spoke to Natasha's boyfriend. He was devastated. They were getting engaged; they were really happy. He couldn't believe she would kill herself. But he did say something interesting," she added.

"What?"

"He said Natasha had been behaving just a little bit odd recently. She had told him that a friend of hers was in danger, and she wanted to help her, so she was doing some detective work to find out more information. He didn't know who the friend was ..."

I paused before answering, "I think that 'friend' was me."

CHAPTER FORTY-FIVE

I really did get off on the danger. It was like a drug. In fact, it took me over. The buzz. The burst of adrenaline.

Early on Steve had taught me how to steal from shops. Just small things. Sweets. Clothes. But it wasn't enough for me. I wanted more. The more dangerous it became, the closer we seemed to become.

So we increased that danger.

Steve stole two Blackberry phones, one for me and one for himself.

I was still a virgin, and he was a desperate fifteen-year-old, so I held all the cards, and I liked that. I liked the power it gave me.

He tried everything to persuade me. But I let him wait and wait because I loved that power so much. He was close to begging me, and I loved that too. He said he'd never felt like this with anyone, and I believed him. He told me I was in safe hands because he said he'd lost his virginity at fourteen to the mother of a schoolmate.

I laughed and said, "Yeah, sure."

"I did, honest," he said.

I laughed in his face and told him to piss off!

But in the end I gave in.

It happened at a weekend. Gavin and Joyce went on a big shop every Saturday afternoon, and they left the older kids in charge.

We did it in Steve's bedroom, and he'd bought some condoms (or rather nicked them from Boots). The experience was only memorable because it was so unremarkable. And within minutes I knew he'd lied about the mother of a mate. He was almost certainly a virgin.

I lay half naked and exposed as he struggled to fit on the condom, swearing and cursing. Then once it was on, he had trouble entering me, prodding, pushing, till somehow he squeezed it in, and I cried out because it hurt so much. A few thrusts, a couple of grunts (he thought I was enjoying it because I was crying out), he came, and it was all over before you could say "premature ejaculation".

Afterwards I said to him, "If you tell anyone about this, I'll fucking kill you."

He never did.

Afterwards I went on the pill, and we both started loving it. We weren't just having sex; we were making love. Sounds corny, but it was true.

We went everywhere together. We were inseparable.

Then it happened, the secret that would bind us together forever.

We were on a night out in Manchester. We'd had a few drinks, we missed the last bus home, and we hadn't enough money for a taxi.

"You said you know how to drive," I said.

"Yeah, course I do," he boasted. "Why?"

"Let's nick a car, and you can drive me home," I suggested.

"Cool."

Of course, we didn't know how to nick a car, so we walked round the streets until we saw this girl in her early twenties opening the door of her Mini. She was on her own, and the street was quiet.

I nodded to Steve, and as she was about to slip into the driving seat, he ran to her, pushed her over and grabbed her keys.

She shouted, "Hey!" but Steve jumped in the driver's seat, and I ran round into the passenger seat. Steve slotted the key into the ignition and turned. The engine started first time. As the girl tugged at the door, I shouted, "Go, go, go!"

And I knew he couldn't really drive when the car kangarooed forward and he promptly stalled it. "Shit!" he screamed as the girl caught us up.

"Bloody hurry up, Steve!" I yelled.

And this time he shot off, a few stutters as he tried to change gear, and we left the girl behind. We both started laughing so loud we nearly wet ourselves.

We were about a mile from home and wondering where to dump the car when it happened.

We were approaching some traffic lights as they changed to red. Steve put his foot hard down on the brake, or he thought it was the brake, but in fact it was the accelerator. We shot straight through the lights. A drunken man in his forties was tottering across the road, and we hit him full on and then slammed into a bollard before coming to a stop.

"Come on!" I screamed as I pulled open the door. Steve followed.

But he stopped as he stared down at the man, who lay unconscious by the kerb.

"Steve!" I dragged at his arm.

"We can't leave him here," he said. *"We just can't."*

"We have to! Come on!" And I dragged Steve away, and hand in hand, we legged it the last mile to the home.

We read about it in the Evening News the next day. A hit and run. The man was in hospital with multiple injuries but was expected to survive. No witnesses. Huge relief.

After a year together I told Steve I wanted a ring. Not some cheap shit but something nice and expensive.

And he presented it to me one night when we were alone in my room. He got down on one knee, opened the ring box and offered it to me.

I laughed at him, but I liked it.

I remember his exact words.

"We'll be together forever," he said. *"Never take this ring off. It's for eternity,"* he told me.

The police came for him about two weeks later. He'd been caught on CCTV. He'd stolen both the ring and a Rolex watch worth several thousand pounds that he'd been flashing around school.

I hid the ring, and they never discovered it, but Steve was arrested, and I cried all night.

I didn't know if I'd see him again, and when I talked to Gavin and Joyce, they said he was likely to be sent to a young offenders' institution, and he certainly wouldn't be returning to the home.

So I asked when I'd see him again, and Gavin said I

wouldn't. That even if Steve escaped a sentence, he wouldn't be allowed back at the home, especially as Social Services thought he was a bad influence on me.

If only they'd known. Steve did everything I told him. I was the bad influence.

CHAPTER FORTY-SIX

PC Griffiths called round just before lunch.

"You've got some news?"

"Yes, I have."

I opened the door wider and led her into the kitchen.

There was a moment's pause before PC Griffiths spoke. "The postmortem has revealed that Natasha died under suspicious circumstances."

"Right. Okay." I wasn't surprised. It was what I'd expected. "Do you know the cause of death?"

"I can't go into that at the moment. But our CID have taken over the case, and the two officers leading the investigation are Detective Inspector Mike Kennedy and Detective Sergeant Immie Harrison. They want to interview you as soon as possible."

"No problem. As you know, I'm home for the next two weeks. And what about Natasha's phone?" I asked.

"Yes, I was getting on to that. We're unable to locate it. We think it's probably been destroyed, at least the SIM card has."

DI KENNEDY WAS in his mid to late thirties, tall, lean but well-toned. His short brown hair was starting to grey at the sides, and he had a couple of crow's feet around his eyes. He had a warmth to his face, and I took to his smile right away.

I noticed his blue suit looked a little crumpled, which also endeared him to me.

His female sidekick, DS Harrison, was around five four, mid to late twenties, with a pretty elfin face and cropped spiky hair. She was also wearing blue: skinny jeans tucked into black leather boots, blue T-shirt and a black leather jacket. In spite of her cute features, there was a steely toughness in her grey eyes.

I took them through to the dining kitchen, and they sat at the table. DI Kennedy pulled out a notebook and spoke first.

"We've been studying this case and looking at the notes regarding the previous visit that our colleagues made. And first off, I'd like to apologise because I don't think we took your call seriously. To be honest, you've been badly served."

His words came as a huge relief to me, and I smiled and nodded a thank you.

"In their defence," I said, "it did look at the time like I was going insane."

"Even so." DI Kennedy shrugged, and I liked him even more.

DS Harrison picked up from her DI.

"Also, having looked at the statements surrounding Natasha Patterson's death, we firmly believe there's a connection to her death and the events that have been happening in your life," she said.

"Yes! Yes, you're absolutely right," I exclaimed excitedly. "That's exactly what I've been saying."

I then told them about Samson, how he'd gone missing and the strange goings-on with the blood and fur. And I wasn't sure if the person who'd taken him had now killed him. They could both see I was very distressed as I talked.

DI Kennedy said, "I'm very sorry about your dog. I mean, it's barbaric."

I nodded. "Yes, it is." I gulped, just managing to hold it together,

He continued, "And I think if we find who is behind both Ms Patterson's death and the events that have been happening to you, we'll find who took your dog." He paused. "And hopefully he's still alive."

"So someone is clearly messing with your head, Dr Thompson," DS Harrison added.

I nodded, glad to be taken seriously at last.

"Anyway, we'd like to clarify what happened regarding you and Natasha Patterson," DS Harrison continued. "She rang you, yes?"

"Yes."

"And told you she had information ... photos that could tell you who's behind this?"

"That's right. She said she had a photo of my husband with another woman, a photo of an ex of mine, Pete, who she thought had been stalking me, and she also mentioned a photo of someone else who she thought was a danger to me."

"How did she know all this?" the DI asked. "Did she tell you?"

"No. I think she'd seen Nick with another woman, so she started keeping tabs on him and then possibly on me." I paused. "Natasha and I were never close friends ... but I think she would have liked to have been."

I went on to describe the complex history between us – Nick's relationship with Natasha, the acrimonious break-up, the stalking that followed; then nothing since we married, until I received the recent phone calls.

I then described the two phone calls in detail.

There was a pause, the two police officers taking in this information, before DI Kennedy started flicking through his notebook.

Eventually, he said, "I'd like to talk about the threatening phone calls you received. You say they've been deleted?"

"So you believe me?" I asked.

"At this stage we're open to every possibility," he said. "So ... if the calls were deleted, it had to be someone who had access to your phone."

"Exactly. That's what I've been thinking."

"And have you come up with a list of people who could have had access?" DI Kennedy asked.

"To be honest, it's difficult." I paused. "Nick, my husband, was away that weekend, so it couldn't have been him. There's really only one I think could possibly have done it ..."

The police shifted in their chairs, leaned in.

"Who?" DS Harrison asked.

And I talked about Pete, who I said was still infatuated with me and hassling me, and the only way the photos of me could have been sent from my phone was if he had access that Saturday evening in the restaurant. He could have deleted the phone calls then.

"Okay," DI Kennedy said sternly. "We'll go and speak with him. And I'll check with the restaurant if he was in around the time you were. Have you got contact details for him and also the name of the restaurant?" he asked.

"I have his phone number. He also works with my husband; they're best friends, actually. Well, I thought they were best friends, but, you know, obviously not ..." I shrugged, tailing off. "And the restaurant is Casa Italia in Didsbury," I added.

"One final thing," DI Kennedy said. "D'you think Natasha was telling the truth ... about these photos of your husband with another woman ...?"

"Yes, I do," I answered firmly.

DI Kennedy followed up with, "It's probably best if we have a chat with your husband, clear a few points up."

I nodded. "I'll ask him to get in touch with you."

"Okay. Well, I think that'll be all for the time being," DI Kennedy said, and they both stood up before he added, "If we find who's been doing this ... the calls, stalking you, coming to the house late at night, then in all probability that person's also Natasha Patterson's killer."

"In the meantime," DS Harrison picked up, "please have a really good think about who would want to do this to you and why. I'm sure you've thought about this already, yes?"

"Many times. But I have no definite idea. I thought at one point it was the father of a patient who died, as he blamed me for his son's death, but I don't think it can be him."

DS Harrison handed me a card. "Text me his details; we need to follow everything up. And, Ellie, may I call you Ellie?"

I nodded and smiled.

"Ring me any time you want. I'm Immie."

"Thank you." I smiled warmly.

"Any time. I mean it," she added.

After they left, my spirits lifted. I didn't feel alone anymore. In DI Kennedy and DS Harrison, I felt like I had found two true allies.

But the question remained:

Who were my enemies?

CHAPTER FORTY-SEVEN

Nick arrived home around six thirty. I was in the kitchen, preparing chicken pesto.

"Just in time," I said as I started to drain the spaghetti.

"How's your day been?" Nick asked as he came over and kissed me briefly on the cheek.

"Interesting," I replied. "I'll bring dinner over and tell you all about it."

"Okay, I'll open a wine," he said.

"There's some already open in the fridge."

Nick snatched the bottle from the fridge and carried it over to the dining area, where I had already set the table.

I spooned the pesto chicken over the two bowls of spaghetti and carried them across to the table.

I'd decided to shock Nick to watch his response, there was no doubt he was a suspect, but could he really have killed Natasha? I found it difficult to believe, but I was about to judge his reaction.

As I placed Nick's bowl in front of him, I said casually, "By the way, Nick, the police want to interview you."

I'd caught him completely off guard, and he looked stunned.

"The police? Want to interview me?" he repeated, incredulous.

"Yes." I nodded as I sat down, starting to twirl spaghetti onto my fork.

"Why would they want to interview me?" He looked across at me in total disbelief.

"It's to do with your ex Natasha," I said, still very calm but carefully watching Nick's responses as I fed him the story, bit by bit.

"Natasha?"

He really did look shocked, I thought.

"Yes. She's been murdered."

I said it so casually it was as if Natasha had simply gone for a walk.

Nick's mouth dropped open, his eyes wide, almost bulging. If this wasn't genuine, he was an excellent actor.

Then I remembered Natasha's words of warning: "Nick is not who you think he is. He's got form. He lies."

"My God! Natasha's been murdered? Honestly?"

I nodded.

"But why ... why would the police want to interview me?" he asked, his face creased in puzzlement. "We haven't been in touch with Natasha since, well, since before me and you got married."

"Ah, well, that's an interesting question," I answered enigmatically. I hesitated before adding, "But she has been in touch with me."

"With you? Why?"

I didn't answer at first. I swallowed my mouthful of food and, as I looked across at Nick, carefully studied his face before telling him, "Natasha wanted to meet up with me. You're not going to like this, Nick, and it's the reason the police want to interview you ..."

I paused, and I could see Nick's back and neck stiffen.

"Go on," he prompted, his voice slightly shaky.

"Natasha said she had photos of you with another woman."

Nick looked genuinely astonished at the news.

"Photos of me? With another woman? You're kidding me?"

"I'm afraid not," I answered, completely cool.

"That's ... that's just ... just ludicrous. Who was it supposed to be? Did you see them?" Nick asked.

I simply shook my head.

"Then it is ludicrous. I can't believe after all this time Natasha was still stalking us. You surely can't believe a word that woman says?" Nick argued.

"But, Nick, the thing is that someone killed her to get to whatever was on her phone. Her phone has gone missing. The police haven't been able to trace it."

Nick slumped back in his seat, face dumbfounded, unable to answer.

His whole face was mapped in disbelief.

Eventually he spoke, a desperate tone to his voice. "So the police think ... do the police really think that I ... do they?"

"Not necessarily, Nick. If you're innocent, you've got nothing to worry about—"

"I am!" Nick answered, nodding his head furiously.

"And Natasha told me other things. She'd seen Pete stalking me—"

"Really?"

"Yes. By the way, did you speak to him today?" I asked.

"No. He was out most of the day in meetings," he answered distractedly.

"Well, don't. The police want to interview him as well. I don't want him being warned off," I told him.

"Ellie, Ellie, please," Nick started to plead, distressed. "Natasha must have been making this up; she must have been lying. I mean, even after all this time, she must still resent me, have a grudge against me somehow …"

"There's also a third suspect that Natasha told me about," I said.

"Who? Did she say who?"

"No. She didn't know the person. In fact, she didn't even tell me if it was a man or a woman. She had photos of them, though. But, Nick, whoever killed Natasha, the police think it's the same person who's been stalking me, who took Samson and possibly killed him, because I know now that it wasn't me. I didn't kill Samson."

"Well, that couldn't be me, then, could it? Stalking you! Come on! Or killing Samson? As if I would do anything to Samson! I loved Samson. You know that!" he cried, and his eyes filled with tears. "I loved Samson as much as you did!" And he picked up a napkin, wiped the tears away and blew his nose. "I'm sorry," he snuffled.

I suddenly felt sorry for him, so I stood up, went across to him, kneeled next to his chair.

"I know you wouldn't hurt Samson," I said as I brushed another tear away from his face with the back of my hand.

I'd been reassured.

That is, until I remembered the smell of an unfamiliar perfume on his pillow.

CHAPTER FORTY-EIGHT

After dinner I felt I needed to untangle my brain, clarify my thoughts. I zipped up a grey fleece jacket, as the night was chilly, and told Nick, "Going to check that the new sensor light works and get a bit of fresh air."

I exited the house via the conservatory door, and immediately I stepped outside, the sensor light activated, flooding the garden in a glow of brilliant white. I walked to the far end of the garden out of the sensor light's beam and sat on the wooden bench.

I breathed in deeply, stared back at the house, then suddenly the sensor light went out, and the garden was cast in eerie shadows from the conservatory lights.

From the house, I would no longer be visible. I stared up at the jet-black sky, only the North Star peeping through, the moon curtained behind lacy clouds. I listened to the hum of traffic along Wilmslow Road.

Mentally I'd crossed Nick off the list.

I believed him. He'd totally convinced me. He just wasn't capable of killing anyone.

But he was still having an affair.

So that left Pete and this mystery third person.

As I looked back at the house, I saw Nick staring out from the conservatory window, his phone to his ear, his mouth moving wordlessly.

He wouldn't be able to see me, I knew that.

Who was he ringing?

I stood and walked slowly back. When I reached the edges of the sensor, I was suddenly flooded and blinded by the light. I shielded my eyes as I walked towards the conservatory entrance, and I saw Nick step back away from the window and quickly end his call.

I felt unnerved.

Whom could he be talking to? Someone he wanted to keep secret?

When I entered the kitchen from the conservatory, Nick had placed his phone on the island, and he was draining the last dregs of wine into his glass.

I asked as casually as possible, "Who was that on the phone?"

And Nick didn't seem thrown, but answered confidently, "Pete. Some boring work stuff."

I didn't follow it up; instead I nodded and said, "I'm off to bed."

"Are you still sleeping in …" he called after me, not needing to finish his sentence.

"Yes," I told him. "I'm still nervous. Just to be on the safe side."

He nodded. "Okay."

"Just make sure your door is locked," I said, and it sounded exactly like a threat.

"See you tomorrow, then, darling."

"Yes."

"Hope you don't have any nightmares."

It was only when I climbed the stairs five minutes later, I remembered.

I could listen to Nick's phone conversation. That was what the audio CCTV in the kitchen was for.

I LAY in bed in the guest room. How long would it take for Nick to fall asleep?

After half an hour, I climbed out of the bed, opened my bedroom door on to the landing, edged silently towards the main bedroom.

I listened, and I could hear Nick's deep breathing, the gentle wheeze from his nostrils.

I crept down the stairs into my office – a windowless space off the hallway, not much bigger than a store cupboard, and only room enough for my desk, which was squeezed against the far wall.

My laptop lay on the desk. I clicked on the file for the CCTV before opening the footage for the kitchen camera. I forwarded it, paused to watch as Nick and I were eating. Forwarded again to the moment I left to go into the garden. I then let the footage run at its normal speed. I saw Nick pick up the dishes from the table, move towards the camera, before his head disappeared as he bent down to slot the dishes into the dishwasher.

He stood, turned. His phone was lying on the island. He picked it up, stabbed in a contact, then walked away from the camera eye towards the conservatory windows, peering out to the garden.

The other person must have answered, and I listened as Nick said, "Hi. How are you?"

I sat at my computer for over an hour, playing and replaying the recording.

I went into the kitchen, poured myself a glass of water, and was about to return to bed around 1 a.m., when I saw Nick's phone lying on the island.

I picked it up and scanned his recent calls.

When I went back to bed, I couldn't sleep. And I was unlikely to sleep.

I knew the woman Nick had been talking to.

I had no choice but to listen as their conversation played and replayed on a loop inside my head.

CHAPTER FORTY-NINE

It was half seven when Nick came down the stairs, wearing his grey Ted Baker suit, hair slick but still damp. As he reached the hallway, he called out, "Morning, Ellie."

And I called back from the kitchen, "In here."

Nick entered the kitchen and saw me sitting at the island, my laptop in front of me. He couldn't see what was on my screen, and he was about to plant a morning kiss on my cheek when I pressed a key on my laptop, and he froze.

He could see himself on the screen. As I pressed the start button, he came alive. He was on his phone.

"What the—?" he said before he was interrupted by his own voice.

"Oh hi, how are you? No, Ellie's in the garden. Look, I don't want to talk on the phone, but we have to stop this now. It can't go any further. I mean it. Got to go; Ellie's coming in."

I stopped the recording and swung round on my stool to face an astonished Nick.

"So you were speaking to Pete, were you?" I asked.

"What is this? You put a camera in here without telling me? What the fuck, Ellie? For Christ's sake!"

I stayed calm. I took a step towards him, and looking directly into his eyes, I spoke softly, underscoring each word. "You lied to me, Nick! You lied to me. And I know exactly who you were speaking to."

Nick's eyes blinked; his head flinched back as if the words had hit him.

I continued to speak calmly as I took another step towards Nick so that we were now almost nose-to-nose. "I know you're having an affair, and I know who with."

Nick didn't answer. His cheeks flushed, and before he could muster any form of defence, I picked up the phone that lay next to my laptop.

"Is that my phone?" Nick asked. I didn't answer. "Give it to me, please." He held out his hand.

"No," I answered calmly. "I checked your phone call from last night."

Nick looked furious. "You had no right!"

And he reached and tried to grasp it from me, but I pulled it away.

"Give me my bloody phone back!" he demanded.

He grasped for it again, and I moved away before turning back to face him.

"Here it is. The exact time I was in the garden. Oh, and look, the call's not to Pete." My voice was light, taunting. I held the phone up. Nick stepped closer to me, tried to grab the phone, and I swung it away in an arc. "It's to 'PA'."

Nick's face was a collage of bewildered astonishment, his eyes wide and startled, mouth slightly ajar, unable to speak.

Then my voice rose, a fierce but controlled anger. I'd

been playing this scene out in my head all night, and I knew exactly what I was going to say and what I intended to do.

"So tell me, Nick, how long have you been having an affair with your PA? I mean, I've known for years that Ursula's obsessed with you, but how long has this been going on?"

Nick's jaw dropped even further, but his face seemed more perplexed than aghast, as I continued, "All those times you pleaded and lied that you loved me, that you would never have an affair, when all the time you were seeing bloody Ursula!"

"No. No, no, no! You've got this all wrong," Nick answered forcefully.

"Oh, have I?"

"Will you let me explain? Please, Ellie." I didn't interrupt as Nick asked again, "Please?"

I nodded once, then stepped back from him, never taking my eyes off him.

"First, I'm not having an affair with Ursula—" This time I was about to interrupt, but Nick held up his hand. "Please. Let me finish. I am not having an affair with Ursula, but something did happen between us at the Birmingham conference."

I recoiled but didn't interject.

"We both got drunk. I know it's no excuse, but I was feeling ... well, it hadn't been great between me and you for ... a few weeks or more. You wouldn't talk about it ..." And he quickly added, "I'm not blaming you. And, of course, our sex life ... again I'm not making excuses for my behaviour, but ... but ... I was feeling lonely and ... and Ursula, I knew she'd always fancied me, and, well, we finished up spending the night together. It's why I switched off my phone. But, Ellie, the honest truth, the following morning I felt so bad, so guilty. And I made it plain to Ursula that it was a mistake, and it couldn't happen again. Trouble is, she won't accept it. So I was ringing her last night to make it plain one final time that it couldn't go any further."

He stopped, stared at me, his puppy eyes imploring for my forgiveness.

And what could I say? Nick's behaviour had totally mirrored my behaviour on the exact same night. But in some ways, I should feel guiltier because I knew I had genuine feelings for James.

I stood there for several seconds as Nick stared at me, eyebrows arched, appealing.

Finally I went up close to him and spoke softly.

"Okay. Thank you for telling me the truth." I paused before asking, "Nick, what do you want ... from our relationship?"

"I want us to work it out," he replied.

I wasn't sure what I wanted.

And so I turned my head away, avoiding a response.

CHAPTER FIFTY

It was soon after Nick left for work that my phone rang. It was James.

Ironic.

I had been thinking of ringing him; in fact, I was constantly thinking of him. He was always there, lurking at the back of my mind. And after what Nick had just told me, I felt like such a hypocrite, yet I still couldn't get James out of my head. And why was I keeping Nick at a distance both physically and emotionally? Was it because of my feelings for James?

As soon as I heard his warm voice, I relaxed.

"James, how are you?" I asked.

"Hi, Ellie, I was about to ask you the same thing. Are you okay?"

"Yeah, I'm good," I lied.

"We're all missing you," he said.

And in my head, I asked, "What about you, are you missing me?"

Instead I said, "That's nice to know."

"Look, Ellie, I've got to go into surgery in a minute, so I haven't got much time, but I should be out by lunchtime if you fancy catching up and talking properly."

I could feel my heart quicken. "Okay, yeah, that would be nice," I answered as casually as possible. "I'll drive into town, and I'll pick you up outside A&E if you like?"

"That'd be great. Should be around one. If I get held up, I'll text you."

"Okay, James. Look forward to it."

"And me."

I had just showered and dressed when my phone rang again. It was Penny this time.

"Ellie, how are you?" she asked.

"Yeah, I'm good," I lied again.

"Look, I was thinking about what you said about you and Nick ... and just wondered ... how are things with you two now?"

"Well, they're not great," I answered honestly.

"And is he having an affair?" she asked.

"Hmm ... it's a long story." Then I asked as a diversion, "What about you and Tom?"

"That's one of the reasons I was ringing. He's moving in with me ... this weekend, actually," she announced.

"Oh, that's great."

"And I'd like you guys to meet him. I was thinking we could have dinner together this Saturday."

"Yeah, that'd be great," I said.

"I was thinking of asking you over here, but, to be honest, we're gonna start decorating, so it'll be a bit of a mess and ..."

"Why don't you come here for dinner?" I asked.

"Are you sure? I know it's a bit cheeky—"

"Don't be daft. No, Penny, I'd like you to come here."

"That's brilliant. Okay, look after yourself, Ellie, and we'll see you Saturday. Hope you like him."

I HAD to wait only ten minutes for James. He came running out the hospital entrance, jumped in the car, said, "Sorry I'm a bit late."

"No problem. Surprised you could even make it. How long have you got?" I asked.

"Have to be back by two; shall we just grab a sandwich somewhere close?"

"Sure. How about the Gemini Café on Oxford Road?" I suggested.

It was bustling inside the café, but we managed to squeeze on to a window table. James insisted on buying the sandwiches and coffees.

Once we'd settled into the seats and we were munching on tuna salad baguettes, James asked, "Okay, be straight with me; how've you been?"

"Like I said on the phone …" James raised an eyebrow, and I shrugged. "Okay, not great."

I went on to tell him about Samson, Natasha, the police visit; I told him about the phone call from the neighbour who'd seen Samson being taken away, but I didn't tell him that that call had saved my life.

And James listened, astonished, and when I finished, he shook his head in disbelief. "What you've been through, it's … you should have got in touch, Ellie," he said. "Really you should."

"I thought about it, but, well, I didn't want to bother you," I explained.

"Bother me! Ellie, come on ..."

"Sorry." I shrugged.

"And I hope Nick's been supportive through all this, yeah?"

I paused just long enough for James to pick up on it. He gave me a sharp look. "Er, yeah," I said eventually.

"Have things been okay between you both?" He paused before adding, "I still feel guilty about what happened."

I smiled. "Yes. So do I."

But then James leaned in across the table and whispered, "I feel guilty ... but I don't regret it."

I laughed before eventually confessing, "And to answer your question, no, things haven't been great ... but not because of you."

I went on to describe the tension between us, my certainty that Nick was having an affair, then his confession that he'd had a one-night stand at his conference in Birmingham. He'd felt guilty afterwards and had said he was sorry.

James raised a meaningful eyebrow. "Yes, I know. The irony."

James's eyes twinkled. "Again, I reiterate, I don't regret it."

I knew James wanted me to agree with him and say I didn't regret it either, but instead I said, "Something isn't right between me and Nick, but ..." I shrugged. "I don't know what it is."

I pushed my empty plate away, glanced at my phone. "God, have you seen the time?"

"Oh bloody hell. I'm going to have to dash. I'll be in touch in the next day or so."

"Please."

And he stood up, leaned in, kissed me on the cheek. As he ran out of the café, he turned and waved. I waved back.

I smiled to myself. I'd missed him.

I walked slowly back to the car. The afternoon still lay ahead of me. I was finding it difficult to fill my time, as the hours seemed to drag.

I had just reached the turning for the car park when ahead of me I noticed a white Qashqai pulling out and turning left towards Oxford Road.

Each time I saw a white Qashqai or Kia Sportage, I had a lurching tension in my chest, and I always glanced at the driver.

I did the same now.

I was stunned.

The driver was Rick Walker's dad, Ray. He did have a Qashqai after all. Which meant, when I saw him before, the Qashqai must have been in for repairs to the front bumper from when he shunted my car.

I caught a glimpse of the front passenger, and I gasped.

I couldn't believe it.

The passenger was Ben. Dr Ben Carson.

CHAPTER FIFTY-ONE

As soon as the Qashqai had passed me, I darted up the street, shot into the car park. Fortunately I was wearing jeans and trainers, and it was the quickest I'd run in months.

I ran towards my BMW, arm outstretched, holding the fob, and the lights flashed as the doors opened. I jumped in, the engine roared into life, and I sped out, tyres screeching. I turned left up to Oxford Road, and two hundred metres ahead of me, I saw the Qashqai indicating and turning left away from the city centre towards Rusholme.

At the junction I had to wait for two buses to pass before I could pull out. The bus ahead of me indicated it was pulling up at the next stop, and I overtook it, but now I was stuck behind the second bus. Traffic lights were coming up, and I cursed as the lights changed to red, and I was still behind the bus. I opened my window, bobbed my head out, scanned the stream of traffic beyond the lights, but I could see no sign of the Qashqai. I cursed and wondered whether it had turned left and I hadn't seen it because of the obstruction from the buses.

I considered turning, but made the decision to carry on into Rusholme.

It was the right decision, because as I drove past the line of curry houses, I saw the Qashqai parked up on the left. I drove past it and backed into the only parking space available.

I presumed they had come for a late lunch at one of the restaurants.

As I parked up, my mind was spinning with thoughts and theories.

Why was Dr Carson with Ray Walker? What was their connection? Was Dr Carson passing on information about our sessions to him? If so, why? Dr Carson knew all my nightmares. I'd thought early on that Rick Walker was the perpetrator, but I couldn't figure out how he could recreate my nightmares. Now I knew. Dr Ben Carson had told him.

But why would Dr Carson do that? What was his motive?

One thing was certain: Ray Walker was the mystery third person, the one Natasha had photographed as he stalked me.

As I climbed out of the car, I crossed the others off my list of suspects.

Pete was in the clear.

And poor old Nick. I'd been tough on him, given him a hard time. For a while I'd pencilled him in as a possibility; now I felt guilty.

One other thought struck me. How could Ray Walker be connected to Natasha's murder? The only conclusion I came to was that maybe Natasha had observed Walker following me, taken photos and then confronted him.

If that was the case, and he was Natasha's murderer,

then he was a dangerous man. Maybe I should ring DS Immie Harrison now. Then I thought, why not confront them both in the restaurant; they wouldn't dare do anything in public. I wanted to find out the truth before I rang DS Harrison.

I walked back along the row of curry houses, glancing through restaurant windows, but there was no sign of them. I passed Ray Walker's car, paused; then I saw them. They were sitting at a window table.

They were studying menus so didn't see me as I entered the restaurant. A waiter approached me. "Table for one?" he asked.

"No, I'm ..." And I indicated Dr Carson and Ray Walker's table. He nodded and stepped away.

The restaurant was quite busy, which was a relief to me. It made me feel safe.

Neither of them saw me as I advanced to their table. I was nervous but not frightened; I felt steely, determined.

"I didn't know you two knew each other," I said casually.

They both looked up from their menus at the sound of my voice, and when they saw who it was, their faces instantly transformed into a kaleidoscope of surprise, shock and confusion.

"Er, an answer, please?" I prompted.

They seemed stumped for words until Ben Carson said, "Ellie, this is ... this is a surprise."

"I'm sure it is," I shot back. "So what's going on? What's the story?"

Ray Walker looked away, clearly embarrassed as I stared from one to the other. I was looking down on Dr Carson's squat frame, his bald dome reflecting the light.

"I ... I'm sorry, Ellie, I should've told you."

"Told me what?"

"I was going to, when you first came to see me, but then I got totally immersed in your case—"

"Told me what?" I repeated with emphasis.

"Ray and I ... we're ... we're cousins."

I was shocked. "What!"

"Ellie, I'm sorry."

My head was whirling, taking in all the implications.

"You're ... you're cousins?!"

He nodded. Ray Walker still couldn't look me in the eye.

"And you never told me!"

"I was ... I was in a dilemma. I wanted to help you but ..." he stumbled.

"You've been pulling my strings from the second I started my sessions with you," I accused.

"No ..."

And I remembered some of our early conversations.

"You even brought up your cousin's complaint against me!" My eyes darted towards Ray Walker, but his head was still bent. "Asking me something like, do you worry about making the wrong decisions, wrong diagnosis? Didn't you?"

Dr Carson shrugged. "You were under stress; I wouldn't have been doing my job properly if I hadn't asked—"

I interrupted him as another thought hit me. "And you planted the idea I was crazy ..."

"That is not true."

"You suggested what was happening in my real life could be hallucinations. That my nightmares coming alive ... it was all going on in my head? You said that."

"I believed that was a strong possibility. And I still do." Dr Carson defended himself.

I turned to Ray Walker. "And that car I saw you in, it was a hire car while yours was being repaired, wasn't it?"

Walker shrugged, not committing himself.

With each question, each accusation, my voice rose angrily, and now people in the restaurant were throwing glances across at us.

"You told him about my nightmares, didn't you?"

Dr Carson now stood up, pushing his chair back and shaking his head vigorously. "No. No, of course not. What do you take me for?"

I suddenly panicked as he moved towards me, and I shouted, "Don't come near me!"

And the whole restaurant hushed.

"You breached patient confidentiality," I accused.

"I did not."

"Maybe you planned it together?" I suggested.

I pointed a finger at Walker, who was still hunched in his chair.

"You took my dog!" I accused. "Did you kill him, you sick bastard?"

Walker looked up, face confused, and he spoke for the first time. "I don't know what you're talking about."

I needed to escape; I needed fresh air; I needed to contact the police. I turned from them, then over my shoulder, I called to Walker, "The police want to interview you. They want to talk to you."

Dr Carson called after me anxiously, "What are you going to do? Ellie!"

But I swept out of the restaurant. As I dashed towards my car, I took out my phone. I'd added DS Immie Harrison's number to my contacts. I scrolled down, found her contact, and pressed to ring her.

I was by my car and climbing in when the call went through to voicemail.

"Hi, DS Harrison, it's Dr Thompson here. Ellie. Can you give me a ring when you pick this up? Thanks."

I switched on the engine, flicked on the right indicator, and a white van slowed and flashed me to come out. As I eased out, raising a hand to thank the van driver, I glanced in my mirror and saw Dr Carson and Ray Walker dashing out of the restaurant towards their car.

There was a constant stream of traffic along Wilmslow Road through Rusholme and Fallowfield, so I couldn't put my foot down. I kept glancing in my mirror, and I could see the white Qashqai about three cars back. I overtook a Fiat Punto, but I was slowed by a delivery van.

By the time I was approaching Didsbury, the Qashqai was only two cars behind me. As I reached my turning, I accelerated up my road, turning a fast right into my drive.

I didn't open the garage; it was quicker to leave the car on the drive. I jumped out, locked the car as I ran to my door, my hand separating out the door key from the car key.

I heard their car enter the drive, glanced over my shoulder and saw the Qashqai was parking next to my BMW. I turned back to the door, hand shaking so much I almost dropped my keys.

I could hear footsteps running towards me. Glancing over my shoulder again, I could see Ben Carson wobbling towards me, only yards away, his cousin a step behind. I pushed open the door and stepped inside. I was about to slam the door shut behind me when Dr Carson's foot lodged between the door and the frame.

"Get away!" I screamed. "I've called the police."

"Please don't report me. I can explain," he pleaded.

As he spoke, he pushed his rotund frame against the door, and I put my shoulder against it, but when Ray Walker added his weight against the door, I knew I couldn't hold them. It slowly inched open, so I stepped back, the door flew open, and Dr Carson and Walker stumbled onto their knees.

I shot into the kitchen. I ran to the island and snatched the unicorn knife from the block. I turned to face them as both men entered the kitchen, dashing towards me, but Dr Carson stopped in his tracks as I held out the knife at arm's length, an inch away from Dr Carson's throat.

"Don't come any closer. Get out!" I spoke, voice shaky but firm. "Just get out."

Dr Carson was unfit, breathing hard. He held up both arms.

"Ellie, please listen. I'm sorry we forced ourselves in, but I have to explain."

"I don't want any explanation," I snapped. "I just want you out of my house."

Walker, who was standing behind Dr Carson, put arm on Carson's shoulder and said, "Come on, let's leave it."

Dr Carson shook his head. "No. I can't lose my job over this." He waited for a second until his breathing evened. "Ellie, it's not me and it's not Ray who's been doing this to you."

"Just get out."

"I found out what Ray had been doing. Stalking you. And I stopped him. He admitted to me that he was following you. He admitted that he drove into the back of you in the car park. I explained that he couldn't and shouldn't blame you for his son's death and that he had to back off."

Behind him Walker nodded. "He did. And I'm sorry, Dr Thompson."

"He also told me he'd slashed two of your tyres and did something to your exhaust. I was appalled."

I nodded. I still wasn't sure whether to believe Dr Carson.

"Ellie, I know it's no excuse for what Ray did," Dr Carson continued, "but he has been under a huge amount of stress, he's been overwhelmed with grief, and he lost all rational sense …"

I listened, but I didn't respond, nor did I remove the knife from Dr Carson's throat.

"And, Dr Thompson, I'm happy to pay for all the damage to your car," Walker said.

"Too late, it's been repaired," I answered coolly before asking Walker, "And do you know Natasha Patterson?"

"Who?" he asked. "Never heard of her."

"She took photos of you stalking me. And she's been murdered. That's why the police want to interview you."

Walker looked appalled. "What? I don't know a Natasha Patterson. I've never heard of her," he assured me.

"And did you come round to my house last weekend to terrorise me? Did you make threatening phone calls?"

"No. No, really, I didn't," he denied. "Honestly I didn't."

"He didn't, Ellie," Dr Carson said. "Last weekend he was with me. I took him to Portugal for a golfing weekend, thought it might help him just to get away. In fact …" Dr Carson fumbled into his inside jacket pocket. "I think I've still got our boarding passes."

He withdrew them, handed them to me. I looked at the names and the date of travel on each boarding pass, and it confirmed what Ben had said.

I nodded, lowered the knife, placed it back on the island, and Dr Carson said, "I swear, Ellie, I swear I never mentioned or revealed anything about your nightmares to Ray."

"I didn't even know you were seeing Ben," Ray added. "Until today. He just filled me in now as we followed you."

Suddenly my mobile rang, and all three of us jumped. I dug it out of my handbag. It was DS Harrison returning my call.

"It's the police," I said to Dr Carson.

"What are you going to tell them?" he asked, his face anxious, strained.

I didn't answer.

Both Dr Carson and Walker were watching me closely, their gaze edgy.

"Are you okay, Ellie?" DS Harrison asked.

I hesitated before answering, "Yes. Yes. I was just ringing for a catch-up, see how you're getting on."

And the tension in Ben's face relaxed; his stiff shoulders visibly loosened.

"Well, we spoke to Peter Evans. We've eliminated him as a possible suspect. The night your house was attacked, he admitted he'd been round earlier, but then he went for a drink in Didsbury, met a woman in the pub and went back to her place. She's corroborated his alibi."

Typical, I thought.

"There's also nothing to connect him with Natasha's murder. We've got the CCTV footage in the areas around Natasha's flat, which we've been checking."

"Okay. Thanks, Immie. That's great." Then, glancing at Walker, "What about Ray Walker?" I asked.

"We've not had time to contact him yet," Harrison said.

"I have his number. I'll text it to you," I told her.

"Thanks, Ellie. And we'll keep you informed if there's further developments."

When I finished the call, I looked up, and both Ben and Ray were staring at me. Ben nodded. "Thank you."

I said simply, "I think you'd better go," before adding as I looked at Walker, "I'll need your phone number. They still need to interview you."

A second before Walker nodded. And Ben Carson intervened, "I'll text it to you, Ellie."

"Make sure you do," I threatened.

They nodded in unison like a comic double act, one small and squat, the other rangy and thin. At the door, Walker paused and turned. "Thank you. And I am really sorry."

"And I'm sorry for your son's death."

He nodded, tried a smile, but it didn't work. His eyes were dead. I couldn't help feeling sorry for him.

"Ben—"

He stopped and turned back.

"You have no excuse," I told him. "Your behaviour was totally unprofessional."

He was about to protest.

"Just leave," I ordered.

After I heard Ray Walker's car pull out of the drive, I released a huge sigh. When they'd forced their way in, I'd believed my life was in danger.

I pulled myself up on a stool at the island, my mind flitting back through the mental list of suspects.

Could I now cross Ray Walker off the list? If so, whom did that leave? Who else knew the details of my nightmares, knew them well enough to recreate them?

There were only three people now.

Nick. Penny. James. I immediately dismissed the idea of two of them.

CHAPTER FIFTY-TWO

I suppose some people would have called it karma. It happened soon after Steve was arrested.

I was shopping in town, and I decided to call into the police station, to try to find out what had happened to Steve, as no one would tell me where he was.

But again they wouldn't tell me anything.

So I just walked and walked all round town. My head wasn't right. I looked at faces thinking they were Steve. I knew they weren't, but I still kept looking for him.

I don't know how long I walked or where I went, but when I decided to go home, it was late and dark, and it had started to rain.

I caught a bus home.

I stepped off the bus and walked back to the traffic lights to cross over, even though there wasn't much traffic at that time of night. I pressed the button and waited till the green man flashed up, then crossed.

I didn't hear or see the blue car that was travelling at over sixty miles an hour as it sped through the red light. When it hit me, I flew in the air and landed by the kerbside, my body all twisted.

It was karma, because the drunken man Steve and I had knocked over never did leave hospital. He'd died of his injuries.

Steve was devastated. He was soft like that. It was a weakness he'd never lose.

I woke up in hospital three days later. My head was bandaged; both legs were in plaster to my knees, one of them sticking up in the air in traction. I'd fractured my pelvis and was suffering from concussion. I was lucky to be alive.

The nurses and doctors were all brilliant. My favourite was Dr Carlyle. He was in his thirties, good looking, charming, and I had a huge crush on him. I knew he was married with two children. It wasn't like how I felt for Steve; it was a crush, nothing more.

My recovery took a long time.

But it changed my life, because for the first time ever, I was totally helpless, and I had to rely on other people, the nurses, doctors and physiotherapists.

So that when I was discharged, I'd seen and felt their love and care, the dedication, and it was more than enough to convince me about what I wanted for my future. I'd had none of that in my life. They showed me care that I didn't even know existed, and they wanted nothing in return.

I knew I had to move on from the person I was, I had needed to be selfish and to think only of myself in order to survive, but that wasn't the way forward any longer. And if I gave something back, maybe I would be happy.

I would train to become a doctor.

CHAPTER FIFTY-THREE

Penny rang late Saturday afternoon with the news.

"Tom told his wife, and she's surprisingly okay. I think their relationship was pretty dead anyway. So we're both really looking forward to seeing you guys tonight."

"And me. Can't wait to meet him, Penny!"

"Think you'll like him."

"If *you* do, then I'm sure I will."

"But that's not the real reason I'm ringing," Penny said.

"Oh?"

"It's ... well, my head's all over the place after something that happened at work yesterday," Penny explained.

"Why, what happened?" I asked, concerned.

"Okay, well, I was filling in on A&E for the day, and this woman was brought in. Minor car accident, but it looked like she might have broken her arm. So I was taking her temperature and blood pressure, and she said to me, 'D'you know Dr James Underwood?' So I told her yes, I knew him very well and usually worked in theatre with him. And I asked why.

And she said she was best friends with James's late wife, Hilary."

"Really?"

"Yeah. So I was a bit thrown at first, but then I said something like, 'Oh, I am so sorry. It was such a tragedy.' And the friend, she was called Bella, Bella Godwin, replied, 'Yes, it was. Except it wasn't suicide.'"

"No!" I was genuinely shocked. "What did you say to that?"

"Well, before I could say anything, she said, 'James killed her.'"

"Oh my God!"

"At first I thought she was making some sick joke, and I sort of forced out a laugh. 'Oh yes?' but she then went on, didn't stop, said Hilary had no reason to kill herself. She wasn't depressed, and in fact she was really positive about her future because she was about to leave James."

"Seriously?" I frowned, before adding, "No, I'm sorry, that's ridiculous."

"That's what I said. But she said Hilary had been planning to leave for some time. She wanted out; she wanted a divorce because James wasn't like he appeared to the outside world. He wasn't this lovely, charming man; he was a control freak—"

"Oh come on, please," I exclaimed.

"She said he was emotionally abusive. He was also hugely jealous. Hilary was never allowed out on her own; he treated her like a prisoner. But she'd planned her escape, and she was moving in with Bella. James found out about it ... and killed her, made it look like suicide."

"Did this Bella have a concussion or something?" I asked, my tone sarcastic.

"No ... I know it sounds absurd," Penny conceded. "I asked her if she'd gone to the police with this ... this absurd theory, and Bella said she had, but of course they didn't believe her cos he's a doctor, seems so charming, and there was no evidence of murder—"

"Exactly!"

"Agreed. But it really shook me up, and I haven't been able to get it out of my head. I mean, I keep thinking it's ridiculous, but then next minute I'm thinking, what if it is true?" Penny said before continuing, "And then as I'm going over it in my head, I'm thinking, if it IS true, and I know he fancies you ... what if he's behind everything that's happened to you?"

"Oh come on, Penny!" I immediately dismissed her suggestion.

"Ellie, there's no doubt he does fancy you," Penny said.

"Even if he did ... and I'm not saying he does, but if he did, why would he try to frighten me? Why would he do all these things to me ... I mean, even taking Samson. Why?"

"I dunno, maybe ... maybe he wants you frightened so he can be there for you – like a brave knight riding into battle to save you."

"Penny, do you really believe all that?" I asked, sceptical.

"No, I don't. I'm just ... well ... throwing it out there. Has he actually tried it on with you?"

I could feel my face flushing, and I was glad Penny couldn't see me. "No, no, of course not," I lied.

But I thought back to our night together, then to the times James suddenly seemed to be there – in the car park when my car wouldn't start and then at the supermarket when I had two flat tyres. But it had to be a coincidence; Ray Walker had confessed to both of those. Could James have been the threatening intruder, and then, when I rang him on the Friday night, he was waiting in his car near my house, ready to ride in and save me? And maybe that night he purposely left his phone behind as an excuse to call round the next day. And overnight he had plenty of opportunity to delete the threatening calls.

But how could he have taken Samson? Maybe he was the one who left the conservatory doors open, and when I walked into Didsbury village, he popped back for Samson.

I shuddered at the thought before rationalising how ludicrous it was.

Or was it?

Penny broke the silence. "Well, what d'you think?"

"I think it's laughable. I think this woman must have had some sort of agenda that we don't know about," I surmised.

"I think you're probably right," Penny agreed. "Anyway. Really looking forward to seeing you."

"Yeah, see you later. Nick's doing the cooking tonight."

"We'll bring some indigestion tablets with us, then!"

And we were both laughing as I rang off.

It was just after four thirty, and Nick was due back any minute. He'd offered to not only cook the meal but also do the weekly shop. He was a good cook, but he mostly left it to me during the week. I often thought he only offered to be the chef at dinner parties just to impress our guests. He never mentioned round the dinner table that he rarely lifted a pan the rest of the week.

I was relaxing in the conservatory, still pondering on Penny's call, both perplexed and confused, when my phone vibrated as it lay on the bamboo sofa cushion.

It was James.

I grabbed it, stared at it, in a dilemma. I was about to

dismiss Penny's warning and tap the green answer button when the call went to voicemail. I waited to see if James had left a message.

He had. I tapped to listen to it.

I had just the one new message and three saved messages; then I heard James's anxious voice. "Ellie, when you pick up this message, please give me a call right away. It's important."

What could be so urgent that James wanted me to call back?

In the end, with Penny's conversation playing in my head, I decided not to return the call.

But five minutes later, James rang again.

I was in a quandary. Should I answer?

I let it ring and ring.

But just before the call was about to finish, I answered.

"James, just got your message. What was so urgent?"

"Thank God!" he said, his voice full of anxiety. "Ellie, I know who's doing this to you. I know who's behind it all."

My heart surged. "Who?" I asked.

"You're not going to believe this ..." He paused.

"James, who?"

"It's ... it's Penny and Nick," he told me.

I waited a moment to take this in, then laughed. "Yeah, yeah. Very funny, James."

"Ellie, I'm serious. I saw them together yesterday. And they looked ... they looked very close. Like lovers."

He waited. But I never answered. I was too confused.

"Is Nick there now?" he asked eventually.

"Hmm, no."

And as soon as I said it, I regretted it.

"Shall I come round, Ellie? I'll come round now, yes?"

"No. No, James. I need to think through what you've said," I explained.

"But you're in danger!" he insisted.

And I thought, *Yes, maybe I'm in danger from you.*

"James, I'm fine. I'm not in danger. In fact, Penny is coming round tonight with her boyfriend, Tom. So I'm sure you've got all this wrong," I told him. "But thanks for thinking of me. I need to go now."

"Ellie, please ... if Tom doesn't turn up, contact me. Yes?"

I rang off.

The thought of Nick and Penny plotting together as a couple seemed utterly absurd. However, what now seemed less absurd, after James's phone call, was the possibility that Bella was telling the truth. He seemed so insistent on coming round, and so convinced that Penny and Nick were having an affair.

Should I ring DS Harrison and ask the police to question James? I'd think about it over the weekend.

It was at this moment that I heard the garage doors groaning open, and I went into the hall, then into the garage, where Nick was opening the boot.

"Everything okay?" I asked him.

"Yeah. Think I got everything. Bloody busy in there," he said.

"You should have let me come with you," I said.

"Your rest day. No shopping, no cooking. But you can give me a hand with the bags," he told me.

As we carried the bags upstairs, I said casually, "Just had a call from Penny."

"Not cancelling, is she?" he asked, slightly apprehensive.

"No, no. Just confirming," I answered, not wishing to go into the details regarding James.

"And Tom's still coming?"

"Tom's still coming."

"Good. By the way, forgot to say, I bumped into Penny last night as I was coming out of the office," Nick said casually.

"Oh right. She never said."

"She was out shopping for something to wear for tonight. Didn't chat. Quick hug and a kiss on the cheek and that was it. She seemed a bit ... well, a bit distracted."

She would be distracted, I thought, her head preoccupied with Bella's accusation about James.

And it suddenly made sense – the friendly hug and kiss between Nick and Penny – that was what James had observed. Maybe he'd deliberately misinterpreted it, to divert any suspicion from him and onto Nick and Penny.

Was he playing me? Had he been playing me all along?

If James really was a control freak and an emotional abuser, I shuddered at the thought of the night I spent with him. He'd engineered the whole thing. He'd slowly been working on me, using that charm, reeling me in.

Yes, he'd been playing me. And I felt such a fool for being so naïve and falling for that false charm.

CHAPTER FIFTY-FOUR

Penny arrived bang on seven o'clock. Her hair was pulled back into a half-pony that made her look about ten years younger. I opened the door, and she greeted me with a big hug; then I edged away from her, as I couldn't see Tom.

"Where's Tom?" I asked, a hint of anxiety in my voice.

"You're not going to believe this. We were just leaving the apartment, and he got a call from his wife. She has a leak. He told her where to switch it off, but she's so useless he's had to pop round there."

Penny could see my reaction, my face dropping, alarm bells ringing in my head, and she smiled. "Don't worry, he'll be round in half an hour max. And if the dinner's ready, he said to start without him."

I forced my face to relax. "Great! That's no problem!"

But still I felt a sense of unease.

As Penny closed the door behind her, she linked my arm and said, "Come on, let's go into the conservatory, have a nice G&T."

As we entered the kitchen, Penny broke away from me

and crossed to Nick, who was chopping onions at the island. "Hello, chef," she said. "Ellie and I would like two large gin and tonics served in the conservatory if you don't mind."

Nick laughed, and he and Penny hugged and kissed briefly on the cheek.

"Just told Ellie," Penny said to Nick, "Tom's going to be half an hour late."

"Oh, that's okay. No problem."

Penny followed me into the conservatory and sat opposite me in the armchair as I curled my legs up on to the sofa.

"Thought any more about James and those accusations?" she asked.

"It's been playing on my mind all afternoon," I told her.

"I bet it has. And mine. Any conclusions?"

"I'm worried ... that what ... Bella, was it?"

Penny nodded.

"That what Bella said, I'm worried she was telling the truth."

"So am I."

I pondered whether to tell Penny that James had rung and was insisting on coming round, but I decided against it. Nor would I mention that James had accused Nick and Penny of having an affair.

My instinctive uneasiness was due to my innate sense that I could trust no one. Only when Tom turned up in half an hour would I be able to relax.

Nick approached with two very large gin and tonics. "Here you are, ladies." And he placed them on the coffee table.

Penny picked up her glass, raised it. "Cheers."

As Penny took a sip, I did the same.

FORTY MINUTES LATER, after a second gin and tonic, Nick called out from the kitchen, "Finish your drinks, just dishing out the mushroom soup and opening a bottle of Sauvignon."

"Shall we wait for Tom?" I suggested. "Shouldn't he be here by now?"

"He said not to wait for him. I'm sure he'll be here soon," Penny said.

Penny knocked back her drink as Nick carried the bowls of soup to the table.

I left most of my second G&T. I was already feeling unnaturally woozy.

Penny stood first, and when I tried to stand, I almost lost my balance, wobbling to one side, and Penny had to grab my hand across the coffee table to steady me.

"Are you okay?" she asked.

"Whoa. Bit dizzy. How much gin did you put in these, Nick?" I asked, my words slightly slurred.

"Sorry," he called over as he forced a laugh. "Hand slipped."

I was a little unsteady as I swayed towards the dining table, and Penny took my arm, helped me to the chair and eased me down.

"You'll be fine with some food to soak up the alcohol," she said.

Once we were seated around the table, Nick at the end, Penny and I either side of him, Penny said, "This soup's delicious, Nick."

"Thanks."

"Simple and quick," he said.

"One of Nick's specialities," I added, my words echoing in my head.

We'd almost finished the soup when my phone rang. It was lying on the coffee table, and Penny jumped up.

"It's okay, Ellie; don't stand up. I'll get that."

She strode across to the phone, picked it up. "It's James."

"Oh. Really. James. Why's he ringing me again?" I slurred.

"Why? Has he rung you already today?" Penny asked.

"Er, yes. Yes. It was … it was nothing."

It was like I was grasping for the words in my head and they were just out of reach.

The phone stopped ringing.

"Oh, he's leaving a message. I'll listen to it."

"No, it's er, it's, er, okay, Penny; bring it here," I continued to slur.

However foggy my head was, I was worried James would repeat his accusation about Penny and Nick in his message.

But I was more worried that there was no sign of Tom. The thirty minutes had stretched to fifty, and he hadn't even rung.

And the thought struck me. Maybe James was right. Tom would never arrive because there was no Tom. Maybe there had never been a Tom.

I looked across and realised that Penny was already listening in to James's message.

I watched as, once the message stopped, Penny pressed "3" to delete it.

"Let me listen," I said, reaching out my hand for the phone as Penny returned to the table.

"Oh, sorry, I've deleted it. You don't want to listen to it,

Ellie; it sounds like he's pestering you. We should be worried about him after all," she said.

"What's going on here?" Nick asked.

"Okay, shall I tell him?" Penny asked me. I could only shrug.

"James, you know James who we work with?"

Nick nodded.

"He's got a thing for Ellie. In fact, I think it's an obsession; he's started to pester her. But there's worse—"

"That's untrue!" I protested. "He hasn't, he hasn't got a thing for me, and he's not been, he's not been pestering me. How can you say that, Penny?"

I caught Penny and Nick exchanging looks.

I stood up unsteadily. "I need some, to get some, some fresh air," I stuttered. "I need to, need to clear, to clear my head."

As I stood, I grasped hold of my phone, which Penny had placed on the dining table, and walked groggily towards the conservatory, slid open the door, half staggered out, then closed it behind me.

As I took a wobbly step from the patio onto the grass, the sensor lights flooded on.

I took only two swaying steps before I slumped down on to the damp grass, knees curled up to my chin, my back to the conservatory.

My phone started ringing again. I glanced round. They were staring at me from the conservatory, their faces anxious and uncertain. Again, I let it ring until it went to voicemail.

The sensor lights went out, and I felt myself disappear into the darkness. They wouldn't be able to see me at all; they couldn't see what I was doing. I hardly moved. Just enough to stay in the darkness. Kept very still, and the sensor lights didn't come back on.

I heard the patio door slide open. So I moved. I could now move, and as I eased onto my knees, pushing myself up like an old woman, the lights blazed back on.

As I walked towards the conservatory, swaying slightly, Penny and Nick hurried back to the table, and when I entered, they were sitting casually, Nick topping up the three glasses of wine.

I slid the patio door across.

I didn't lock it.

As I weaved towards the table, Nick said brightly, "Feeling better, Ellie?"

"Not really." I nodded. "Think I'll go for a lie-down. Sorry, Nick, I just don't feel very hungry."

As I moved towards the kitchen, Penny jumped up. "Who was that on the phone?" she asked sharply.

"Wrong number," I managed.

I was trying to hurry away from them, but somehow my legs felt like lead, and Penny was by my side as I reached the kitchen.

"Let me see, please," Penny said, and before I could object, she snatched the phone from my hand.

"Hey," I managed.

Penny looked at the phone. "Oh, it looks like the caller left you a message, Ellie. Shall we see who it's from?"

"No ..." I reached out my arm, but Penny stepped back.

She pressed to play the message, then held the phone in the air away from my reach and put it on speaker.

James's voice started to fill the silence.

"Ellie, did Tom turn up? I bet he didn't. You need to ring

me back. Urgently. I've been doing some research on Penny. On her past. She's dangerous. You're in danger."

And the message finished.

There was total silence in the room. An unspeakable, edgy atmosphere as if the revelation was so momentous that any words would be inadequate.

I focused my eyes first on Nick, then back at Penny. I shook my head in disbelief.

"No. No. No …"

"I'm so sorry, Ellie, I really am," Penny said, sounding genuinely apologetic. "You're a good friend, sort of … but there's nothing we could do."

A moment before I asked, "So there is no … no Tom?"

"No. Nick is Tom." She shrugged, again almost contrite. "He wasn't late. He was already here."

"How long … how long have …?" I tailed off.

"How long have we been seeing each other?"

I could only nod my head once.

"Well, the first time we slept together, we were only fifteen."

My face must have looked a crumpled map of confusion.

CHAPTER FIFTY-FIVE

"Penny, I'd like you to meet Nick. Nick, this is Penny, my very best friend."

That was the moment that changed everything for me.

As soon as I saw him, I knew who Nick really was. It had been nearly twenty years since the day he'd been arrested. His eyes were the same, maybe not as twinkly, the smile not as broad, and his black hair no longer tousled, it was short and neatly styled, and he was taller.

But I recognised him immediately.

And I could see by the startled expression in his eyes as we shook hands that he also recognised me. Ellie didn't pick up on it.

He offered to buy me a drink, and Ellie and I moved to a table in the snug.

"Well, what d'you think?" she asked once we'd sat down.

"Where did you find him?" I asked. "He's lovely."

"He works with my ex, Pete."

"Really?"

I was amazed that Steve worked in an office. How could that have happened? And why had he changed his name?

As the evening progressed and the conversation flowed easily, I couldn't connect the Steve I'd known with the person who sat opposite me. He was much calmer, laid-back, confident, yes, but he had none of Steve's swagger, the natural charisma. Of course, I also knew the person Steve had projected to the world was not really him. It was all a show. I knew how nervous he'd been to ask me out, and he'd always been more sensitive and vulnerable than he'd ever admit.

But when Nick laughed, throwing his head back, a big, infectious, throaty guffaw, the memories of Steve's laugh came flooding back.

Ellie popped off to the toilet, and we nervously stared at each other; then simultaneously we started laughing.

I can remember every single detail of that conversation. I can see and hear it now as I sit here.

He said, "I can't believe it!"

And I repeated his exact words. "I can't believe it! Where's Steve? What happened to Steve? And Nick? Who's Nick? And this job! The last time I saw you, I'd just taught you to read."

He glanced at my right hand.

"You're still wearing that ring!"

"Of course. I never take it off. It's for eternity, remember."

I had so many questions to ask him.

"I'd rather Ellie didn't know about my past, but if you fancy meeting up for a drink after work, we can catch up properly, and I'll tell you all about it?" he asked, as if he'd read my mind, his eyebrow rising quizzically.

"I'd like that." I smiled.

WE MET up in Wetherspoons in Piccadilly. We didn't want to bump into Ellie, and I knew she'd never go into Wetherspoons.

Once we'd settled at a table, we just stared at each other, smiling, saying nothing, occasionally shaking our heads in disbelief. It was during those wordless few moments that I knew this wasn't just coincidence.

It was Fate. It was inevitable.

But I could never have guessed the dangerous road down which it would take us.

Nick/Steve broke the moment first. He raised his pint and said, "Cheers."

I did the same before asking, "Right ... Steve to Nick ... explain."

He nodded. "Okay. Well, how much do you know about what happened to me after I was arrested?" he asked.

"Nothing. Absolutely nothing. They wouldn't tell me anything."

And so he told me his story. He'd been sentenced to twelve months in a young offenders' institution. He survived it because he was good at survival. When he came out, he was on probation for another year. He was told he must never go back to the home. And never to contact me. He said he ignored the rules and wrote several letters to me.

I was furious. "You did! Those bastards never passed them on to me!"

Anyway, after he came out, the probation officer found him a place in a hostel. But it was horrible, and after two nights, he left, slept on the streets for a couple of nights, begging. Over the twelve months inside, he'd had lots of time to think. But mostly he was thinking what a dick he had been to blow it with me ...

And I said, "Yeah, I couldn't believe it when you robbed that jeweller's shop and you didn't disguise yourself! Idiot!"

He said it was on impulse, and he wanted to please me. But then he said back then ... nearly twenty years ago ... everything about him was fake, a sham. And I told him I knew that, and then I reminded him about the time he bought me, or rather nicked, that book about birds.

Nick covered his face and laughed. It was only years later when he read To Kill A Mockingbird he knew what he'd done.

We both laughed.

Anyway, Steve told me how he'd got a job helping in a corner shop in Rusholme, one of those that sold everything. And there was this old guy in there, Asian guy, on his own. So he asked if he had a vacancy, and it just so happened that his wife had died the previous month, and he needed help in the shop, as he was struggling. He didn't ask Steve any questions, not his age, nor where he was from, nothing. Just trusted him. He even found a room for him above the shop.

The only thing the shopkeeper had asked him was his name that first day, and he thought, I don't want to be Steve. I don't want to be that person anymore. I was ashamed of who I was. So the name "Nick" just popped into his head.

I asked him how long he stayed there, and he said he was there for four years. That meant we'd been just down the road from each other all the time I was training to be a nurse.

Maybe if we'd met then, maybe things would have worked out differently. I could have been going out with Steve instead of Ellie.

Anyway ... no use going there.

He said he constantly thought about me and what I'd done for him, teaching him to read and not laughing at him, and telling him he was bright and clever, and that was one of the reasons he started going to college but still worked in the evenings and weekends, and he passed five GCSEs. And he went on to do his A levels, got three. He didn't go to uni but got a job in an advertising office, cos he was still good at blagging ... and it started from there.

I asked him if Ellie knew about his past. She didn't. By the time he met Ellie, he'd invented a whole new story. That his parents were quite old, and they'd died when he was in his late teens.

"I left Steve behind," *he said.*

"I loved Steve," *I told him, and I wasn't sure from where that popped out, but I could feel my cheeks burning as soon as I said it.*

And he leaned across the table, took my hand and said, "And I loved Penny."

He released my hand almost immediately, looking embarrassed. He sat back in his chair, smiled awkwardly. We stared at each other, remembered those moments together when we were different people, before my lips twitched, and I said, "And I want to thank you for teaching me everything about how satisfying sex could be."

A laugh exploded from him, erupting into a coughing fit so that he had to take a drink to clear his throat, and he eventually told me he was a total bullshitter and he'd been a virgin!

"I'd never have guessed," *I said sarcastically.*

And he laughed again, a little more controlled. He said his whole life had been bullshit, and he was embarrassed to think back to how he was. And then he said, "And now you're a nurse."

"Yes," I told him. "But I wanted to be a doctor."

And I knew he could see the bitterness in my face and hear it in my voice. So I changed the subject.

"Did you know Ellie was orphaned quite young?" I asked. He did. "But it wasn't like us. Did she tell you how?"

He shook his head.

"She was ten. Her parents were both consultants, top in their particular fields; they also had personal wealth, were very rich. They were killed in a car accident. But unlike us, Ellie was one of the lucky ones in two ways. She was adopted quite quickly and stayed with them and was happy and loved. Secondly, her birth parents' savings, including the sale of their large house, was put in a trust for her, and when she was eighteen, she was suddenly extremely rich."

Nick looked astonished. He knew Ellie was quite well off, but he didn't realise she was that rich.

"The house Ellie owns in Didsbury ... how much is it worth? A million maybe? There's no mortgage on it. And I struggle to pay the mortgage on my two-bedroom city centre flat!"

As I talked about Ellie, I realised how jealous I was of her and how deep-seated was my actual resentment. Yes, we'd both lost parents, but I had suffered as a child. I was unloved, mistreated and had to fight for my survival, whereas she had been loved from the moment she was born, and she continued to be loved.

And while Ellie's inheritance had made her rich, I was still drowning in student debt. I knew life was never fair, but the final straw, she was not only dating my first love, she was a doctor. I wanted to be a doctor. Not a nurse. A doctor. I resented her so much it hurt, it hurt inside my head.

She had the life I craved. I wanted that life.

With such emotions swimming around in my head, I asked Nick, "Do you love her?" and I watched his reaction closely.

He hesitated before answering, "I do now!" and he let out a huge roar of laughter.

I joined in, but when we stopped, we looked at each other, staring, deep in thought, and it was in that exact moment our lives were altered for good or bad.

He said, "Shall we go?" and I nodded, and as we made our way between the tables, he took my hand.

We stepped outside into the cold air and turned to each other, and as he stared at me, I realised that although we had become different people, deep inside we were still the same; up to this point, we'd been fooling ourselves. We were still dangerous, still attracted to danger, and ultimately we could do nothing about it.

I only lived five minutes away.

We didn't need to speak. He took my hand, and we started running across Piccadilly and down Portland Street. As Steve dragged me along, I immediately regretted wearing the highest heels and the tightest, shortest denim skirt from my wardrobe. I should have worn skinny jeans and low-heeled boots.

In the lift to my fourth-floor apartment, we started kissing. It was ferocious, desperate, and when the doors opened and we spilled out into the corridor, I grabbed his hand, pulled him three doors up, and we fell into the room, kicking the door behind me. And it was then that I was glad I wasn't wearing tight jeans as we tore off each other's clothes, hands *everywhere, breathing hard, so desperate that we had sex against the wall just inside the door.*

Later, we made love again, on the bed, slowly, gently, caringly. And afterwards as we lay on our backs, holding hands, I said, "That was almost as good as our first time!"

And we nearly fell off the bed laughing.

When we stopped, he stared at me, his face serious.

"What?" I asked.

"Do you ... do you ever think of the time we stole that car ... and the man ... the man I knocked down?"

"No." I shook my head. "It was a long time ago. Do you?"

He nodded, and I reached across and put both arms tightly around him.

Much later, in the early hours, I watched as he dressed himself and wondered in my head what was going to happen now.

And I could see Nick was going through the same thought processes because once he was dressed, he turned to me and said, "Well, what now?"

And that was when we made the big decision. We had to be together. We were soulmates. We had no choice in the matter.

We planned everything a few days later when we met up again for a night together in the Midland Hotel.

Nick/Steve talked about finishing things with Ellie so that he could be with me, but I convinced him of another way.

He would marry Ellie and move into her huge, detached house, and he would live with her long enough to get a decent divorce settlement and in the meantime siphon off chunks of her money into a personal account.

But eventually, even that wasn't good enough for me. I was determined to take over Ellie's life completely.

CHAPTER FIFTY-SIX

I was propping myself up by the island, my eyes wide with utter disbelief and shock at the appalling revelations. Penny appeared to take huge pleasure in describing each long-term deceit.

I knew it wasn't just the drink. I'd been drugged. I thought it was fentanyl.

I'd tried to keep a clear head by asking questions, forcing myself to concentrate on the horrific answers, but my head was clouding fast, overcoming thought processes, the voices of Penny and Nick sounding like distant echoes on a bad telephone line.

I had kept the conversation going for over half an hour. Surely James and the police should be arriving soon. How much longer did I have before I passed out?

I'd guessed something wasn't right even before Penny jumped up to answer my phone and delete James's voice-mail, because there was no way my head would be so fuzzy after only one drink. And I'd also caught Nick and Penny sharing a glance. It confused me but also made me wary. What could be going on?

When Tom didn't turn up, I knew.

I needed to escape the dinner table, needed to clear my head, clean out the confusion.

As soon as I flopped onto the damp grass and my phone rang, I saw it was James. I wanted to answer but instinctively I felt I was being watched. I let the call go through to voicemail.

When the sensor light snapped off and I was plunged into darkness, I listened to James's message with my phone hidden inside my jumper so it gave off no glow. As I listened, my body started to shiver and shake, part from the chill in the air but also from the cold fear created by James's message. I thought about ringing him back, or better still, ringing DS Harrison, but as soon as I moved, the sensor would flash back on, and Penny and James would see what I was doing, and they'd be out the conservatory door before I could make the call. I also thought about running out the side gate, but again, with the alcohol, the drugs, I was too unsteady on my feet, and I probably wouldn't make it to the gate before they caught me.

So instead, from inside the top of my jumper, I managed to text James:

> Need help. Call police. Been drugged.
> Think fentanyl. Don't ring me.
> Conservatory door unlocked.

I sent it, then stood up, and the sensor lights blazed on. As I staggered up towards the conservatory, I saw Penny and Nick moving quickly away from the window.

I hoped to God they wouldn't think of checking my text messages.

WHEN PENNY FINISHED TALKING, I looked from one to the other, both of them hazy shadows of themselves, before my unfocused gaze settled on Nick. I was grasping for words, trying to form them into a coherent response.

I spoke bitterly to Nick. "How stupid I've been! All this year!" I stopped, rubbed my eyes. My mouth was dry as if dehydrated from a long night's drinking session. I thought back to only recently when I'd accused Nick of having an affair with his PA, Ursula.

"PA," I said. "Didn't think. Didn't think. PA. Penny Austin. My best friend Penny Austin!" I almost spat the words out.

Penny shrugged. "Yes. That phone call to me when you were in the garden. Nick was getting cold feet. He wanted to call it off. Didn't want to take it any further. But it was too late. Once we'd killed Natasha, it was way too late."

Nick and Penny were staring at me, watching and waiting for the moment when I would collapse to the floor.

But I wasn't giving in. I was fighting.

I remembered that the CCTV was recording this conversation.

But as if Penny could read my mind, she held out her arm, opened her fist, and the three camera eyes rested in her palm. I shrugged.

My eyes narrowed at Nick, trying to focus on his ghost-like outline. "How could you ... how could you ... do this to me? For over a year. Married. Married over a year."

Nick looked down. Did I sense a hint of guilt? Maybe I could appeal to him. Somehow. If there was still one tiny decent part within him, could I appeal to that?

"Must've been difficult … for you … fourteen months … pretending … pretending you loved me, cared for me."

Nick took a minute to answer. "Not really. Because I did care for you. At first. It was when I met Penny again I realised I didn't love you … couldn't love you like I needed to … I'm sorry." Nick tailed off, and he looked like he meant the apology.

And then the image of Samson popped into my head. "Which one of you took Samson?"

Penny smiled, a cruel smile. "I did."

"And where is he? Is he still alive?" I pleaded. "Please tell me … tell me he's …"

"I'm sorry. I had to kill him. He knew everything. I couldn't risk him barking out the truth!" And she roared with laughter at her sick joke. Then she stepped forward. "Enough of this. Ellie hasn't got long before she passes out; we need to get her upstairs and into bed—"

I shook my head violently, and as Nick took a step towards me, I screamed, "No! Don't come near me!"

Nick stopped. He looked in two minds.

"Get hold of her, Steve, and carry her upstairs," Penny ordered.

Then Nick shook his head. "I can't. I can't do this. We have to stop."

"Steve, we are so close. You need to be brave. We've come this far, just this one final step," Penny pleaded. "I can't carry her upstairs on my own; we need to do this together."

She took hold of Steve and started to push him towards me.

"Don't. Please. I can't do it," he begged.

My back was pressed tight against the island, and almost in slow motion I swivelled round, grabbed the unicorn knife from its block, spun back round to face Nick, his figure now blurred and indistinct.

Penny pushed Nick really hard one final time towards me, but then she must have seen the knife in my hand, and she tried to tug him back, but his foot slipped on the tiles. He half stumbled forwards, and as my trembling arm held the knife out in front of me, in one awful motion he fell forward.

He fell onto the knife, and it buried itself deep into his chest.

There was a look of complete surprise in his eyes, followed by one of horror as both hands grasped at the knife, and he stared down at it in disbelief.

He tumbled from his knees, onto his side, as Penny ran forward screeching, "No! No! NO!" as she bent down over him. "Steve!" she cried. "Steve, don't die, please don't die!"

But I knew, I knew when I saw where the knife had penetrated that there was no hope. Blood started oozing from Nick's mouth, and he started to choke. His eyes clouded and became vacant as Penny cradled his head.

It was as if I were watching the end of a gruesome movie, but watching it through a gauze veil. The effort of defending myself had drained all my energy, and I slowly slumped to my knees, my legs too weak, collapsing like a puppet whose strings had been cut.

My eyelids were heavy; I couldn't keep my eyes open; I needed to sleep. Penny's shrieks and cries were disappearing into the distance like an ambulance siren fading as it entered a tunnel.

Just before my eyes shut completely, I saw a vague outline of a man bursting into the conservatory, shouting my name, followed by sirens, tyres screeching, bellowing urgent voices, and then the outside world closed down.

CHAPTER FIFTY-SEVEN

James stopped just inside the conservatory when he saw the tragic tableau – Nick's body, Penny wailing over him, Ellie slumped next to them.

Was Ellie also dead? Was he too late?

Penny looked up at the sound of the conservatory door opening, saw James, his eyes wide, shocked, his body as still as a waxwork, and her face changed rapidly from grief to fierce anger. She took hold of the knife sticking from Nick's chest and dragged it out, Excalibur-like, its blade glistening and dripping with blood.

James was about to run to Ellie when Penny screamed out, "Don't come any nearer!" and she bent over Ellie's unconscious body with the knife held to Ellie's throat.

James froze, unsure, as DI Kennedy and DS Harrison burst through the open conservatory door, followed by three more uniformed officers.

DI Kennedy took in the scene and instructed, "Step away, please. We'll deal with this now."

James eased slowly back, letting DI Kennedy and DS

Harrison edge forward before Penny waved the knife at them, then pointed it back towards Ellie's throat: "I said don't come any closer!"

DI Kennedy nodded, stopped and spoke softly. "It's Penny, isn't it? Penny Austin. Penny, please put down that knife. It's over. It's over, Penny. There's nothing you can do. So please don't hurt your friend Ellie."

Penny's body stiffened at the word "friend".

"Put the knife down and step away, Penny. Place the knife on the floor and step away," DI Kennedy continued.

Penny didn't move. No one moved. No one dared move. There was total silence in the room. As if a spell had been cast over them, they were all as frozen and still as Sleeping Beauty.

DI Kennedy stared across at Penny, who stared back.

Neither spoke.

The silence seemed to last forever, and it was only penetrated when another police siren screeched into the drive. This sound broke the spell, and suddenly Penny raised the knife high above her.

James gasped, "No!"

But Penny didn't plunge it into Ellie's body.

Instead, she smiled at DI Kennedy, an inward smile, as if to herself; then she sliced the knife brutally across her own neck.

As the blood seeped out in a thickening red line, she stared down at Nick lying next to her. Then from deep within her there erupted a desperate howl, and she threw herself across Nick's body.

She lay there, quite still, hugging tightly on to him, as if this were the tragic climactic scene of an opera by Verdi.

AS SOON AS Penny collapsed on top of Nick, James dashed forward to Ellie. He kneeled to check her vital signs. He listened for Ellie's respiration rate, but she was hardly breathing. He rubbed his knuckles hard over her chest bone, but still she didn't respond.

Where was the ambulance? He'd called them at the same time as the police and asked specifically that they bring the antidote to fentanyl, as he didn't have a supply at home. They should have been here by now.

He tilted Ellie's head back, lifted her chin and pinched her nose. He bent over to perform mouth-to-mouth, giving her two quick breaths, then one long breath every five seconds. After a few minutes he heard the ambulance siren drawing closer.

He shouted to the uniformed police officers, "Go let them in the front door!"

The two detectives were next to him; DI Kennedy was kneeling down over the bodies of Penny and Nick while DS Harrison was watching James, and she asked, "Is she going to be okay?"

"I hope so." James nodded grimly.

He heard the front door slam open, and two paramedics ran in, carrying their equipment. One was a woman, short but robust in her thirties, and the other was a large man in his forties.

"Have you got the naloxone?" James shouted as he saw that the woman already had it in her hands, ready to pass it on. James didn't bother slipping on latex gloves; this needed to be administered immediately. The paramedic broke open the syringe from its plastic and passed James both the small bottle of naloxone and then the ready-to-use syringe. He inserted the syringe into the lid of the bottle, drew the antidote out, then swiftly plunged the needle into Ellie's arm.

DS Harrison was watching him, and as James looked up, he said, "This usually works in around two or three minutes. She'll regain consciousness; then we'll need to get her into hospital."

The paramedics now kneeled over Penny, trying to stifle the flow of blood from her neck, but both of them had the sense that she was a lost cause.

And precisely three minutes later, a very long three minutes, Ellie opened her eyes, saw James staring down at her.

"You're going to be okay, Ellie," he said, smiling warmly.

CHAPTER FIFTY-EIGHT

I stayed in the Royal for three days. James popped in to see me on a regular basis in between his shifts or in his few breaks.

"You saved my life," I told him.

James shrugged modestly. "You were very brave, doing what you did."

I wanted to know what had happened to Nick and Penny because the events that played in my head, prior to losing consciousness, were so vague and shadowy. James described the moment from when he entered the house via the conservatory.

Inside, I felt devastated. The two people I'd been closest to had betrayed me. I found it emotionally hard to process the long-term deceit.

After the third day, I remembered James's message where he'd told me he had found disturbing information about Penny's past life.

"So what did you find out?" I asked.

"Okay. It didn't take much research to find that Penny

had been living in a Children's Home since she was eleven or twelve. I located the home and spoke to Gavin and Joyce Davies. They're in their late sixties now, but still taking kids in."

Gavin and Joyce had told James about Penny's history from eleven to when she left the home.

"After the accident and with Steve gone, Penny went into a depression, tried to take her own life and finished up having a breakdown. They said she was desperate to become a doctor, but she didn't pass the required A levels, and that's why she went into nursing even though she was obsessed with being a doctor."

I took all this in, thought about it, before saying, "God … God, James, that is so tragic. I feel … I feel sorry for her …"

"Ellie, she tried to kill you! They both did. They plotted against you for over a year!"

"I know, I know, but even so …"

James took hold of my hand, squeezed it. "You're a good person, Ellie."

I shrugged. "I never knew Nick, did I? Funny thing is, I feel I knew Penny better than I knew Nick." I paused. "Their relationship, it's monstrous, but it's also like a tragic love story."

By the second day, I was clear of the fentanyl, and although I was still weak and exhausted, on the third day I was allowed to go home.

James was due to pick me up at the end of the day when he finished his shift.

But there was still one thing bugging me.

Did Penny lie to me about Bella? Or was she telling the truth? Did James kill his wife? I was pretty sure of the answer, but I needed it confirmed. I needed to know I could trust James fully.

Once I was fully dressed and my small suitcase packed, I still had an hour before James was due to pick me up, so I rang through to A&E.

"Good afternoon, it's Dr Ellie Thompson here …"

"Oh hi, Dr Thompson, how are you now? We've all been so worried about you."

The Royal might have had a large medical community, but gossip and scandal spread as quickly as a viral video. There was genuine disbelief and horror regarding Penny, sympathy and compassion for me (I'd received a small avalanche of "get well" cards from my colleagues), and James was viewed as the heroic saviour.

I recognised the receptionist's voice. It was Olwyn; in her fifties, she was known for being friendly but firm.

"Oh, thanks for asking, Olwyn. I'm fine now. In fact, I'm being discharged today," I told her.

"That's great news. Anyway, what can I do for you?"

"Okay, I have a couple of strange requests. First, can you check back to Friday to see if a Bella Godwin was brought into A&E, minor car accident, broken arm?" I asked.

"No problem. Just bear with me."

The line went dead for a minute before Olwyn picked up. "Dr Thompson, we've no record of a Bella Godwin attending A&E any time last Friday."

I breathed out slowly. "Thank you. One final thing …" I hesitated before continuing, "Did … did Penny … Penny Austin …" I could hear a slight intake of breath from Olwyn. "Was Penny working in A&E for the day on Friday?" I finished firmly.

The answer came back quickly. "No. No, definitely not, Dr Thompson."

"Thanks, Olwyn."

And I finished the call, overwhelmed by a huge sense of relief.

I could trust James.

But I was saddened by Penny's shocking level of deviousness.

THE NURSES WAVED me off as James carried my case to his car, all the time keeping a reassuring, comforting arm around my shoulder. He eased me into the passenger seat before placing my case in his boot.

"I've got a surprise for you when we get home," he said, smiling.

"What sort of surprise?"

"You'll soon find out." His eyes twinkled.

We didn't speak for the rest of the journey home, but James kept glancing at me, checking I was okay.

As we drove into my drive, I felt quite nervous. I shivered at the thought that the blood from Nick and Penny might still be staining the kitchen tiles.

But James, reading my thoughts, said, "I arranged for a deep clean in your kitchen. It's looking spotless."

"Thank you." I nodded.

When we entered the hall, the big surprise was waiting for me.

As soon as he saw me, Samson came running at me, barking in excitement. I couldn't believe it. I kneeled, and he jumped straight into my arms and started licking my face, even the salty tears of joy that were now flowing.

I looked to James, who was smiling at me and Samson. "How did ... I mean where ...?"

"When the police went round to search Penny's flat, Samson was locked in one of the bedrooms."

"Aww, no. And look at him, poor thing," I said, still crying.

There were large bald patches where Penny had sliced off clumps of Samson's fur. But there were no cuts, no scratches on his bare skin.

James then said firmly, "Why don't you take Samson up with you to the bedroom? I think you need to rest."

And I did still feel drained with little energy, not just from the drugs but from the accumulated trauma and emotional exhaustion.

The person I thought was my best friend had betrayed me. My husband had betrayed me. The level of deceit and duplicity was difficult for me to comprehend. And the pair's long-term, cold-hearted planning to take over my life was beyond anything I could understand.

I didn't want to think about it.

"I'll bring you a drink up, okay?" James offered.

"A decent cup of coffee would be great," I said. I'd missed fresh coffee after drinking the weak, instant coffee served up to patients at the Royal.

James went into the kitchen while I climbed the stairs, Samson still in my arms.

"Won't be long," he told me.

However, five minutes later, when James brought up the fresh coffee in a mug, my eyes were drooping. Samson was nestled close, his head on my chest, but I managed a tiny smile.

"Thank you."

James sat on the edge of the bed and took my hand.

He spoke softly. "Ellie, I think you'll have a lot of dark days ahead after what you've been through. You're bound to. But you're strong. So strong. And you've got lots of friends, more than you ever knew."

He'd brought up a bag filled with the cards I'd received from my colleagues.

As he held the bag up, he said, "You're greatly loved. And if you have dark days, I promise I'll be around to brighten up those days." He smiled before adding, "Sorry, that sounds so cheesy."

"Totally cheesy." I smiled, squeezing James's hand.

But I liked cheesy. It was what I needed.

JAMES STAYED with me that night.

And when I woke, screaming, with nightmare images of Penny and Nick and the bloody knife as it plunged into Nick's chest, James was there. He was smiling, a warm, generous smile, eyes bright and reassuring. He gently stroked my hair.

"It's okay, Ellie, it's okay," he whispered. "It'll take time, but you'll come through this."

I smiled back at him. I believed him.

Everything was going to be okay.

EPILOGUE

After Ellie and Steve/Nick married, I found it painful to watch them together, and I felt the resentment against Ellie really building. I kept telling myself I had to stop thinking like this. I had to be patient, and when the divorce came through, Steve and I would be together ... for eternity.

I was never unfaithful to Steve. I couldn't be, because I was so obsessed with him. However, as Ellie was always pushing me to find the "right man", I had to invent relationships with guys who never existed, and we always "broke up" just at the point when Ellie insisted on meeting him.

When the year had passed and Steve was no closer to getting a divorce, I lost patience. I told him we had to do something. I wouldn't wait any longer. I wanted everything that Ellie had. I deserved it.

But we only formed a proper plan when Ellie's regular nightmares became more disturbing and real, when Ellie's life and dreams became almost ... indistinguishable to her, and she started talking about the nightmares coming alive.

We both thought Ellie was deranged and delusional to

actually believe such utter nonsense. However, maybe, if we actually recreated her worst nightmares, we could push her one step nearer the edge, to the point where she genuinely thought she was insane and felt so crazy that she committed suicide.

It was never our initial intention to kill Ellie ourselves.

Our intention was for her to kill herself.

And it was all going to plan, better than we could have hoped. Ray Walker, by stalking Ellie and damaging her car, helped us without knowing it. Dr Ben Carson, the creepy psychiatrist Ellie was seeing, suggested Ellie could be hallucinating, and that really helped.

We bought a professional voice changer from Spy Shops, plus several mobile phones, and when I rang Ellie as her "nightmare", each time from a different mobile, my voice not only sounded like a man's, it sounded spooky and weird.

And it felt, for both of us, like a game. An exciting game. A game where we were in complete control.

It was when Ellie told us about the nightmare where she killed her dog, Samson, that we got the idea of taking Samson. Steve had given me a spare set of keys to their house. I was watching the house and saw James leave, and I thought, you deceitful little cow, Ellie. Then I saw Ellie draw the curtain in her bedroom after James left. She was going back to bed. This was my chance. I waited till I was sure she'd be asleep, and I let myself in. Oh, and she had left her phone downstairs, so I killed two birds with one stone by deleting all the threatening anonymous calls.

I walked Samson out of the conservatory, leaving the door and gate open on purpose. I'd parked on the main road, and I was sure no one would notice as I dragged Samson away.

It was a clever plan that really would tip Ellie over the edge.

Oh, and Ellie's sleepwalking was a gift. Especially when she almost killed Steve. We knew then we were close because if she really did think she had killed Samson in her sleep, that would be it, she'd topple over the edge.

But it didn't quite work.

That was why we had to organise Ellie's death. And it needed to appear like suicide.

Course, our plans really started going wrong when Steve received a phone call from Natasha. She had photos of me and Steve, and she said she would send them to Ellie. She wanted some money for her and her fiancé to go on some expensive holiday or other.

We went round to see her, forced ourselves into the flat. I pushed her over, her head banged on the corner of the coffee table, and she fell unconscious.

We searched for Natasha's phone, and I found it tucked into her back jean pocket. We also found an iPad and a laptop.

Now we had to make Natasha's death look like suicide. Steve wouldn't help; he was useless. I had to run the bath myself, drag Natasha into the bathroom, undress her and sort of ease her into the bath.

I then pushed Natasha's head deep under the water. I'd taken the sharpest knife I could find from the kitchen and sliced both Natasha's wrists lengthways, not across.

But it all went wrong. Just like my life. It's always gone wrong.

Just when we were so close to getting it all. So close – until Ellie killed Steve. Murdered him.

PENNY STOPPED TALKING. She looked across the table at Dr Harlow and took a sip of water from the plastic beaker on the table. Her mouth was constantly dry, and her voice, deep with a broken croak, no longer sounded like the old Penny.

She had been speaking to the psychiatrist for well over an hour.

Dr Kate Harlow had been carrying out a mental assessment for the last two weeks, and they were nearing the end of today's session.

Penny's neck and throat were still bandaged, but the bandages were due to be removed the following day. She wore no make-up, her skin was pale, and her lacklustre blonde hair was tight off her face in a pony, giving her a taut, fierce appearance. Her eyes were dull, but with a spark of defiance.

Penny wore the standard-issue clothing of the psychiatric hospital: light blue trousers, blue top.

Her ring was missing.

The interview room was bare, white walls, no window, one plastic table in the centre and two plastic chairs screwed down, one on each side of the table.

Dr Harlow was in her forties, greying short hair, glasses propped on top of her head.

Standing by the door, arms folded, was Wardle, a male psychiatric nurse. He was over six feet tall, well built, thick forearms, a bald bullet head. He looked more like a bouncer than a nurse.

As Penny placed down her beaker of water, she looked

directly at Dr Harlow and said, "I'm not mad, you know; I'm not insane. After what my parents tried to do to me, I think I'm very normal. Surprisingly normal. You can't blame me for wanting more out of life. Who wouldn't feel they deserved more? I deserved everything. Like Ellie. She had everything. And look at her now! I'm locked up in here, yet Ellie killed my boyfriend, my lover, and she is out there, free as a bird. It's not fair. Not fair at all. Is it? You tell me, Dr Harlow, is that fair?"

But Dr Harlow didn't respond. Instead she stopped the tape.

"Have we finished?" Penny asked.

"For today, yes."

"Good."

Penny glanced beyond Dr Harlow to Wardle, who still stood motionless by the door. He nodded once to Penny, and a tiny smile flickered across his lips.

Wardle would be visiting Penny's room later that night.

Penny couldn't wait. She liked Wardle. He wasn't like Steve. He was stronger, not just physically but mentally. He wouldn't let her down like Steve had done. Wardle would do anything for her. Wardle knew Penny was as sane as he was. And he'd said he'd get Penny out of there. He'd promised.

And Penny would make sure he kept that promise.

THANK YOU FOR READING

Did you enjoy reading *The Sleepwalker*? Please consider leaving a review on Amazon. Your review will help other readers to discover the novel.

ABOUT THE AUTHOR

Ian is an ex teacher, hospital ward orderly and encyclopaedia salesman. He started his writing career with the BBC and has had in excess of 30 radio productions broadcast before moving on to TV where he wrote for *The Bill, Coronation Street, Emmerdale* and more recently a US/Canadian TV romcom movie . In theatre he has had over 20 full length stage plays produced for local Reps, No. 1 tours and a run in the West End. *The Sleepwalker* is his first novel and he's found it far more challenging than writing plays or TV scripts!!

Printed in Great Britain
by Amazon